PRAISE FOR B.

THIS PLACE OF WONDER

"*This Place of Wonder* is a wonderfully moving tale about four women whose journeys are all connected by one shared love: some are romantic, some are familial, but all are deeply complicated. Dealing with loss, love, hidden secrets, and second chances, this stirring tale is utterly engaging and ultimately hopeful. Set along the rugged California coastline, *This Place of Wonder* will sweep you away with the intoxicating scents, bold flavors, and sweeping views of the region and transport you to a world you won't be in any hurry to leave."

—Colleen Hoover, #1 *New York Times* bestselling author

"Kristin Hannah readers will thoroughly enjoy the family dynamic, especially the mother-daughter relationships."

—*Booklist* (starred review)

"Barbara O'Neal's latest novel is simply delicious. Engrossing, empathetic, and profoundly moving, I savored every sentence of this story of several very different women who find solace and second chances in each other after tragedy (though not before facing some hard truths and, yes, a few rock bottoms). *This Place of Wonder* is one of the best books I've read in a long time."

—Camille Pagán, bestselling author of *Everything Must Go*

"I have never much moved in the elevated circles of California farm-to-table cuisine, but O'Neal makes me feel like I'm there. Rather than simply skewering the pretensions, *This Place of Wonder* pinpoints the passions. Some of these characters have been elevated to celebrity, some are newcomers to the scene, but all are drawn together by the sensuality, the excitement, and ultimately the care that food brings them. Elegiac but also forward-looking, this is a book about eating, but more than that, it's a book about hurt and healing and women finding their way together. I loved every moment of it."

—Julie Powell, author of *Julie & Julia* and *Cleaving*

WRITE MY NAME ACROSS THE SKY

"Barbara O'Neal weaves an irresistible tale of creativity, forgery, family, and the FBI in *Write My Name Across the Sky*. Willow and Sam are fascinating, and their aunt Gloria is my dream of an incorrigible, glamorous older woman."

—Nancy Thayer, bestselling author of *Family Reunion*

"*Write My Name Across the Sky* is an exquisitely crafted novel of three remarkable women from two generations grappling with decisions of the past and the consequences of where those young, impetuous choices have led. A heartfelt story of passion, devotion, and family told as only Barbara O'Neal can."

—Suzanne Redfearn, #1 Amazon bestselling author of *In an Instant*

"With its themes of creativity and art, *Write My Name Across the Sky* is itself like a masterfully executed painting. Using refined brushstrokes, O'Neal builds her vivid, complex characters: three independent women in one family who can't quite come to terms with their fierce feelings of love for one another. O'Neal deftly switches between three points of view, adding layers of family history into this intimate and satisfying study of how women make tough choices between love and creativity and family and freedom."

—Glendy Vanderah, *Washington Post* bestselling author of *Where the Forest Meets the Stars*

THE LOST GIRLS OF DEVON

One of *Travel + Leisure*'s most anticipated books of summer 2020

"A woman's strange disappearance brings together four strong women who struggle with their relationships, despite their need for one another. Fans of Sarah Addison Allen will appreciate the emphasis on nature and these women's unique gifts in this latest by the author of *When We Believed in Mermaids*."

—*Library Journal* (starred review)

"*The Lost Girls of Devon* draws us into the lives of four generations of women as they come to terms with their relationships and a mysterious tragedy that brings them together. Written in exquisite prose with the added bonus of the small Devon village as a setting, Barbara O'Neal's book will ensnare the reader from the first page, taking us on an emotional journey of love, loss, and betrayal."

—Rhys Bowen, *New York Times* and #1 Kindle bestselling author of *The Tuscan Child*, *In Farleigh Field*, and the Royal Spyness series

"*The Lost Girls of Devon* is one of those novels that grabs you at the beginning with its imagery and rich language and won't let you go. Four generations of women deal with the pain and betrayal of the past, and Barbara O'Neal skillfully leads us to understand all of their deepest needs and fears. To read a Barbara O'Neal novel is to fall into a different world—a world of beauty and suspense, of tragedy and redemption. This one, like her others, is spellbinding."

—Maddie Dawson, bestselling author of *A Happy Catastrophe*

WHEN WE BELIEVED IN MERMAIDS

"An emotional story about the relationship between two sisters and the difficulty of facing the truth head-on."

—*Today*

"There's a reason Barbara O'Neal is one of the most decorated authors in fiction. With her trademark lyrical style, she's written a page-turner of the first order. From the very first page, I was drawn into the drama and irresistibly teased along as layers of a family's complicated past were artfully peeled away. Don't miss this masterfully told story of sisters and secrets, damage and redemption, hope and healing."

—Susan Wiggs, #1 *New York Times* bestselling author

"More than a mystery, Barbara O'Neal's *When We Believed in Mermaids* is a story of childhood—and innocence—lost, and the long-hidden secrets, lies, and betrayals two sisters must face in order to make themselves whole as adults. Plunge in and enjoy the intriguing depths of this passionate, lustrous novel, and you just might find yourself believing in mermaids."

—Juliet Blackwell, *New York Times* bestselling author of *The Lost Carousel of Provence*, *Letters from Paris*, and *The Paris Key*

"In *When We Believed in Mermaids*, Barbara O'Neal draws us into the story with her crisp prose, well-drawn settings, and compelling characters, in whom we invest our hearts as we experience the full range of human emotion and, ultimately, celebrate their triumph over the past."

—Grace Greene, author of *The Memory of Butterflies* and the Wildflower House series

"*When We Believed in Mermaids* is a deftly woven tale of two sisters, separated by tragedy and reunited by fate, discovering that the past isn't always what it seems. By turns shattering and life affirming, as luminous and mesmerizing as the sea by which it unfolds, this is a book club essential—definitely one for the shelf!"

—Kerry Anne King, bestselling author of *Whisper Me This*

THE ART OF INHERITING SECRETS

"Great writing, terrific characters, food elements, romance, a touch of intrigue, and more than a few surprises to keep readers guessing."

—*Kirkus Reviews*

"Settle in with tea and biscuits for a charming adventure about inheriting an English manor and the means to restore it. Vivid descriptions and characters that read like best friends will stay with you long after this delightful story has ended."

—Cynthia Ellingsen, bestselling author of *The Lighthouse Keeper*

"*The Art of Inheriting Secrets* is the story of one woman's journey to uncovering her family's hidden past. Set against the backdrop of a sprawling English manor, this book is ripe with mystery. It will have you guessing until the end!"

—Nicole Meier, author of *The House of Bradbury* and *The Girl Made of Clay*

"O'Neal's clever title begins an intriguing journey for readers that unfolds layer by surprising layer. Her respected masterful storytelling blends mystery, art, romance, and mayhem in a quaint English village and breathtaking countryside. Brilliant!"

—Patricia Sands, bestselling author of the Love in Provence series

Lady Luck's Map of Vegas

Lady Luck's Map of Vegas

a novel

BARBARA O'NEAL

LAKE UNION
PUBLISHING

Text copyright © 2005, 2014, 2024 by Barbara Samuel
All rights reserved.

Published by Lake Union Publishing, Seattle

www.apub.com

Amazon, the Amazon logo, and Lake Union Publishing are trademarks of Amazon.com, Inc., or its affiliates.

ISBN-13: 9781662521393 (paperback)
ISBN-13: 9781662521386 (digital)

Cover design by Shasti O'Leary Soudant
Cover images: © Miloje, © YuriyZhuravov / Shutterstock; © Raymond Forbes LLC / Stocksy

Printed in the United States of America

For the two women who shaped me—my mother,
Rosalie Putnam Hair, who taught me to be a tiger,
fierce and wary and strong; and my grandmother
Retta Madoline O'Neal Putnam, whose job
it was to convince me I was a genius
at whatever I tried.

PART ONE

CHEYENNE CAÑON INN

Located in Cheyenne Cañon Park. This historic ten-room mission-style mansion was once an upscale bordello and gambling hall. Prices range from $99 to $219 a night.

PROLOGUE

Eldora

I'm on the bus home from Cripple Creek, my purse fat with winnings from the slot machines, when it hits me. I'm staring out at the deep gorge between two mountains, where there's still a lot of snow in the gullies, and I'm thinking about bears and how they stay warm all through the winter, but that's really because I'm worried about my girl, Gypsy, and where she might be sleeping this April night.

But then it hits me, outta nowhere: There isn't a soul on this earth who knows me for who I really am. It's not real pretty, you understand, and I've got a lot to answer for.

Then I think: I'm tired of it. It's a burden when your whole life is a lie. You start getting confused over what's true and what's not.

Staring into those deep canyons, where a person could fall and get lost and not be found for years, I also know there is only one person I can tell. That's India, my other daughter.

India. The only thing I ever really got right. Not the shaping or making of her—she did all that herself—just the letting of her into the world. Providing a space for her to grow in my body, and trying to find a good roof to put over her head. Both their heads, of course, Gypsy and India. You don't love one child more than the other, but let's be realistic here. Some are easier to love than others, and India was my easy one.

It's funny that she drives me around now all the time. When she was about two, she'd never miss a chance to hop in behind the wheel of my Thunderbird. She loved to pretend she was driving!

She was so little, always smaller than her sister, even though they're identical twins—that was a big surprise, let me tell you!—that she'd have to kneel in the seat to reach the steering wheel. I'd climb in beside her, Gypsy sitting outside the car in the grass playing one of her little games. I'd leave the door open so I could keep an eye on her, and me and India would be off. She'd say, "Where you want to go, Mama? Let's go." And off we'd go, driving away in her imagination. To Paris, which she picked up on television. To the store. To anywhere.

Once upon a time my daughter adored me. God, she was the cuddliest child you ever saw, loved curling up in my lap like some little animal, burrowing under my breasts, her plump little arms wrapped around my waist. "Love you, Mama," she would say. I'd stroke her thick black hair and kiss her head. She always smelled so good, my little girl. "Love you, too, baby," I'd say.

Gypsy never was like that. From the minute she was born, she was kinda separate. I guess it makes sense, knowing what we do. I always did feel like she was a little alien girl, though I tried not to show it. She just never would let you get anywhere close, not anybody, except her sister.

Don't know where my India went, really. She started hating me at the usual age, but unlike most girls, she didn't ever get over it. I see it, that barely veiled hostility, but what are you gonna do?

As I'm watching the shadows grow beneath the pines outside the windows of a bus filled with senior citizens, I think she might as well hate me for who I really am.

CHAPTER ONE

India

The sun is setting over Pikes Peak when I get home Tuesday afternoon. The play of pink light is as delicate as a teacup, so beautiful that a muscle in my neck untwists. The mountain feels like a relative. I find myself checking in with it a thousand times a day glancing over to see where the light is, whether the snowy cap is white or gray or pink, whether I can see a hidden valley.

My passion for it surprises me. I grew up with it, after all, looked askance at the tourists crowding into town every summer, shooting endless, endless photos of it. It was, in those days, only a mountain. I didn't understand the appeal. Now its burly steadiness against the horizon is something I can count on, unlike life.

I fit the key into my front door and take one last glance at the Peak before carrying my load inside. The canvas bag of supplies goes on the breakfast bar between the kitchen and the sparse living room that I've not decorated with much of anything because I'm not planning to stay. The mail I hold in my hand, because it is my policy to handle each piece of mail only once. The bills go in one pile, the junk—most of it—in another, the business letters in a third pile.

Two are from clients, and I take the time to open those first. They are checks. One is a retainer for a site I've agreed to design for a Denver photographer, the other a hefty—yes—final payment for an enormous, complicated site for an eccentric old writer. I smile, thinking of him. Paul David Walters, a grizzled adventurer with four ex-wives, led me on a merry chase for three months, changing his mind every ten minutes, but his wits were sharp and his insights into the function of the web were brilliant. It's the best site I've designed in years and it is in my portfolio. The payment, too, is quite sweet. Solvency for another three months, four if I'm frugal.

Tucked between the utility bill and a flyer for a new restaurant down the street is a postcard from my twin sister, Gypsy. I glance involuntarily at the bag of groceries on the counter, then pick up the card for a closer look.

It's an index card with a miniaturized version of one of Gypsy's paintings on the blank side. She works mainly with *descansos*, the roadside crosses planted at the sites of accidents, and graveyards, and this is an abstract graveyard with a blur of pinks and yellows and stylized crosses, so odd and beautiful it draws the eye almost against one's will. Gypsy's paintings invite the viewer to come closer, lean in, hear a secret, a mystery. I stare at this one a long time, wishing I really could.

On the back, where the lines are, is a message scribbled in Gypsy's pointed, spidery hand. Unfortunately, the only thing I can read is my name, India, and the date, which she's written in numbers at the top. Last week. That's a good sign.

The rest is written in a language I wished I remembered, the one we created as babies and used between ourselves until we lost it at around eleven or twelve—which is actually quite late; most twins stop using their secret languages by first or second grade—or rather, I lost it. Gypsy kept it, and when she is delusional, as she is now, it is the only language she uses to communicate with me.

I stare at the words with great concentration, as I always do, sure that the veil between past and present will lift one of these days, and I will suddenly remember the code. I even went to a hypnotist once to see if she could help me. It hadn't worked.

And no miracle occurs now, either. The only clue I can gather from the card is the postmark: Tucumcari, New Mexico. It's something.

I put it down on the counter, take off my coat and hang it in the nearly empty coat closet, then I go back to the kitchen to put away the groceries—a can of Eagle-brand condensed milk, maraschino cherries, paraffin, baking chocolate; chicken breasts and coriander; onions, basmati rice; the whole milk Jack likes in his tea. The cherries, so very red and round, are irresistible, so I open the jar and take three of them by the stem, popping them into my mouth one at a time. Then the bottle goes into the fridge, on the door, next to the olives I keep for my mother. The milk is slightly out of place, and I nudge it into its place beneath the light.

At the back of my neck I feel the lure of Gypsy's card, and close my eyes, trying—in the way of twins, not some new-age fruitcake—to sense her, sense her mind. It's not there.

And there, at the bottom of the grocery bag, is a box, tapping its foot while it waits for me to face it. I'll hear that little tap all evening unless I answer it, so I carry it into the bathroom and close the door. Gypsy once laughed uproariously when she found out I close the door even when I'm alone, but there are some things that just require privacy. I'm not like her and my mother, who don't have a single body secret in the universe. I'm sorry, but I don't need to share or know any of those things.

I read the directions on the box twice to be sure I understand them, then, safe behind the closed door, I follow them. I wash my hands and wait.

It doesn't take very long. In minutes, the lines on the pregnancy test form a distinct, undeniable plus sign.

Pregnant.

Carefully, I wrap up the stick and the box in lengths of toilet paper, as if there is someone else here who might see it in the trash, then carry it out to the kitchen and throw it away safely under the sink.

Pregnant.

I'm swept with an intense dizziness, and put a hand over my belly. It's a weird thing to do, considering my horror, but it's involuntary. Am I trying to sense it? Repulse it?

But instead, for one long, yearning second, I see my lover against the screen of my eyelids, his black hair, his quirky smile—and for one single flash of time, I imagine a daughter with tumbling black curls and a tilt to her eyes.

No.

With a sense of seasickness, I open my eyes, list sideways, and pick up the postcard from Gypsy. It contains all the reasons I cannot take the chance no matter how much I might wish it.

∽

My mother no longer drives, so two hours later, I am sitting in the dark at the parking lot of Winchell's Doughnuts on Eighth Street, waiting for her bus to arrive from Cripple Creek. There is a nearly full moon pouring down on the Peak, making the snow shine. I think again that the mountain is beautiful enough to make up for a lot of things I've had to face about living in Colorado Springs again.

I'm sitting in my mother's car, since she refuses to ride in anything else. It reeks of cigarettes and old leather, and I turn on the heater full blast and roll down the window. A man passing by turns his head and whistles quietly. Over the car, not me. It's a 1957 Thunderbird, turquoise, which Eldora has owned since it rolled off the lot, and it's in cherry condition since one of the last things my father did before he died was restore it, top to bottom. I'm fairly certain my mother loves this car more than she loves me.

I'm a little early, so I spend the time going through my purse, which I'm persnickety about. It's been a day or two since I've had a chance to organize it, make sure everything is in its place. There are three sections and two small, zippered pockets. In one section are my comb, lipstick, a small mirror in a rubberized pocket that keeps it from breaking, a fingernail clipper, and an emery board. All in their places. In the middle section that zips, I keep three pens with caps, a small notepad, and a calculator. The tops are off two of the pens and I replace them firmly, zipping the pocket. In section three is my wallet, and I open it to be sure all the cards are in their places—the grocery store cards in one section, the credit cards in another. I also keep my keys in the third section, but they're currently in the ignition.

In one of the smaller zippered pockets I keep a ChapStick and my cell phone. In the other, inside the bag, are the usual female supplies—I open it and look at the tampons and realize with a shock that I might not need them for a while. What would that be like? A hollow feeling goes through me.

The bus lumbers in. It's the early evening service, so everyone getting off is over the age of fifty. They go to gamble early before the casinos get too smoky and then return home by nine so they can take their evening medications and have a good night's sleep, the binging and ringing of slot machines dancing in their heads. The lucky ones are easy to spot. They're laughing and joking, jingling change in their cotton jackets.

I know when Eldora will be next because there is a handsome, Mediterranean-looking senior, dapper with silver at his temples, who gets off the bus and turns around to hold out his hand to the woman behind him. She steps down carefully in her high heels and slim slacks, her perfect red hair shining beneath the streetlight. Even in the dark, I can see her long acrylic nails, nails she has done every other week by a Vietnamese young man at the local strip mall. Technically, she's a senior like the rest of them, sixty-three, but my mother has been the most glorious female in any room since they laid her in a nursery and all the other fathers wished that she was their baby instead of the plain one they got.

She laughs her throaty laugh at something the man says and lifts a graceful hand in farewell. He'll think about her for weeks.

As she comes toward the car, she waves at me, too, but doesn't hurry her long-legged walk any. In the dark, it would be easy to mistake that body for one thirty years younger. Legs long as a spider's, shoulders straight and square beneath her neat, boxy jacket. A diamond at her throat catches the light and winks at me as she climbs in, smelling of bourbon and Tabu and cigarettes. "I," she says in her whiskey voice, "had a very good day."

"Did you?" I start the car, glare at her when she takes a cigarette out of the pack.

She makes a noise. "I haven't had one for two hours, India! And it is my car."

I put my hand on the gearshift and just look at her. She puts it back, snaps her case closed. "You are such a fuddy-duddy."

"Ah, well. So you won a lot, huh?"

"Six hundred dollars!"

I blink. "Wow. Was it that Monopoly machine?"

"No! That blasted thing isn't paying worth a squat these days. No, this was a quarter machine in the back of the Midnight Rose. It paid and paid and paid, and I finally hit the big one." She fidgets, opens her purse, closes it. "That nice man you saw at the bus was sitting right beside me, bringing me luck."

"Did you give him your phone number?"

"Oh, don't be silly. After Don Redding, all other men are just shadows."

Don is my father, who died six months ago. This pierces me because until he died, I never thought Eldora was particularly besotted, and I feel guilty for hoping she'll find another husband to dote on her so I'm off the hook. "Well, at least you got out and had a good time."

"I did. It was nice."

At a stoplight I hand her the postcard I got in today's mail. "I heard from Gypsy."

My mother looks at it, her mouth working as she tries to decipher it.

"Don't worry," I say, "I don't know what it means, either."

"I can't see the postmark in this light. Is it readable?"

"Tucumcari," I say. The word is layered with meaning. For me, for my mother, and for my poor sister, who suffers from schizophrenia.

Eldora is quiet for a moment. At a red light on Colorado Avenue, not six blocks from the house I grew up in, she says, "You know, I was thinking about her up there. Had a little brainstorm."

"Pray tell."

"You're gonna argue with me, so I don't want you to say yes or no right now, all right?"

"Mom—"

"Don't start arguing before I even say it!"

The light turns green, thank God. If I hurry I can be at her house before she gets it all out, and then I can pretend to forget about it. "Go ahead." I try to sound more patient than I feel.

"I want you to drive me to Las Vegas."

"No."

"I said don't answer yet. Just hear me out."

"No." What I don't say aloud is, *no friggin way*. No way am I driving across the country with my mother and her cigarettes and her penchant for bourbon on some wild quest that will lead nowhere.

"What I was thinking is that maybe we could look for Gypsy."

I ignore her. The house is straight ahead, a plain ranch style in Pleasant Valley, near the Garden of the Gods. My father bought it for her just after my sister and I were born, and it has quadrupled in value since. It's been paid off since 1979, so she's sitting on a small fortune. There is a light in the window, showing a crystal lamp shining on a red-velvet piano shawl that decorates the back of a chair upholstered in deep blue, one of the pockets of beauty that fill my mother's house. It looks welcoming.

Without waiting for her, I get out of the Thunderbird, lock the door, and head toward my own vehicle, a slightly less dramatic dark-blue Toyota sedan. Her high heels tap behind me.

"I can see you're in a bad mood. We can talk about it later." She nudges my arm.

"What?"

She leans her cigarette into the lighter she's had at the ready since she got off the bus, blows a plume of smoke politely away from me, and presses a crisp hundred-dollar bill in my hand. "Go to the spa for a day, sugar. It'll make you feel better."

"Mom!" I try to give it back, but she's already going up the walk, waving a hand behind her. "I don't need your money, I swear!"

"Oh, just take it, baby!" She turns around but keeps walking backward. The tip of her cigarette glows red. "That man's coming in to see you tomorrow, isn't he? Buy something wicked." She waves. "'Night!"

For a long moment, I stand there at the foot of her driveway, the bill in my hand. We all say this, but in my case it's true. My mother is a wacko with absolutely no sense of reality.

Las Vegas. I shudder.

CHAPTER TWO

India

There are no messages on my machine when I get home, just as there have been no calls on my cell this evening. That's because I have no life in Colorado Springs—a place I had vowed never to return.

Until six months ago I had a perfect life. A town house in the Capitol Hill area of Denver, a beautiful old place with twelve-foot ceilings and the original wood moldings, plenty of work pouring in, lots of interesting friends, many of them in the arts or the computer industry—a pungent mix when I stir them together at parties. I'm good at parties, which I say without arrogance. I love them; love the work of getting all the details just right, the food and drinks and people and music and settings. There are often people sleeping on my couch the morning after.

The good old days, I think, flipping through my CDs. There's the Frank Sinatra and Dean Martin I used for a Rat Pack party I threw last summer. We all dressed up in A-line dresses and turquoise eye shadow with false eyelashes and danced to Frank's love songs. It was great. I got the idea from my mother, actually, who'd spent quite a bit of time in the old Las Vegas and loves to share tales of Sammy Davis Jr. and Frank and all the others at the bar of the Sahara or the Sands. That's where she met my father, at the Sands, playing blackjack. I wonder if that's why she wants to go there now.

Tugging my hair into a knot at my neck, I keep flipping through the CDs. I don't want Frank or Dean tonight, and choose a Dido CD that's been a big favorite lately. I'm on a kick with female soloists—Natalie Merchant and Dido and k. d. lang. I tell myself it's because I can do my work while listening to it, not because I'm in love.

At that Rat Pack party last summer, my life had been exactly where I wanted it. Jack and I had had several long weekends together by then, one in Colorado, one in New York City; we were in the very first flush of a love affair—always the best part. My sister, Gypsy, had been stable and on her meds for more than two years. She'd recently been in town for an opening and had sold all but two of her paintings the first night. My father, eighty years old and vigorous enough to walk an hour every day, rain or snow, doted on my mother, leaving me free to live seventy miles away from her oxygen-sucking presence. I spoke to him on the phone the day after the party and he told me about a surprise getaway he was planning for her sixty-third birthday party.

Two days later, he went for his daily walk and collapsed beneath the Kissing Camels, dead from a massive heart attack. We all said the same thing—that if you had to go, that was the way to do it—but the reality has been difficult for me. It proved impossible for Gypsy, who went off her meds and disappeared two months ago, in spite of the fact that I'd seen it coming and tried to get her space in a boarding home for a little while. There wasn't anywhere for her to go—cutbacks in the state budget meant all the private facilities were full to the brim and then some.

And my mother simply retreated into a bottle. She's always been fond of her bourbon, but within a week of the funeral she was disappearing nightly into a fifth. Too much. Since my father once made me promise that I would care for Eldora after his death, I had no choice but to sublet the apartment in Denver and come back to the Springs to get her stabilized.

Which, happily, she appears to be. I've been thinking I can move back to Denver within a month or two. Go back to my perfect life. Work I'm actually crazy about. My beautiful apartment. Weekends once a month with Jack, alternating between New York and Denver, weekends that have been wildly romantic and never too threatening.

I think of the plus sign on the pregnancy test.

With Dido in the background, I sign on to collect email, and there is a satisfyingly huge amount of it. Here is where most of my social life takes place these days—online. There's a note from Jack, but I leave it to last and sort through the rest. Ads for penis enlargement and the latest letter from an alleged African minister begging for help go in the trash. I flag a discussion about writing and designing for the living web, collect all the business-related emails into a file for morning, when I'll be fresh enough to give them the attention they deserve.

There are a couple of chatty emails from friends in Denver. Alice is having a party on the twenty-fifth and wants the pleasure of my company. "C'mon, India," she writes. "We miss you! It's a forty-minute drive!"

There is another from Hannah, my best friend, she of the throaty voice and designer shoes. "What's going on, Redding?" she writes. "You've been ducking me for a week. Call me. Right now. I mean it."

I glance at the clock, pick up the phone. Hannah answers on the third ring. "Okay, what's going on?"

"Hannah, I am so sorry. I've just been swamped. Jack is coming tomorrow and my mother has been having me drive her all over the universe and I've been working my head off. How are you?"

"I don't believe you," she says. "You only do the recluse thing when you're upset about something. Are you depressed about Gypsy?"

It's a good cover, and I leap on it. I can't bear to tell her about the pregnancy test yet. "I am depressed about her," I say, and I realize that it's true. "I really thought she might make it this time, that she wouldn't get delusional anymore. It sometimes happens when people get to their forties and fifties."

"I know, sweetie." Hannah, a gallery owner, had been instrumental in getting Gypsy's work into the world, and she owns several of her paintings. "I think about her a lot."

"I got a postcard from her today, in our twin language. I'll save it for you—there's a pastel drawing that's just fantastic."

"How's Jack? How's your mom?"

"Fine and fine. My life is boring right now, Hannah. Tell me about yours. Have you met any interesting men lately?"

"Well," she purrs. "Now that you mention it, there are a couple of interesting prospects."

I smile. Hannah loves men and they love her back, but the prospects angle is a joke. A man caught her in marriage for three years in her twenties, and afterward she swore off marriage forever. Since she's nearly six feet tall, with red hair and natural, double-D breasts, there probably won't be a shortage of suitors anytime soon. "Tell me," I say.

She does, and I'm happily enfolded in her adventures for a while. By then, I'm ready for bed and the email I've saved for last. It's from Jack and it's only one line: "I am thinking of the red shoes with great pleasure."

I'm seasick again and put my head down on the desk.

~

It's funny how the moments that change your life sneak up on you. The night I met Jack, saucer-size feathers of snow were falling out of a heavy pink sky. I walked to the pub, not minding the kink the moisture would give my hair. There's nothing quite like the soft air of a falling snow. Light from the pub, with a proper Irish name—O'Connell's—spilled yellow onto the sidewalk through a mullioned window. I could hear the rush of voices inside, and there was an agreeable sense of happiness in my chest. New work. That was what I was thinking about.

We'd only communicated by email, Jack and I. He'd seen my web designs and wanted to talk to me about putting together something for his magazine, a publication for adventure travelers. I had a picture in my mind of a jowly Irish American, an Ernest Hemingway type, hard drinking and hard living, with fists like hams and white hair. It was some face my brain sent up from central casting to go with "Jack Shea, magazine publisher and outdoorsman." He'd been skiing at Aspen and had hired a car to bring him into Denver for the night.

All great for me. It was plain he had deep pockets and wanted a substantial site.

I pulled open the heavy wooden doors to the pub. Air heavy with a heady mix of cigarettes and alc, perfume and old nights enveloped me. From the jukebox came the sound of a heavy fast Celtic drum, which lent a sense of excitement to the room. It was crowded, but I'd asked him to meet me by the main taps, and I pushed through the college students and businessmen.

Spying Jack, I knew right away it was him, even though he was so very different from the picture I'd had in my head. He had a pint of something dark in front of him, and he wore a black leather jacket with many years of wear on it, not battered, but comfortable to the last degree. He was digging in the pocket of his jeans for a bill to give the bartender, and a lock of that thick black hair was falling on his face. I had a glimpse of a sharply cut white cheek, and light glanced off the crown of his head, and I swear, it had been years and years, but my heart flipped.

It scared me. I stopped and thought about leaving. I stood there for a minute, waiting for him to raise his head. His nose was strong and straight, that elegant right angle, and his mouth was generous, which is a sort of requirement of mine.

What surprised me was the aura of rough-and-tumble about him. The well-worn boots, the jeans, the scuffs on his leather coat, his too-long hair. Not a bad boy—he was tougher than that. Bad boys were posers where he came from.

And how do you know all that about a person in three seconds? I don't know, but we all do it. And sometimes we know we're right.

I had the advantage when he looked up and saw me. His face didn't show a damn thing, but his eyes—and this was the first time I'd seen them, so clear and even a gray, the exact color of the ocean on a cloudy day—flickered.

He said, "Your picture does you no justice."

"You're Irish Irish," I said without thinking.

One side of his mouth lifted. A thin white scar cut through his left eyebrow. The eyes were spectacular up close, flecked with darker gray. "So I am. Galway."

"Sorry," I said, and stuck out my hand. "That was pretty idiotic. Jack Shea, right? I'm India Redding."

His hand went around mine, white and strong, with scatters of dark hair on the back. His nails were clean, oval, neat; a contrast to his hair, which seemed curiously untended, a little shaggy, too long across his forehead. The blackness pointed up the gray of those eyes, which were having a conversation with me, sweeping my face, my lips, my breasts—but in the right way, admiring without leering.

He looked at me. Not politely. Not with any expectation. Just looked, and I felt it all through me, as if he really could see everything I was, all I'd ever been. After a moment, he lifted his chin. "I am very pleased to meet you, India."

I admit it, the accent slayed me. Who could resist that brogue, ruffling the Rs and frolicking through ordinary words like "very" and "pleased." I gave a passing imitation of someone with a brain, however, and gestured him toward a booth. "It will be quieter over there. We can talk about what you're looking for."

He followed me over. Not so tall, I noticed, but graceful, light on his feet. We settled across from each other, both of us shedding our coats, then leaning forward over the table. There was a moment of collision, almost shocking, when our eyes met. I was arrested for a moment, and the air was thinner—all those things that sound absurd. Wonderful. Terrifying. Electric.

"Well," he said, clasping his hands around his glass, "I'm flummoxed. You're beautiful, and I don't know what to say."

I smiled at that, ease coming back into my chest. "So are you."

"Now that I know is a lie," he replied, and I noticed his finger stroked the scar on his eyebrow. "But it's a nice one, so I thank you."

We made small talk until the waitress brought me an ale. I was going to order Guinness, but I was afraid he would think I was trying to curry favor, and ordered a microbrew instead. The waitress cooed over him.

"I just love that accent," she said.

"Thank you." He smiled at me, and cocked his head a little as she left. "It's Irish Irish, you know."

In my younger days, I would have blushed. Instead, I inclined my head in return, smiling to acknowledge his little insider joke. "Now, how can I help you, Mr. Shea?"

One brow lifted. "Well, Ms. Redding, I'd like a web page."

I had a steno pad and took notes. It was a quick, straightforward exchange; he spoke clearly and directly. I asked for clarification, he gave it. I sketched, he shook his head; I sketched again, he began to nod, tapped the page with his index finger.

I leaned back, poked the page with my pen. "The demographic is not the twenty-something, then. You're looking for a market share among an older set."

"Exactly. A fit fifty-year-old who wants to hike to Machu Picchu or take an adventure cruise in New Zealand."

"Excellent." I sipped the ale, made a note to myself to check some of the other magazines in this age group. "What about the financial demographic?"

"Sensible, not luxury."

"Arthur Frommer, not Condé Nast?"

Again that quirky half smile. "Right."

"Interesting. I think I can come up with a few ideas for this. I'll require a retainer, but it will apply toward the final bill if you hire me."

"Fair enough. I'd also like you to meet some of my staff and get their ideas as well. Is that possible?"

"In New York?"

"Sure. It shouldn't be a long trip, but it should be face-to-face. I'd be happy to put you up—we keep an apartment."

What the heck. I hadn't been anywhere in ages, and it would be tax deductible, and, well, how awful would it be to listen to him talk a little more? "I'm sure I can arrange that."

"Good." He raised a hand for the waitress, and patted the note-book. "End of business, then. We'll just be ourselves now. Is that all right? May I call you India?"

"Please."

When the waitress appeared, he said, "What'll you have?"

"I didn't want to be patronizing before," I said, and grinned, "but I'd really like a Guinness."

A little breeze of surprise over his mouth. "Make it two." When she'd gone, he said in that musical way, "My kind of woman."

"Tell me about yourself," I said, leaning forward. "You're from Galway. How did you get here?"

"That is a long and tangled story, girl."

"All right. Tell me a little bit of it then."

He fingered the scar again, and seemed to notice me noticing. "Beer bottle when I was seventeen." He mimed fisticuffs. "I had a bit of a temper in those days."

"Rakish. You could be a pirate." The pints of Guinness came, black and frothy. I sipped mine and sighed. "They always say it doesn't travel well, but it tastes fine to me. I love it."

"It's better in Ireland, but it's not so bad here." He raised his glass. "Cheers."

I clinked the glass. "So you were a wild young man?"

"Sure, I was," he said. And he spun a tale, cheerful and funny, of his youth in a neighborhood of council houses in Galway. His father worked for the rail yard, his mother as a clerk for the local grocery.

Both were quite religious and dragged him to Mass far too often for his pleasure. There were seven brothers and sisters, of which he was the eldest. "There were too many of us in that house, and I signed on with a freighter going to Australia. Didn't have to go to Mass anymore."

I laughed.

He traveled the world and made his way into travel writing, and made a good living for himself.

The story unrolled in a droll voice that poked fun at himself and his life, and had the ring of an oft-told tale, which I didn't mind. It was funny and punctuated with bits of trivia. On a trip to San Francisco, for example, he fell to drinking with a group of young computer geeks. He did an article on them, and one sent him a thank-you with an offer to invest in a software product they thought would revolutionize certain business practices.

Jack paused, lifted his glass. That heavy lock of black hair fell on his forehead and he tossed it off. "It was a bloody coup. I made a fortune. Bought the magazine, and here I am."

"Never married?"

"Sure, I was married." A darkness crossed his face, the expression I recognized could probably be thunderous. He said, "Everyone marries, don't they? But I prefer not to think about it."

"Fair enough."

"Now your story, India. No husband? No children?"

"Nope. Not interested."

His gaze went through me, seeking the truth of that. I didn't look away. "Unusual."

I told him then, up front. "I have a twin sister who suffers from schizophrenia. It seems wiser not to have a child."

"I see."

Something was drawing me under his spell again. The agreeable atmosphere, the shimmer of those gray eyes, the lure of putting my hands in his hair. I wanted to touch him, very badly. I wanted even more to kiss him. He looked at my mouth.

Bad idea.

"I think I'm going to have to get going," I said lightly.

"So soon?"

"Early morning," I lied. I was afraid if I stayed I would end up sleeping with him. A very bad idea, considering how much I wanted the contract to design his web pages. I stood, held out my hand. "It's been wonderful talking to you, Jack. Really."

He dropped some bills on the table. "I'll walk you out."

So we put on our coats and went out into the saucer-size snow-flakes, falling like fake snow to lie in little fluffy piles in corners. I held out my hand to shake his, and he gave me that little half smile as he accepted it.

Then he drew me forward, closer and closer, just our hands held, and he lifted up his other hand and cupped it on my face.

And kissed me. His mouth was hot as a bubbling dessert, sweet as blackberries. A voice in the back of my mind said, *Be cool, be cool,* but instead I moved a little into a more comfortable position, and put my arm around his shoulder, and we kissed some more.

I finally raised my head. "Um . . . I have to go."

He moved his thumb over my lower lip. "I'll see you again, India. Good night."

CHAPTER THREE

India

The next morning, I'm sitting on my balcony drinking a cup of tea to settle my stomach. It is not my imagination that it's upset and morning sickness-ish, because that was one of the reasons I bought the pregnancy test. Sick every morning the past week, which started to be difficult to ignore.

It's early April, and there is spring along the edges of the world, a hint of green in the valleys, a certain thinning of the brilliant winter white of snow on the Peak. I have to wear a jacket and my fuzzy socks, but the air is so clear and light, it's worth it.

Not that I'm particularly happy about the view.

I'm absolutely furious this morning. Furious at my body, furious at the breakdown of contraceptives, just plain freaking furious. It's not like I haven't been trying to prevent it—and not without a fairly high cost, I must say. I am unable to tolerate hormones—birth control pills gave me bruises; Depo gave me the endless period from hell, and after that they wouldn't let me try Norplant. I'd had an IUD, quite happily, for some years, but I developed an allergy to copper and they had to take it out. In the meantime, I have been struggling to find something that would work reliably until they let me have a new one. I had even considered getting my tubes tied, but in the end decided not to. A friend had asked me at one point why I didn't just give up sex if I was so worried about it, and she had a point. But that's not fair, either, is it? Not to mention unrealistic.

The only thing left was a cervical cap, and it seemed to be doing a good job.

Until now. But that's always the way, isn't it? They're fine until they're not.

The phone is lying beside me on the table. When it shrills in the quiet morning, it scares twelve years from my life. I check caller ID. My mother, but I answer it anyway. "Hey, Mom. What's up?"

"Did you have a good night's sleep, sweetheart?"

I roll my eyes at the sound of her dulcet tones and settle back to be wheedled and cajoled. "Good enough, I guess. How about you?"

"Like a baby!"

"Good."

"Did you think any more about my trip idea?"

"No. I told you last night I'm not going."

"Will you at least hear me out? I thought about it some more, and this could be good for you."

"Really."

"Don't sound so skeptical."

I can hear her exhaling into the cold morning, imagine I can see her leatherette cigarette case beside her on the railing. Suddenly, I have no patience. "Mom, what's this about, really? Why can't you gamble in Cripple Creek?"

"I just want to go. I want to remember. Is that so bad?"

"No. It's sweet, actually. But why don't you just let me put you on a plane?"

"I want to go in the Thunderbird. You won't let me drive by myself, and I have to tell you, darlin', that I don't really want to go alone."

"I don't have time right now. I'm behind on my work as it is."

"Hmm," she says. Inhales. "I think you might need a break, to tell you the truth. It could be fun, India. You've never been there, have you?"

Why would I want to? I think, but aloud I say only "I'm not a gambler, Mom."

"I could show you around the old Las Vegas—we could go to the Sahara and the Riviera. Just hang out."

"Hmph."

The rest of her pitch comes out in a rush: "And I really would like to look for Gypsy and I'd like to get away, and I think you need a break, and you're always talking about needing to get new ideas for colors and layouts and designs. Maybe it would be good for you to fill the well."

For one long moment I'm tempted, remembering the trip we made together—my mother, Gypsy, and I—in 1973. I think of Gypsy's paintings—tin crosses and plastic flowers, splashes of turquoise, and that vivid fuchsia and neon. A pressure in my chest makes it hard to breathe and I say, "No, I don't think so."

"You know she always turns up down there." She pauses, uncharacteristically, and when she speaks again, her voice is quieter. "Maybe, just once, we can find her and bring her home before something terrible happens."

A fool's errand. We'll look and look and never find her and break our hearts wondering where she is, if she's warm, if there is anyone taking care of her. But how can I just say no? "I'll think about it. Right now, I have to get off the phone and get ready."

"Oh, that's right!" she says, and I know very well she hasn't forgotten. "Jack is coming in this weekend, isn't he? Will you have time to come by and let me meet him this time?"

"Mom, it's not that serious. I don't want to give him the wrong impression."

"Oh, it doesn't have to be anything like that. Good God. I'll just serve cocktails and you can be on your way. He just sounds kind of interesting." A coquette's laughter rolls through the line. "It's been a while since I had a chance to flirt a little bit."

"Yeah, since yesterday."

"Oh, but he was old."

"Gotta go, Mom."

"All right, all right. Think about it, okay?"

"Yep."

CHAPTER FOUR

India

I love this part of my love affair: getting ready.

On Friday morning, I begin by cleaning the apartment, putting fresh flowers on the table, scenting the air with incense, and making sure all the candles are properly placed for later ambience. I've made chocolate-covered cherries from scratch, something my father and I used to do for Valentine's Day. Jack loves them. There is a fire laid, ready to be lit with a single long match, and I have a bowl of sweet grass to sprinkle over it when the coals are low. We'll have a chicken curry for supper, one of his favorites, and the fridge is stocked with the brown ale he prefers.

Now I shower, washing my hair and removing every stray hair on my body. My legs are as sleek as wax, my eyebrows elegantly arched. I rub scented lotion from my neck to my toes. On my ordinary body, which is growing a little thicker through the middle than I would like but seems to be a function of encroaching years—or perhaps sitting for hours unending at a computer screen—I wear black lace undergarments. The bra is French, very low cut, the panties as brief as a comma, the slinky chemise as gossamer as a dragonfly's wing.

Over all that, I wear a simple red sweater and jeans and the red high heels that make me feel tall and lean and spider-legged, like my mother, even if it's a long, long way from the truth.

And then I'm standing in the airport waiting for him, and every molecule in my body is primed for the first glimpse. My heart leaps every time I see a black leather jacket or glimpse a dark head in the crowd.

The rush never changes. It's been so heady that I've told all my friends they need to find a long-distance lover—it's all the good of a relationship: the romance and flowers and sexual rush, and none of the bad: the power struggles and push for commitment and bouts of flu.

I've decided not to tell him about the pregnancy test. Not while he's here this time, anyway. I haven't seen him in thirty-two days and we only have twenty-four hours, and I'm not going to waste any of it. It will be less volatile through email, anyway. I won't have to watch his face close, watch a wall rise between us, putting him forever on the other side.

It makes me want to cry. But the rules between us have been very clear from the beginning: no ties, no commitments, no discussions of our relationship, no probing questions about other lovers. I set it up that way, as I always do, and Jack, who had a terrible divorce five years ago, agreed quite heartily.

On the concourse in the airport, I spy his figure and it hits me all over again. I don't fall in love, but I am in serious lust with Jack Shea, and judging by the longing looks thrown at him by passing women, I am not alone. And it's funny, but it's not that he's so devastatingly handsome. He's forty-seven, after all, and every minute of that shows on his craggy face. He's not particularly tall, either, only a few inches taller than me, and not even that when I'm wearing the red shoes.

But there he is, walking up the ramp toward the waiting area, a man with black wavy hair, dressed in slacks and a well-worn black leather jacket, a bag casually thrown over his shoulder. I love the way he moves, the easy glide of his steps, the way he smoothly sees the little girl dashing in front of him and reaches down to touch her shoulder before she falls.

Then he catches sight of me, and his face brightens. Even from a distance, it seems I can see the ocean-gray of his eyes, the lift of one side of his mouth, the pleasure he finds in looking at me, imperfect as I am. As he comes closer, he makes a play of looking at my feet, and winks at me.

Then he's there, taking my hand, leaning close to smell my neck, making a long, warm sound in his throat. "God, you look beautiful," he says, and there's the killer voice, that Irish accent and vibrant tenor. The smell of him, like a morning wind, wraps me close, and my heart is swelling twelve times its size. I kiss his cheek, discreetly. Public shows of affection embarrass him, but what I'd love to do is throw my arms around him.

I can't wait until we're at the car, and we've settled his bag in the trunk of my Toyota. Then he glances over his shoulder, mischief in his eyes, and says, "Come here, and let me kiss you."

And this, too, is a good part of having a long-distance lover. That first kiss after parting—the lingering drink of the longed-for lips, the soft cries of surprise and hunger. His arms around me, mine around him, my discovery, so rich every time, that he fits me exactly right. My hips are soft by the time we're done. He lifts his head, his hands close on the small of my back. There's a twinkle in his eye. "You wore your red shoes."

"Just for you."

"And what else?" His hand moves upward, under my jacket.

"You'll have to wait and see."

"Is it black?"

"Maybe." I chuckle, brush hair from his forehead, liking even the feeling of his brow against my fingers. "You are so predictable."

"Mmm," he says, and takes my hand. "Then you should know what I'm thinking now."

I laugh. "Does it have anything to do with piles of pillows?"

His fingers tighten. "Yes, sweetheart."

In the car, he holds my hand, his thumb moving over the heart of my palm. We talk of inconsequential things, his flight, some work details. He asks about my mother and I ask about his secretary, who had pneumonia.

Inside the door of my apartment, he reaches for me, and we're kissing like sixteen-year-olds, deeply and with great pleasure. One difference: Jack is ever so much more skilled than a sixteen-year-old. I thought I knew all there was to know about sex after twenty years of it. From the very first kiss, I felt it in him—a particular passion, intent, something. I have puzzled over it a thousand times and still can't name it.

And I don't have to. He walks me backward into my bedroom and we leave a trail of clothing—his shirt, my sweater, his belt, my jeans. He halts by the bed to admire and touch the black garments, looks with huge enjoyment at my feet in the red shoes that I've left on for him, and raises his head. "God, I love being with you," he says, and then shows me how much.

I put my hands in his thick hair, smelling the scent of him, wondering if this is our last weekend together. If I will have to give him up. Perhaps because of that it's all the sweeter, touching him, being with him. I press details into my memory—the silky length of his back, the whiteness of his lower belly, the look of his face when he lies beside me, his hair a tumble, his eyes closed. He doesn't fling himself away after sex as so many men I've known will do, but always holds on, as if that, too, is part of the pleasure. I've not yet slept a single night with him that I didn't wake up and find his body wrapped around mine.

～

Once our initial lusts have been slaked, we shower lazily together, then head for the kitchen to make supper. He's happy with the ale I've stocked. "You don't want one?" he asks in surprise.

"I've had a little bug or something." I had decided upon the lie to both hide my reluctance to drink until I make up my mind what I'm going to do, and to cover the possibility that I might be ill in the morning again. "Alcohol is not agreeing with me."

He leans close in concern, touching my head. "It was likely a fever for me, sweeping you away."

I chuckle. "Ah, that's it."

He puts The Corrs on the CD player and cuts the chicken up for me, since cutting meat seems to be one of those things that makes my hands hurt these days. Too much keyboarding, though I'm careful to protect my hands as much as possible. I chop the onions.

When they're simmering in the curry mix, he opens another ale and spies the card from Gypsy. "Isn't this your sister's work? Do you mind?"

"Go ahead." I cross my arms as he studies the painting.

"Extraordinary how she sees."

"It is. I often wonder if it's her illness that makes her vision so unique. And if it is, then—" I lift a shoulder, leaving the thought incomplete.

His eyes are steady on my face. He nods, then flips the card over. "What language is she writing in? I don't recognize it."

"No one does," I say with a smile, "we made it up when we were little."

"No kidding? I've heard of that, but I've never known anyone who'd done it. Can you speak a little to me?"

"I don't remember it. Wish I could."

He puts the card down and brings his body close, his arms on either side of me against the counter. "It isn't your fault, you know." He kisses me, softly. "Not remembering."

"I know."

He closes his eyes, kisses me again, murmurs, "I'll be remembering this next week when I'm in all those wretched meetings."

"Me, too." And I will. I'll be in the middle of something next Wednesday and his face, in just this moment, with the pale gray kitchen light falling on his eyelids, his black lashes, his craggy cheekbones, will come to me. I'll think of the taste of his mouth, which never hurries away from mine. I'll think of this slow, lovely, meditative way he has of kissing me, and I'll want him with me, doing it again. Impulsively, I hug him. "You are really something, you know that?"

"I do," he says lightly and we part to change the music.

An hour later, I'm getting ready to make the rice when my doorbell rings. Since I really only know one person in Colorado Springs, I don't have to guess who it is, and I look up at Jack and roll my eyes.

"What is it?"

"Not a what. A who." The bell rings again and I give him a wry smile. "My mother has decided she's going to see you for herself."

"Lovely," he says, and it's not sarcastic. "I've wanted to meet her."

"That's what you think." I go to the door, and pull it open. She's standing there, looking innocent, every inch of her perfectly groomed. "Hi, Mom. How did you get here?"

"My friend Candace dropped me off," she says without a trace of guilt, and she holds up a bottle of Irish whiskey. "I brought a present."

It's classic Eldora, and I have to grin. "Come on in," I say, and wave her into the living room. Jack, standing by the table, drying his hands on a cup towel, blinks, just once. I've seen it a zillion times.

Men love my mother.

Eldora smiles her dazzling smile, blinks her Elizabeth Taylor eyes, and in her throaty, rich, sexual voice, says, "Hello! You must be Jack. I brought you a little present. I hope that's all right. Americans always get things wrong, don't they, but I asked what the best Irish whiskey was, and the man seemed to know what he was talking about."

He accepts the bottle, tossing that lock of hair from his forehead, and says with great approval, "Very nicely done."

"Jack, this is my mother, Eldora Redding. Mom, this is Jack Shea."

"I've heard so much about you," Eldora says.

"All good I hope." He meets my eyes, and I see his are twinkling. Brightly.

"Oh, yes," she says, putting her oversize purse on the table.

"I need to get the rice on," I say. "Let me get you some glasses and you two can have a cocktail. We're going to eat in about twenty minutes, Mother. Would you like to stay?"

She shimmies out of her elegantly cut wool jacket, displaying a green silk blouse that somehow makes the most of her pretty shoulders and long neck. "No, thank you, sweetie. Candace is coming back in a half hour, and we're going to see a movie."

From the kitchen cupboard, I fetch two highball glasses. "You want water?" I ask Jack. He waves a hand.

Eldora pours a generous measure for each of them, and lifts her glass. "Cheers," she says with a smile, and taps his glass.

He gives her the lopsided grin I love so much, and toasts her in return. "To a beautiful lady."

He's in good hands and I go back to the kitchen, half listening as she questions him in the most charming possible way. "Tell me about Ireland, Jack," she says. "I've never been there. Would I like it?"

And of course, he's hooked, spinning tales for her of his Galway, which anyone who knows him for more than three minutes knows he misses like an amputated leg. I measure cold water and rice and set them to boil, leaning on the counter, listening.

Eldora weaves her special magic, with her purring, cigarette- and whiskey-ruined voice, her low, appreciative laughter. Jack leans one elbow on the table and tells a story of the mythical princess, Galva, who drowned in the River Corrib and gave the city its name. My mother listens intently. Jack responds with wider gestures, a broader accent. That lock of dark hair falls on his forehead, and he gets the glow. The Glow.

For one tiny second, I'm eight and there is a cocktail party in the living room. My mother is dressed in a green sheath that cuts a daring V in the back, showing her smooth skin and slender shape. Gypsy and I will soon be hustled off to bed by the teenager hired for the chore, but for the moment, we, too, are dressed up in white patent leather sandals and matching floral-print summer dresses—hers yellow, mine blue. There are ribbons in our hair and we have been allowed to have a plate from the goodies my mother is passing around, cocktail wieners and one-inch sandwiches with some meat paste inside and Ritz crackers with tiny folds of ham on them.

I'm fixated on my mother, who is luminous and shining in a way I can never quite put my finger on. She stops and makes everyone feel good. I see how they smile at her, how she pats an arm, compliments a hairdo, how their eyes follow her—men and women alike—when she carries her tray to the next set. She halts before Gypsy and me, squatting in a ladylike way to offer us a little more. Her perfume wafts over us, and she winks. "How are the prettiest girls in the room?" she whispers. "Have some chocolate, babies. Don't forget to kiss me goodnight before you go to bed."

She's off again before we reply. Gypsy waits until she's gone and puts the chocolate-covered cherries on my plate, along with the Ritz cracker. She doesn't eat round food.

In my dining room, Jack lets go of a burst of laughter over a joke my mother's made. Drawn by the sight of him, by the fertile sound of his laughter, I drift around the breakfast bar and settle on a stool, on the edges of their conversation.

Eldora looks at me over her shoulder, raises one perfectly arched brow. "Have you ever been to Las Vegas, Jack?"

"Not yet."

"I lived there, you know, back when it was still Sin City. Oh, the stories I could tell you!" She sips her whiskey. "I've been trying to talk India into driving there with me. She doesn't seem to think it would be an adventure."

Jack sends a glance my way, sees my set face. "Ah," he says.

"Are you a fan of classic cars, Jack?"

"A bit," he says.

"My mother," I cut in, "has a 1957 Thunderbird, her pride and joy."

She is unperturbed by my stealing her punch line. "Do you know the model? This one is turquoise, completely restored, headlights to whitewalls."

"A beautiful car for a beautiful lady."

"India won't let me drive it, though."

"Mother," I warn. This is an area into which I do not want to venture. She hadn't driven in years—something to do with her eyesight, though I've never been sure exactly what—but after my father died, I took away her keys when I caught her driving drunk.

"Well," she says, straightening. "I'm hoping to convince her that a drive to Las Vegas would be just the thing to refresh her. Especially in that beautiful car."

The doorbell rings. "That'll be Candace," Eldora says, and takes a last swig of her whiskey as she stands up. I go to the door to let Candace in, a small, round Black woman of indeterminate age. They worked together for years as secretaries for Hewlett-Packard. "Hey, baby," she says to me, and gives me a kiss on the cheek.

"Why don't you go to Las Vegas with her?" I ask.

She gives me a look. "Not in this lifetime."

CHAPTER FIVE

India

We have our supper in front of the fire, Jack and I, and make love some more in the orange-flecked dark. Afterward, we lie skin-to-skin and talk, as we always do. About an imaginary house on a cliff overlooking the sea in Ireland, where we have border collies for him and a cat for me. It's an old game, never serious, but for the first time, I see myself with that black-ringleted girl on my hip, looking through kitchen windows to the rocky Irish coast.

Jack tucks a lock of hair behind my ear. "You're very quiet."

I take a breath, banish the imaginary child. "I was thinking of Gypsy, wondering where she is tonight."

"You don't seem to worry about her as much as I think I would," he says slowly. "How can you not go look for her?"

He means well—he's only known her when she's relatively healthy— and I roll up on one elbow. "She's done this so many times—the first time was when she was seventeen. She ran away from home and didn't show up again for five months. I was sick the whole time, couldn't sleep, couldn't eat. I ended up graduating from high school late because of it."

His eyes are still, his fingers twisting through a lock of my hair. "So it's survival for you. To keep it at a distance."

I lift a shoulder. "Pretty much. If I could save her, I would, but when you love someone who is as ill as she is, you have to make peace with some parts of it or you ruin your own life."

"Well, then," he says. "I'll light a candle for her. Saint Anthony of lost things, hmm?" He smiles, but I know he'll do it.

A lump grows in my belly. That's the other sad angle to all of this pregnancy business. Jack is Catholic. Not wildly, not going to Mass every Sunday or even once a month, but it's a steady thread through his life and world. It intrigues and bewilders me—I've never dated a man with religious leanings. But all I say is, "That would be nice."

His eyes crinkle. "Your mother is quite a character."

"Yeah, that's one way to put it."

"Was she a showgirl?"

I snort. "She'd love everyone to think so, but I'm pretty sure she was a cocktail waitress at the Sands."

"You don't know?"

"She tells a lot of stories, but her part in them is pretty vague." I shrug again. "It doesn't hurt anything to let her keep her little fantasies, right? And who knows, maybe she was having some luck getting into shows before she met my dad. Then she got pregnant and married him and they moved here."

"I liked her."

"Of course you did. You're male."

He draws a line down my cheek. "I liked her because there's much of her in you."

"That might get you killed, Jack Shea."

"She's charming and beautiful and outgoing. Just as you are."

I squeeze my eyes tight. "Trust me, the appeal wanes with time."

"You should go with her, India. Parents don't live forever."

His parents have not been gone long—his father three years ago, his mother a year later. I touch his craggy face. "I know."

"Let's go to bed where I can hold you properly."

This, too, is one of my favorite parts, lying in the quiet dark with him after our passion has been spent. Lying in my warm bed, with the quilts over us, his skin close against my own, he says, "I wish there would be a blizzard to snow us in together."

"Me, too. We could have fires all day and night."

His mouth brushes against my temple. "I could sleep with you for days."

He falls asleep, lulled by Irish whiskey and the quiet, and I lie there in the glow of the very small lamp, looking at him. His hand rests over my side, and I stroke his hair idly, memorizing his face. That strong, straight nose, the stubble that shows some silver, the creases around his eyes, and his black, black lashes.

Jack, I think, and fall asleep with my hand on his chest.

～

His flight leaves at three p.m., taking him on to California for those meetings he talked about yesterday. We laze around through the morning, making love one more time before we get up, amble through a big breakfast, then walk it off in a nearby mountain park, full of hills and valleys. It's rugged and wonderful, and it's one of my treats to myself to walk there, one of the few pleasures of being back in Colorado Springs.

A golden retriever escapes his leash and bounds up to us joyfully and sloppily greeting us. His master, a woman around my age, is running behind, crying out his name to no avail. Jack catches the dog's collar, chuckling, until she can catch up. "I'm sorry," she says, breathlessly. "He's a rescue and I haven't managed to get him trained yet."

"That's all right," Jack says, smiling. "He's a good fellow at heart." He rubs the dog's ears, receives a slobbering, adoring kiss for his effort. "Aren't you, boy?"

The woman hears the accent and—I've seen it a thousand times— perks up. "You're British, aren't you?"

"Not quite," he says with the same patient smile he's given the thousand others I've heard ask the question. Nothing charms Americans like accents. "Irish."

"Oh!" She smiles at me, to more or less include me, but then her bright blue eyes are back on his face. "Are you two living around here? I'm in a Celtic band. You should come listen to us."

"He's just visiting," I say. "I live close by."

"Oh, good. You should come hear us, at Killian's Pub. Thursday nights, eight o'clock."

"I'll look forward to it."

"I'm Irish, too," she says to Jack.

I swallow a smile, knowing he will ask, "Oh, really? From what town?"

"Well, we don't really know. We're Kennedys and O'Haras. My mother's done some research, but none of us have managed to get over there."

"You should go," he says politely, and we make a move to go around, but she keeps talking.

"I really want to."

Jack nods. "You should." He takes my hand and we make our way back up the hill. He gives me a secret smile and squeezes my fingers. "I'm a god," he says, his nostrils flaring. "Irish Irish."

"Indeed."

All too soon, it's time to take him back to the airport. We stand in my living room, hugging. Kissing a long goodbye, then hugging some more. "I hate this part," I whisper.

"So do I." He combs his fingers through my hair. "I wish . . ."

I pull back. "Wish what?"

For a long moment, he watches his fingers pulling through my hair, rubbing some between his thumb and forefinger. His eyes are changeable, a very cloudy color just now. He smiles slightly, then shakes his head. "Nothing." His arms go around me again. "Here we are, saying goodbye."

"Here we are."

"I'll call you tonight."

"I'll look forward to it."

"Maybe we don't have to leave so much time between every month, hmmm?"

I think of my secret. "Let's talk about that."

He sighs, kisses my ear. "I'd better go."

It's our habit that I should leave him at the departure gates, rather than pay for parking. He pauses for a moment, tossing that lock of dark hair from his forehead. "You should go with your mother to Las Vegas, India. You will never regret it."

"Except while I'm doing it."

He touches my neck. "I'm serious."

I nod. "I'll think about it, okay? I promise."

He's still hesitating. A car honks behind us, wanting into my spot, but I ignore it. It occurs to me that I might not see him anymore, not ever, and in case it might be true, I take three seconds to press all the details into my mind—the shine of light over the crown of his black hair, the angle of his tanned cheekbones, the cut of his mouth. He's looking back at me, his hand skimming my hair. There are silent words in the air, their weight heavy with their intent.

I love you, we say without speaking it. Then he kisses me quickly. "Be careful," he says, and he's gone.

～

This is the worst part of a long-distance affair—the night after he leaves. The rooms are not only just dull now, they're hollow with his absence. I fix a salad for my supper and watch the news with my plate in my lap, since there is no one to share the table with. Beneath the sound of the television is an echoey silence where I can hear a ghostly memory of Jack's laughter.

It starts to snow, big fat flakes, and the sight makes my heart feel empty with longing. I stand by the glass doors and watch it swirl out of the air, thinking of last night, and the fire, and Jack's broad chest. I wonder where he is now, if he's made it to his hotel yet, if he thinks of me on airplanes, or if I slip out of his thoughts the minute he leaves me. I wonder if there are other women in his life. Because he's going to be in San Francisco, I torture myself with a vision of a sophisticated brunette, a single businesswoman who travels so much she has frequent-flier miles on all the airlines, Marriott and Hilton honor cards in her wallet.

I fold my hands over my changed middle. No, he doesn't have other women, any more than I have other men. I don't know how I know it, I just do. He probably does think of me in my red shoes when he's on planes, when he's alone in hotel rooms.

That's also the beauty of a long-distance relationship. It keeps things electric.

The phone rings. With hope, I snatch it up, but it's my mother. "Hi, sweetie. Did Jack get on the plane all right?"

"Yeah, Mom. It's not exactly rocket science."

"Meow," she says. "Missing him, are you?"

I notice a bit of a headache behind my eyes. "I'm just tired. What's up?"

"Nothing, really. I just called to chitchat." There's a liquid purr to her voice, not yet blurred, but going there.

"I'm just about to take a bath and go to bed, Mom. Let's chat in the morning."

"Good God, India, it's not even eight o'clock." She lets go of an earthy laugh. "But I guess if I had such a sexy man around, I'd be tired, too."

"Mother!"

"Sorry," she says, but there's no regret in the word. "I did want to tell you that he's terrific, India. Really a nice man. You should hang on to this one."

"Mmm."

"You're grumpy."

"And you've been drinking."

"That's true, but I've been sticking to the three drinks rule, and then I'm going to bed." Ice clinks softly in the background. "D'you think any more about Las Vegas?"

"I don't have to think about it, Mom. I'm not going."

"You haven't even given it any real thought." She clears her throat. "I'm asking you for a favor."

I take a breath. "I know. Look, I really am tired and cranky and this isn't the best time to have this conversation. I'll call you in the morning, okay?"

"Will you think about it meantime?"

"Yes. I promise I'll think about it."

"All right then, sweetie. Go get some rest."

I hang up and carry my plate to the kitchen. I pass the spot where Jack and I stood last night, touching, kissing. My feet cross the place where his were standing.

I need to tell him that I'm pregnant. Soon. It makes me feel sick to my stomach again. In sudden inspiration, I sign on to the internet to check some facts.

By my calculations, I'm seven, maybe eight, weeks pregnant. That gives me three or four to decide what I'm going to do. Jack should be allowed to participate in the decision, but I have a week or so to continue to consider my options on my own first. I feel so conflicted right now that I'm not sure I can stand to have his conflicts on top of mine. Not just yet.

In my hand, the phone rings. The security screen shows 007, and I grin. "Hello, James," I say in a silky, throaty voice. "Mission accomplished?"

"I'm here, anyway. It was a miserable flight." His tongue rolls through the syllables, buttery and soft. "Overbooked, packed, and I couldn't get an upgrade."

I smile to myself, thinking it's funny that I can hear a man complaining and still love the sound of it. "Poor dear, flying coach like the rest of us cattle." I lean a hip on the counter, close my eyes. "How's the room?"

"Quite nice, really." His voice drops a little. "I'd like it better if you were here in the bed."

"Mmm. And what would I be wearing in that bed?"

"Red shoes."

I close my eyes, see myself as I imagine he must be thinking of me now, naked except for my shoes, and I think of the way his eyes glint at such moments. "And what would you do?"

"Are you lying down?"

"Not yet." I carry the phone with me toward my bedroom. "I'm lighting a candle."

"Hold on." The phone clatters down and I know what he's doing. I do it, too—strip out of my clothes and slide into the bed that still smells of him. The phone clatters and I smile. "Are you there?" he says, low.

"Yes."

"Naked?"

"Mmm-hmm. Wearing red shoes."

"Good. Now would you like to hear what I'm going to do to you?"

"Oh, yes."

And he tells me. In great, exact, luscious detail.

CHAPTER SIX

India

My mother is a Gemini, which means her mind lights on things for about three seconds at a time, then moves on to the next. There is no mention of Las Vegas when I call her the next morning. Instead she says, "Darlin', how busy are you?"

"Why?" I return suspiciously.

"I broke two nails last night going through my closet, and it's time for a pedicure, anyway. I got out my sandals. Remember the gold ones with the beads around the big toe from last year? I just thought of your dad so much when I put them on. I might want to get a new pair, really. It was pretty sad and—"

"So you want me to take you to the nail salon?"

"Only if you're not too busy."

"I can drop you off and come back." It takes hours for the full treatment, I've noticed. Once every three weeks. I shudder to imagine spending that much time and money doing nails.

"Mmm."

"What? You didn't expect me to sit and wait, did you?"

"Well, no, not really. I was hoping to give you a little treat, sweetie. Why don't you come in with me and have a paraffin treatment? I noticed you were rubbing your hands again the other night. They're hurting, aren't they?"

My hands always ache the slightest bit lately, a side effect of the constant keyboarding. And the paraffin treatments are heaven. "I don't really have time this morning, Mom. I have to get a rough outline of a site done by the end of the week."

"Well, then, how about late this afternoon? Knock off an hour early and we can go to the salon and I'll fix us some supper back here."

I think of Jack, telling me that parents don't live forever. I think of my father, asking me to take good care of her. I hear myself say, "Okay. I'll come for you around three-thirty. Make an appointment, though, so we don't have to sit around waiting."

"Aye, aye, Cap'n."

~

At the nail salon, my mother greets the shop at large in Vietnamese. They speak back to her in the same language, and a girl who looks about twelve, with tiny hips and tiny shoulders and tiny breasts, ushers Eldora to the pedicure chair. Everyone greets her. She asks about one's new marriage, another's cousin from California. They're eager to tell her everything.

Because I am Eldora's daughter, I'm also given a queen's welcome. Unlike her, however, I find the accent painfully difficult to decipher when the young man who is to take care of me tries to make small talk. It distresses me that I have to keep saying "Pardon me?" and I take refuge in silence.

Eldora has her toes done in fire-engine red, her nails in an extravagant french manicure that makes the most of her long fingers. She does have beautiful hands, I think, as we stand outside afterward and she smokes a cigarette. She wears several rings—a diamond engagement ring that glitters in the low afternoon sunlight, a ruby the size of a peanut, even a delicate thumb ring made of lacy white gold. "Would you mind," she asks, "if we ran an errand on the way home?"

"Not at all." The paraffin treatment has left my hands feeling loose and relaxed, and the rest of me seems to have followed. Not even the acrid smell of her cigarette is annoying just this moment. Nobody else's smoking particularly bothers me, actually. Only hers. "What do you need?"

"Well!" She blows out a plume of smoke, and gets a look of mischief around her eyes. "I've had the most wonderful idea!"

Thinking it's about Las Vegas, I give her a noncommittal, "Oh?"

"Yes." Her voice is breathy in that Marilyn Monroe way. "I have, well, I'd rather show you. I have some things in storage."

"All right." When she finishes her cigarette we pile into the Thunderbird and drive to the U-Store-It. It's fenced and bleak, and I nervously eye a pair of rough-looking characters at the end of the strip. Probably drug dealers, stashing bodies. "Mom, why do you have stuff in here?"

"Oh." She waves a vague hand. "It's just stuff I brought with me from Las Vegas. Never really knew what to do with it."

"Did my dad know?"

She's digging the keys out of her purse. "More or less. We didn't talk much about my life before he and I met."

I'm not sure I want to go there, but my mouth says for me, "Why not?"

She fits the key into the lock, her gold bracelet sliding around with a heft of diamond. "Some things are just better left behind." The door swings open. "Here we go."

There's not much inside except stacks of large, flat plastic storage boxes, the kind you can put under your bed. Through the pale-green plastic walls of the boxes I can see swaths of fabric—the hem of a green brocade, a fluff of what looks to be fur. "God, Mom!" I squat to peer at it more closely. "Is this mink?"

Her mouth turns up in a secret smile. "Yes, it is."

"Wow." I stand up, brush my palms off. "What do you want to take?"

"All of them, if they'll fit. If not, we can come back."

"What are you going to do with them?"

"Sell them!" Her long blue eyes glint happily. "I was looking on eBay the other night, and I just had a brainstorm! All that stuff from the sixties has come back into style, you know? The hairstyles and the drinks"—she waves a hand—"everything. On eBay they had a few vintage dresses, but nothing like these." She grabs a box, and the size is awkward enough she has to tilt her head around it. "Let's load up and I'll show them to you. You might even want first dibs."

In the end, it takes three round trips to get the boxes transported to my mother's house. We stack them in the living room, go back and get another load, and now stand in the lowering darkness of evening, our hands on our hips. "There must be dozens!" I say.

Eldora inclines her head, brushes the top of one box. "Fifty-two."

Everything I know about my mother seems suddenly thin as chiffon. "Fifty-two dresses."

She raises one elegantly arched brow. "Fifty-two cocktail dresses."

"What in the world did you need with so many cocktail outfits?"

"It wasn't like now, India," she says with a hint of censure. "Women didn't go out to the casinos in just any old thing. They dressed up. Always. That was my world, and I couldn't go out in the same ones all the time, now could I?"

"I guess not." I reach for the box on top. "Let's see 'em, then!"

"Wait!" She holds up her hands. "Let's do it right."

"Right?"

"Yeah. Let's see . . ." She snaps her fingers. "Martinis, and Frank Sinatra."

In spite of myself, I smile. She does love setting the mood. "You make the martinis and I'll put on the music."

She wiggles her shoulders happily and trots off to the kitchen. I bend over the prodigious number of CDs alongside the stereo, everything from Vivaldi to Patsy Cline to Frank, Miles Davis to Mendelssohn, all of them alphabetized. She seems a ditzy sort, my mother, but her taste in music is as vast and varied as her taste in books, and there is an entire bedroom devoted to her collection of books.

My fingers walk through the Sinatras, and I pull out a "Best of" collection, slide in the CD. As the smooth voice and tinkling piano pour into the room, I smile. "They call you Lady Luck . . ."

From the kitchen, my mother calls out, "Olives or onions, sweetie?"

And I remember that I can't drink anything. "Um . . ." It'll break her heart if I don't have at least one martini. But if—

"Onions, please." I'll pretend to drink with her. Pretend to sip, then pour it out into . . . what? I look around. There's an African violet in full, passionate pink bloom. Not there. "I need some water, too, if you wouldn't mind." I'll dump sips into the water glass.

Dancing slightly, I peer at the sides of the boxes. I see a splendiferous array of color and glittery fabrics.

I am seven, standing in my mother's bedroom, adorned in one of her beautiful negligees and a pair of rhinestone clip-on earrings and a pair of red high heels. In the full-length mirror, I am beautiful, as beautiful as my mother, and I incline my head the way she would.

Then, suddenly, she's behind me, and I start, whirling around, afraid she'll be mad. Instead, she smiles, sways toward me and tilts her head. "I think you need a necklace with that," she says, and plucks out a long rope of faux pearls from the treasure chest of her jewelry box.

"Here we are," she sings now, and hands me a perfectly chilled martini with three onions on a cocktail sword. Only my mother would have actual swords in her cupboard. She sips her drink and gives a sigh of satisfaction. "I'm not crazy about gin, but there's something so perfect about a good martini once in a while!"

"It's a Gibson if you put onions in it."

She waves a hand. "Whatever." Settling her glass carefully on a coaster, she puts her hands on her hips. "Now, where shall we start?" She bends over the boxes, running her long index fingernail along the sides, clearly cataloging which dresses are where. "Ah! This one." She takes the top two boxes off and puts them aside, and opens the lid of the third.

I'm struck by the expression on her face as she lifts out the dress on top. Her eyes are soft, misty, and the smallest of smiles turns up her mouth.

Then the dress itself steals my attention. It's sleeveless hot-pink silk, empire style, with a scoop neck. Literally thousands of tiny crystal beads cover it in a shimmer of light. "Oh, my God, Mother!" I cry, my hands reaching for it. "This is gorgeous!"

She puts it up to her body. "Wonder if they still fit me?"

"Oh, go try it on!"

Quickly she shakes her head, smoothes a hand down the skirt. "Not now." She holds it out to me. "Want to try it yourself?"

"I will if you will."

Her eyes glitter. "Dress-up?"

"Yeah."

So we open all the boxes and look at every last dress. I feel dizzy with the beauty of them, dazzled by sapphire and teal, by silk taffeta and chiffon. There is a dress in every color from ivory to black, mostly in bombshell styles that would have shown off her fabulous figure brilliantly, but also more demure numbers. One of my favorites is a bronzy design over silver lamé. The front is simple, fitted, and the back drops to a dramatic V. "You had a green dress like this."

"Yes, your father bought it for me. I was wearing this one when I met him."

"Really." I finger it. "Try this one on, then. Let me see you in it!"

She lifts a shoulder. "No, not that one. I don't think I can get into it."

It's difficult to choose which one I want to try, particularly because some of the waist sizes are positively minuscule, but I settle on an aqua taffeta. The fabric shimmers when it catches the light, turning blue and aqua and forest green by turns. The scoop neck is crossed over with a little flap of a collar and the skirt is modestly full. "That was always one of my favorites," my mother says approvingly. "It will look wonderful on you."

There are others, too. A black crepe with a chiffon neckline and satin trim, with the designer's name inside: Don Loper. "Isn't he the one on the Lucy show?" I ask.

Eldora, absorbed in shaking out a brilliant, Chinese red silk with a Mandarin collar, says, "Mmm-hmm. A lot of these are designer originals. You could get them at the end of the season pretty cheap if you watched."

She opens the last box and says, "Ah. This one." It's a soft blue-and-cream princess line, with a sweetheart neckline and floaty chiffon skirt. A scarf wraps around the bodice and joins the skirt. It's Pussy Galore through and through. I start to laugh. "They had to fall over dead when you wore that dress."

"You better believe it." She holds it against her. "I absolutely loved this dress. I wore it one night to the Sands." Her limpid eyes go misty as she looks back in time. "Frank was playing."

"The Frank, I assume?"

"Naturally." She sways, and the skirt floats around her legs. "I had some gold high-heeled sandals, and it was summer and I had a good tan, so I wore it without stockings." She closes her eyes, lets her head fall back. "That was some night."

For a second, I feel again that slight sense of disorientation over the woman standing in front of me, but there's another part of me skittering away from the vision. We're pretending here. "Put it on!" I say. "I'll try this one."

"Oh, India, I don't know." She touches her face. "I wasn't thinking of putting them on. I just thought I'd try selling them on eBay so somebody could maybe get some pleasure out of them. I thought you'd look nice in some of them, too."

"Just one?" I bend my knees, stand up again, like the little girl I was once. "Please?"

She grins. "Oh, all right. Don't ask me to look in the mirror at my age spots, though." She skims off her shirt right there, but I rush away into the bathroom and close the door.

The taffeta rustles as I pull it over my head. It smells faintly of some perfume I can't name. The bodice falls into place and I skim out of my jeans beneath the dress, pull up the side zipper. I tug a little at the waist, shift my breasts more fully into the magnificent bodice, and pull my hair into a knot before I turn around and look in the mirror.

Magic. I laugh aloud at the vision of myself—white shoulders luminous against the green-water shimmer of the fabric, creamy breasts framed like plump melons in the sweetheart neckline. But it's not slutty. It's Elizabeth Taylor—sensual elegance.

I can only imagine how my mother looked in this dress. She'd been what—twenty-two, twenty-three—when she wore it?

God.

I dance out of the bathroom on my tiptoes, imitating high heels, and my mother is struggling with the back zipper of her dress. I ballet-dance over, taffeta swishing around my knees, and pull it up for her. It slides up easily. If she's gained two pounds since then, I'd be surprised.

She turns around slowly, fussing a little with the scarf at the bodice, adjusting the fall of it. I can see she's embarrassed, which is a total rarity for her. "Oh, India, I feel silly. I haven't worn this dress in forty years. No woman my age needs to be in a cocktail dress like this." Her hand falls protectively over the top of her chest. "I have wrinkles in places that never occurred to me in those days."

But there in front of me is the mother I remember from my childhood—her slim shoulders, her prodigious bosom, her tiny waist, and pretty long legs. I take her hand, and hold it out, and curtsy before her. "Mom," I say, smiling, "you are still the most beautiful woman in any room."

"You're sweet," she says, but I see a dangerous emotionalism in her eyes. It's not booze-induced, either. She's been good tonight.

Then she blinks. "Oh, look at you, India!" she cries. "You'll have to take that one and wear it out to dinner sometime when you go to New York City."

Jack. He would love this dress. I feel a rush of excitement, followed by the big gut-drop of remembering my secret. I swallow. "Maybe I will," I say. "Let's put this one aside, anyway. And Mom, I've just had a great idea. Rather than putting the dresses on eBay why don't you let me design a website for you? We could write little stories about each of the dresses, maybe link to eBay if you want, but have it all go to your website."

"You would do that?"

I hate it that she really is surprised, that I've been so mean-spirited about things that she's honestly shocked when I want to do something nice for her. "It would be a blast, Mom. Truly."

She smiles. "All right, then. It'll be our little project."

CHAPTER SEVEN

Eldora, 1959

When India leaves, I pull out all of my favorite dresses and spread them over the couch, pour myself a new martini, and try them on, one by one. I can't bear to see myself in the mirror, but it pleases me that they still fit. The smell of Joy perfume comes out of the seams, bringing ghosts crowding into the room with me.

It gets to be a burden when your whole life is a lie. You start getting confused over what's true and what's not, what really happened and what didn't, which sins need addressing and which ones can be let go.

There isn't a soul on this earth who knows my real story. It's beginning to weigh on me. It's not that it's pretty—far from it. I have a lot to answer for, but even murderers need to confess, don't they?

I start the Frank Sinatra CD over again. Hear that? It sends an arrow right through me, every time.

It was such a different world then. I guess there were a lot of things wrong—I can see that. It's not such a great thing that the Black folks were living on one side of town and we were living on another. That Las Vegas was so racist back then. There were social problems. There always are.

But the world in those days wasn't nearly as grim as it is now. We were so innocent in so many ways. We were trying to get into space, and there was a sense of possibility, a sense that anything could happen.

Listen . . . you hear that light, lilting happiness in there, in his voice, in that piano? God, there's nothing like it.

Now, come with me, back in time.

We're sitting in the Copa Room at the Sands, and it's not some imitator, it's really Frank singing. It's dark and a cloud of blue cigarette smoke hangs over it all; in the background is the sound of the barman clanking bottles. I'm drinking a martini, with two olives. It's served so cold there's condensation on the outside of the glass, and each time I take a tiny crisp sip of it, a little bitty river of moisture makes a line through the frost.

I'm wearing a cocktail dress—a Castillo, bronzy over silver lamé. It leaves my shoulders and a nice swell of bosom bare. My hair is swept up into a french twist and around my neck is a single, winking diamond my prince gave me because I loved the one Elizabeth Taylor wore in Cat on a Hot Tin Roof. *I know, when I walk through the room, everyone is admiring me, men and women alike. It's a heady feeling. I sometimes just walk through the room to feel their eyes sliding over me, licking at the turn of my neck and the smell of my perfume.*

But tonight is different. Tonight there is a man with dark eyes who is staring at me and I am trying to ignore him. For one thing, he is much too handsome—thick dark hair swept away from his forehead, a strong nose, cheekbones flying upward, a bold jaw and clean chin. A beautiful, full-lipped mouth. He's wearing a white tuxedo jacket and black slacks, something of a uniform, I will learn, because the white sets off his darkness so beautifully.

And I know, looking at him across the room, that he knows the power of beauty, too. That sometimes he, too, takes a walk across a room just to revel in that gaze. I think of how I will look next to him, round and redheaded and white-skinned. There will be no one who cannot stare at us. I think of how our bodies will look together naked, and my knees go weak.

I cannot allow such a man into my life, but of course I do, and of course it is my undoing. As it is his.

I can close my eyes and see us now, his smooth dark chest with its beautiful scattering of dark hair, my breasts, white and plump with the tips so redly aroused. I see my flat white belly ending in red hair and my legs opening for him. I see him entering me, a strong healthy root of power, see his face flushed and dark with the moment, and—

Alex, Alex, Alex. God, I loved him. I never had another lover like him. For three years, we devoured each other. We were obsessed with it—with each other, with the delirium of our heady combination, with our passion, with having sex together. A thousand ways, a thousand places, a greed of fantasy and desire.

It was impossible to stop it once it began. It was impossible that we should not have come to a bad end. Real love needs grounding, some moments of ordinariness, or it burns like gasoline, hotter and hotter and hotter until everything is cinders.

But he's only one part of the lie that's my life. Just one. Layers and layers of them, and maybe, for me, I need to remember what's true and what's not.

Standing there in that Castillo, forty years later, I think of India with a pinch in my heart. She needs to hear my story. The real truth, and I truly do not know how she'll take it.

CHAPTER EIGHT

India

There is a message on my machine when I arrive home. It's Gypsy, a fact I can only make out because it's her voice. The message itself is unintelligible—the singsongy language of our childhood that seems to trigger nothing in me but frustration and confusion. It's long, probably five minutes, and I feel the pressure in my chest building and building and building the longer she talks. When it's finished, I play it again, closing my eyes tight and listening as carefully as I can to see if I can make out some meaning in her words.

I can't. I save the message, though. It's the first time she's spoken to an answering machine in the language, and maybe if I listen to it enough over the next few days, I might begin to remember. Or maybe someone else—a linguistics person, maybe?—would hear some pattern that will provide a key to deciphering it.

In the meantime, I can tell she's all right. Delusional, certainly, but cognizant enough to call, and although there's a certain excited sound to her message, it's more the excitement of happiness than the frenetic blur that would signal her "bad" voices are talking to her. She even laughed at one point, as if she'd told me something great or beautiful or even just amusing. Like, "I saw the most amazing canyon this afternoon! Wish you could have been here with me."

I think about calling my mother to let her know, but I could tell when I left that she was heading to her inner world and I don't want to talk to her when she goes there, shielded from the outside by her booze and cigarettes. It'll wait until morning.

It's odd that Gypsy is keeping in touch, I think, kicking off my shoes and going into my office to check email. There have been times she disappeared for months and we didn't know if she was dead or alive until she surfaced somewhere. This time, it's like she's on a vacation, her contact the normal sort of thing anyone on vacation would do: postcards, phone calls.

Maybe, I think with a stab of guilt, she wants us to come find her this time. She'd been stable on her meds for a long stretch before this disappearance. I was, in fact, foolishly convinced that she was cured, that she would be one of those people who just start getting better as they age, and never get delusional again.

As I flip through the queue of email messages, I find that I'm squinting at the screen, my eyes dry and tired. My whole body is tired, really. I could drop down a well of sleep and never reemerge. Jack hasn't called, which means he's likely in late meetings, and I don't want to end the day without talking to him for a few minutes at least. I flip through the CDs and put Natalie Merchant into the disc player, settle on the couch, and put my feet on the table. My hands fall on my lower tummy. It feels the same from the outside. Maybe a little harder or something. Taut.

Closing my eyes, I wonder how to tell Jack, but I haven't even formed the first theoretical method of telling him when a flash of gold lamé floats over my eyes. Then green-and-cream chiffon, black velvet, hot-pink taffeta, beaded turquoise silk.

I can see my mother in any one of them. Wearing stiletto heels and bare legs in the Las Vegas night, her skin smelling of Tabu perfume. No, not Tabu. That was something she wore for my father. Whatever it was that came out of the seams of those dresses is much more elegant.

The website could be fun. I can decorate it with paper doll images from the fifties and sixties, advertising art cut from ads featuring pink appliances. Drifting sleepily, I let images rise—those starburst shapes, a background of pink and gray. I want some neon, I think, in soft tones.

Suddenly, I see the whole thing, the full frame of the page, Eldora's Cocktail Hour in pinkish neon script against the pink and gray of a magazine layout. No, not quite. Maybe . . . Lady Luck's Cocktail Hour.

When the phone rings right beside me, my head jerks up out of a full sleep, and I blink heavily, trying to see the button to answer. "Hi," I say.

"Ah, have I wakened you?"

"Jack! No." My voice is too croaky to hide, though, so I say, "Yes. I must have fallen asleep on the couch. What time is it?"

"Ten. Are you all right?"

"Just a long day. I helped my mother get some dresses out of storage. They're amazing." I tell him about the designer cocktail dresses. "There are fifty-two of them. I cannot imagine how she afforded them."

"Not if your theory is true about her being a cocktail waitress."

I frown, seeing ripples of chiffon. "You know, she's never really said that's what she did. There's a general spirit of cheerfulness, and she spent a lot of time at the Sands and she had a woman friend who was a showgirl and was helping my mother audition."

"Surely, if she'd been a showgirl, she would have said so."

Suddenly, I consider my father's part in all this, the fact that she said they hadn't talked much about her life before they met. "Well, maybe. But she might have been in one of the early topless shows. My father would not have particularly appreciated that."

"She certainly has the figure for it."

A blip of jealousy zooms over my nerves, and I tamp it down. How ridiculous is it for me to be jealous of my sixty-three-year-old mother? Except that it's been this way my entire life, me living in her bigger-than-life shadow. Once in a while you just want to be the star yourself.

My silence must have stretched a little longer than I imagined, because Jack says, "What does she say about it?"

"I know she wanted to be an actress, and went to Hollywood. It didn't work out for some reason." I've heard the story a hundred times. "She was a small-town Texas girl—prettiest one, cheerleader, dance lessons, all that." I stand up and carry the phone with me into the kitchen, put the kettle on for a cup of herb tea. "She doesn't say she was the prettiest one, of course. She's not that vain."

Jack chuckles.

"I'm sorry." I take milk out of the fridge, set a cup on the plain white counter. "I don't mean to be rambling on and on about my mother. I'm just blown away by those dresses."

"Truly, it's the most interesting story I've heard today. I don't mind."

"So they were boring meetings?"

"You have no idea." In the background, I can hear him open a can, probably beer. "I'd rather hear about your mother going to Hollywood."

"All right. The story goes that she and another girl were recruited to a camp, a dance camp or acting camp, something like that, and Eldora's mother, who was a strict Southern Baptist or maybe Adventist, was very much against it. So my mother and her friend hopped on a Greyhound bus and ran away from home when they were seventeen. The family disowned her and she never went back."

"So you've never known her family at all?"

"Nope."

"It sounds like a movie."

The kettle begins to gurgle, and I dig through the stack of herbal teas. "On a side note, I just want you to know I'm being heretical here tonight. Red Zinger."

He makes a noise of horror. "Primitive. On with the story. She went to Hollywood, then . . . ?"

"I'm not sure exactly why she decided Hollywood wasn't going to work out, but she and her buddy started going to Las Vegas on these little junkets, and there were lots of opportunities. So they moved there."

The kettle starts to whistle and I grab it, frowning as the picture I've had in my head all these years wavers in light of those dresses. You could get them on sale if you watched, she'd said to me. "Hmmm."

"Yes?"

I frown. Poke the red tea bag with my spoon and watch it bounce back to the top of the water. "Designer dresses. That's all. How much would a designer dress cost on sale, even at the end of the season?"

"On that I have no opinion, sweetheart."

"Yeah, well, I'm a champion shopper, and I've never found a designer dress I could bear to purchase. Not a designer cocktail dress."

"Perhaps she had admirers."

"Oh, no doubt. There's the car, too, which she says a promoter gave her." A sudden thought pierces me. "Oh, God, Jack! What if she was a call girl? I mean a really high-class one, or something, but—" Then I think of my father. No way he would have fallen for a call girl, even the highest of the high class. "No, that's not it, either."

"Perhaps she was acting and dancing. Why have you always assumed that she didn't?"

"I'm not sure." I'm *not* sure. I mean, she has the body for it, that's for sure—all legs and chest—but she's not a dancer. She doesn't seem to really know about the shows. "Maybe I'm just being mean to her. Maybe I don't want to give her the benefit of the doubt."

"Mmm. Well, I expected someone different, after all the stories."

This sends a bristle up the back of my neck. Annoyance, irritation. Even my lover, who has till now claimed I was the most fascinating woman he's ever met, finds my mother more fascinating than me. "The stories are all true, you know." I stir my tea more violently than necessary. "It's just that men can never see her clearly because they're besotted on sight."

He laughs. "I believe, India, that you might be a little jealous."

"Jealous? Of a bombshell has-been who can't recognize she's old? Who still flirts with every man in sight—at the grocery store, the nail parlor—where, I might add, she has learned some Vietnamese in order to flirt more effectively with the staff there—even driving along the road?"

He says nothing into my pause, and I sip the tea, burning my lip. "Shit. I burned my lip."

"And so you should have," he says with a hint of laughter in his voice.

He's good at this, teasing me into a better humor. It's possible that I am . . . somewhat difficult, as Hannah has often said to me. I'd like to be nicer, better, different, but how do you change that?

"All right, you wretch. You're right. Maybe I am jealous, and catty because of it. But she's also a pain in the neck in a lot of ways."

"I know." His voice lowers. "You know what I think you need?"

"What?"

"My hands on your shoulders."

"Yeah? Lips on my neck, too, maybe?"

"Not for a while. Perhaps I'd even brush your hair."

I make a noise of longing. "Oh, you wicked, wicked man. Tell me about it."

"I would use a natural bristle brush," he begins, "and start at the crown."

"Mmm-hmm." I settle down on the couch and close my eyes, imagining as he describes it, how it would feel to have him brushing my hair.

⁓

In the middle of the night, I awaken suddenly and sharply. I blink in the darkness, trying to get my bearings. Coyotes are singing right outside, and I think it must be their voices that yanked me out of sleep. Intrigued by their proximity, I get up to see if I can see them. I pull the blind and peer into the darkness.

And catch my breath. Just below the streetlight in the parking lot, next to a red Ford Taurus, is a trio of them. They're smaller than I imagined, shaggy and dun-colored. One has a rabbit in his jaws, and one of the others lifts his narrow nose and howls at the sky. From a distance comes an answering yip—a sound of laughter.

Then they're gone, disappearing into the wilds of a field between houses. I have goose bumps on my arms.

Gypsy. I was dreaming of Gypsy when the coyotes called me.

She was standing in a graveyard, flinging her arms open to indicate the scene. "Look, India," she said to me. "Look at all this beauty!" And when I looked around, she was right. The sky over us was soft purple with coming rain, making the mountains on the horizon a rich blue. The graveyard was on a hill and the graves were piled high with flowers—all kinds of flowers, real and plastic, in orange and pink, white and blue. Pinwheels spun in the breeze, and the dolls and stuffed animals on the children's graves got up and danced. It was Day of the Dead, I knew suddenly. The crosses shone with some inner light, and even the shadows had a glitter like the lamé on my mother's dresses. "Gypsy," I said, but she just spun around in a private dance with teddy bears and baby dolls, her hair blowing in the wind.

There are tears flowing down my face now. She would tell me the coyotes had come to dance and sing for me, just as she was dancing in the graveyard.

Letting my head fall forward to touch the cold glass, I close my eyes and let myself miss her. I know where the graveyard is—high in the mountains of New Mexico, near a tiny village called Truchas. She's painted it a thousand times. We saw it the first time when we took our odd vacation with my mother in her too-small Thunderbird the year we were eleven.

In the distance, the coyotes celebrate the night. I raise my head. "Okay, Gypsy. I'm coming."

CHAPTER NINE

India

In the morning, I call my mother. "Can you be ready to go first thing tomorrow morning?"

"Go?" Her voice sounds raw, like she's smoked five billion cigarettes overnight.

"To Las Vegas? Have you forgotten?"

"No! Really, India? You'll drive with me? In my car?"

"Yeah. And we'll look for Gypsy. I had a phone call from her last night, a message in our language. I couldn't tell what she was saying, but I looked up the number on the internet, and it was a pay phone in Las Vegas." I pause, then add, "New Mexico."

"Did she sound okay?"

"Honestly, she sounds happy, Mom. Like she's on vacation."

"Maybe she is." She clears her throat. "I'll get ready. I'll need to get to the bank."

"All right. Figure out what errands you'll need to run, and I'll come over around three or so, and we can get it all done then."

There isn't a lot that can't be put on hold for a few days. I tend to work too much, a leftover from the too-hungry days when I was trying to get established and make a name for myself. I now have more than thirty regular clients, with new business coming in all the time, and lately I've thought an assistant to do some of the scut work would be nice. Just this minute, I'm caught up on most of the updates, except for one that I should be able to accomplish on the road via laptop. I'll have my evenings free, after all. My mother most often dives into a bourbon by seven at the latest, and is snoring by nine.

There is a new site I'm designing, but my deadline is weeks away. I'll bring the work with me and fiddle with it if the mood strikes, but as my mother pointed out, I've been tired and maybe need some creative meandering time.

In preparation for the trip, I pull up maps on the internet and print them out to study, circling the places we know Gypsy wanders. The names are lyrical and odd: Truchas and Tucumcari, Santa Fe and Espanola and Acoma. Twice, she has surfaced at a homeless shelter in Gallup. Once it was Tucumcari. And I know she goes to Truchas and Espanola, because she paints them, traveling a crooked, twisting route from Raton, through the mountains, into Santa Fe because she loves *descansos*. There are a lot of *descansos* on those high narrow roads.

Her travels echo the vacation we took with my mother when we were eleven. I remember the trip well, though I've never quite understood why it made such a deep impression on Gypsy. Why is it the root of both her distinctive paintings and her psychosis?

What surprises me, when I look at the route of that old trip on a map, is how nonlinear it is. I've never realized that Tucumcari is so far out of the way—miles and miles to the east of I-25, or even the tiny State 76 that we took through the mountains to Santa Fe. I try to figure out the best way to drive it all, and I have a headache trying to make it into any kind of sense.

"What the heck were we doing?" I say aloud to the empty room.

The map screen flashes advertising for Route 66, showing where Tucumcari stands on the old road. I notice that Tucumcari to Gallup is along the old Route 66. Much of it would still have been in place when we took our trip—or would it? A stir of excitement touches me, a lost world, one that touches my life, my sister, my mother. Paper place mats, diners, neon, all of it surges up from some lost box of memories.

Did I have a book of paper dolls from Route 66? I can't quite grab the vision and it slips away.

And it has no relevance to the planning of this trip, anyway. How had we gone in those days? I can't remember. It had been, in some ways, a miserable trip—squeezed between the seats, the sun beating through the windows, my mother smoking and smoking. I have a flash of her jaw, set hard, and Gypsy and I exchanging looks as we stopped at a gas station.

I shake my head. Where will we have the most luck finding Gypsy? That's where we should go first. Then on to Las Vegas.

Nevada, that is.

Slightly nauseous, I take a break to fix some cinnamon toast and stand at the counter, looking out my glass doors toward Pikes Peak. This afternoon it looks like a movie set, painted in blue and gray and white against a piece of plywood propped against the sky. The scent of the toasting bread curls out to tease my tummy. The sleep and the hunger at least make sense to me now—for a while there, I was afraid I was dying of some dread disease.

Instead, I am only pregnant.

Only.

Once a day, I let it in, the panic. What am I going to do? I have to make some choices, and soon, before there are no choices open to me. I have to tell Jack, too. I could, if he were someone else, have an abortion and never say anything about it. But I'd have to be someone else, too. Whatever happens, he needs to know.

It makes me miss him acutely.

Enough panic. I put the dish with its toast crumbs into the dishwasher, brush off my hands, and go back to planning the drive. As I do, I set a deadline: By the time I come back, I will have to decide what I'm going to do about the . . . situation.

~

By the time Jack calls that evening, however, the primary subject on my mind is the trip itself. I'd sent him an email earlier in the day, letting him know our basic plans.

"I'm insane," I say without preamble. "Insane. This is the stupidest idea I've ever had in my life. What in the world made me think this would be okay?"

His chuckle is low and soft, and immediately the tense muscles in my neck ease the slightest bit. "You'll be thankful later."

"Yeah, way later. Can I complain for a few minutes about this wretched route?"

"Surely."

"For God knows what reason, we have to go billions of miles out of the way to Tucumcari, which is in the wilds of eastern New Mexico, where nothing lives except walking stick cactuses and coyotes. Then we have to go up to the mountains to this weird, scary little town in a part of New Mexico where the bloodlines go back to the conquistadors and they speak a weird variation of Spanish that's as archaic as the English in the Appalachians. Then we'll have to stop in Espanola, which is a mean, unfriendly place."

"Maybe you'll find her in Tucumcari."

"Maybe." A headache burns at the base of my skull. "Ugh. This is crazy."

"Take it one day at a time, sweetheart. Just one step at a time."

I nod. "Right. God, it's good to hear your voice. How was your day?"

He makes a dismissive noise. "Boring meetings. I'm tired of the road, of hotel rooms, of restaurant food. I would rather be there, sleeping with you tonight."

"I'd like that, too." And I remember something he'll like. "I saw the coyotes last night! It was so cool."

"You saw them? What were they doing?"

I tell him the whole story. "It was magical."

"I wish I'd been there." His voice is sincere. He adores everything about the west. Even tumbleweeds, which I tease him about. Anyone who has ever had a pile of tumbleweeds collect in a corner, grabbing every stray bit of paper in the universe, or tried to yank one out of the ground while still living, has no illusions about the noxiousness of the creatures. But Jack loves western images. Tumbleweeds, coyotes, gunfighters, saloon girls. Everything. I smile to myself. "I'll bring you souvenirs, shall I? A six-gun in a holster, an Indian headband?"

"I would like that, sweetheart."

We talk for a little longer, and I feel the weight of my secret growing, tugging at my longing for him, my yearning to keep it just as it is, never cross that line. But I feel guilty, too. I see his craggy face, the gray threads at the temples of his hair, the way it gets too long because he gets busy.

What I want to say is, Jack, did you know I've fallen in love with you? Instead I say, "Jack?"

"India?" he says, lightly mocking.

"I need to tell you something."

A pause. "Is it bad?"

I'm not sure how to answer. "Um."

"You've met someone." He says it matter-of-factly. Without expression.

"No." There's a close knot in my throat. "That's not it."

"I'm listening."

I squeeze my eyes tight. "I'm afraid I've had a biological accident."

"What?"

"I'm pregnant, Jack. And I know this doesn't figure into anything we've ever discussed and we don't have to talk about it tonight. I just wanted to tell you that I am, that I'm thinking about what to do. And I don't know."

I run out of words and halt.

The silence from the other end of the phone is deafening. I hear it down the line, and echoing into the apartment around me. Echoing the dullness and emptiness of what my life will be like post-Jack. Starting over. Again. I can't quite get a good breath.

Finally, he says, "I see."

And I realize I was hoping for something else. Perhaps I'd imagined that he'd be happy, and his pleasure would make me feel more optimistic.

"I'm sorry, Jack," I say. "Do you want to just think about it for a day or two?"

Still a hush. Finally he says, "I'm sorry, India. I'm flummoxed."

I nod. "It's okay. Me, too."

"You know I'm Catholic, India."

"Yeah, well, I mean, yes, I do, but what does that mean?"

"I cannot give my blessing for an abortion."

"Jack! That's not fair. You know the circumstances here. You know why I never wanted to have a child."

He's quiet. "Yes. Bloody bad luck, this."

"Let's just think about it for a day or two, huh?" I rub the spot between my eyebrows, the Gulf of Sorrows opening up in my chest. "We'll talk when I get back."

"India—"

I wait.

He says only, "I'm sorry, India."

"Me, too, Jack."

PART TWO

THE BLUE SWALLOW MOTEL

An authentic Route 66 establishment awaits you! Built in 1939 and listed on the National and State Historic Registers, it continues to provide cozy accommodations at budget prices.

CHAPTER TEN

India

Eldora opens the door with a flourish the next morning. She is dressed in a pair of slim black slacks, black high heels, and her emerald green blouse. Her sunglasses are black cat eyes with teeny rhinestones on the swooping top piece. She wears them along with a green chiffon head-scarf without a hint of irony.

"Off we go on our adventure!" she sings. Her Tabu slams my lingering morning sickness like a fist to the gut. I have to step back, take a gulp of April morning.

"Are you all right, India?" she asks, touching my forehead. "You're pale as a ghost."

No, I want to say. My life sucks and this is the stupidest idea I've ever had. "Fine," I say, leaning away from the perfume. "Let's get you loaded up."

"Oh, let me get that, sweetheart," she says, shifting a Life Saver around in her mouth. "It's pretty heavy."

I raise an eyebrow at the enormous suitcase. "Is that even going to fit in the trunk?"

"Sure! I've done it before."

I shrug, and let her drag it on its wheels down the sloping driveway. Everything about her irritates me—the high-heeled sandals, the sound they make as the case gathers momentum and she's tippy-tapping down to catch up. Her stupid glasses. Her perfume. She stands at the car for me to come unlock the trunk, and takes out a cigarette and her lighter. "Can't you wait?" I say with a scowl.

"I'm just getting it out." She takes hold of one end of the suitcase. "Ready? It'll take us both to lift it."

I don't suppose she's considered that I might have some luggage, too. But then, being an ordinary sort of woman, I won't require the props Eldora needs for staging her life.

Meow, meow.

It fits surprisingly well, and my mother, no dummy, steps away from me a few paces. "I'll just smoke this right quick and we can get going. Do you need anything? Some water or something?"

Which is shorthand for something she wants to stop and get. "I'm all right. Did you have something in mind?"

She exhales. "I wouldn't mind a nice Starbucks. We could go through the drive-up." This is a concession, because she usually insists on going inside and having flirting time with the counter people.

I nod, my arms crossed over my tender stomach. Maybe steamed milk would be soothing.

I am miserable from more than the morning sickness, of course.

There was nothing from Jack in email this morning. I'd thought he might try to call me, too, but he hadn't. Who knows when I'll have a chance to check my email next?

"All right," my mother says. "Let's hit the road, Jack."

She doesn't know what she's saying.

I'll let her live for another hour. Maybe. Especially as she hands me a piece of Juicy Fruit gum, and miracle of miracles, it settles my stomach.

∼

The day is crisp and fine driving south on I-25. The Spanish Peaks rise like blue hips from the dun and green of the high plains, scatters of thin white clouds form scarves across their tips. The sky is fiercely blue. We're listening to the radio, and the car has a satisfying amount of power, not to mention a certain cachet. My mother in her dark glasses looks like she's headed for Vegas. It's not so bad.

Eldora is not in one of her chatty moods, and once I adjust to the perfume, it's peaceful enough.

But I'm still startled to be doing this. Why am I, again?

One thing about driving—you can't run away from your thoughts. And my thoughts this morning are all about Jack. There's a sore spot in the middle of my chest, like a goat head is stuck there.

I tell myself that he's not a young man, after all, and it was sudden, springing my pregnancy on him like that. I've had some time to adjust—that sneaking suspicion for at least a month before I let myself even start to fret, then a week or two of strong worry, then the confirmation and a week since then.

Nonetheless, I'm knocked out a little by his reaction. Not just his disappointment, which I'd expected, but his line in the sand over the possibility of abortion. Did that mean he would not condone it and be angry with me and get over it, or would the sin be so serious it would end our relationship?

The goat head digs deeper into my heart.

The rhythmic sound of the car wheels sets my mind to wandering, back through time. To the second time I saw Jack, in New York.

~

It was only a few weeks after that night at the pub that I saw Jack a second time. We corresponded via email a few times, talked twice on the phone, then I made arrangements to fly out and meet his staff to get their input. I was to fly in on a Tuesday, out on Thursday, giving us the full day on Wednesday to meet with his staff.

I'd never been to New York City before, and although I was trying to be cool, I was giddy with excitement, craning my neck and biting back exclamations of delight as we circled the city—so distinctive even at night from the air, that skyline poking so tall into the darkness. All those floors of offices and apartments and hotels, so many people, so many little containers of life, stacked up so high! I could see landmarks and water, river and bay, tiny twinkling lights in a dazzling display. Gypsy, I thought, would love this.

And all the way there, I admit, I was thinking about Jack with a burn in my chest. His gray eyes, that lock of dark hair on his forehead, his generous smile.

That kiss. Blackberry sweetness.

I was trying to tell myself it was unprofessional, that I needed the contract, that it would help me establish myself, but when I saw him standing in the faintly green, dingy light of the airport, all sensibility went out the window. He wore his worn leather jacket, and his hair was even shaggier, so straight and black, that scar standing out against his brow.

What slayed me was the way his face brightened when he saw me. I hurried up to him, not sure what to expect. He took my hand, leaned close to me. "Hello, India," he said, low and close.

I was lost. "Hello, Mr. Shea."

"I am not Mr. Shea right now," he said.

"Jack, then." His fingers laced between mine, and I clasped my purse close to my body, a gesture of defensiveness, gathering myself so I could look up without revealing everything too fast. "It was beautiful flying in."

"It's going to snow," he said. "Tomorrow, after our meeting, I'll show you a little of the city. Would you like that?"

"Yes."

Outside, next to his car, he paused. "I have thought of nothing all day but kissing you."

"Oh, thank goodness," I whispered, and let him gather me up, like a doll into the blanket of his arms, bend his head, that lock of hair just brushing my forehead as he kissed me.

It wasn't just nice. It was like biting into hot berries—little blasts of surprising heat and sweetness. I touched his face, the leanness of his jaw, felt the faint prick of his beard against my fingertips. His breath soughed over the corner of my mouth, and I know I made a sound. He pulled me tighter, plunged a hand through my hair, and I felt myself wanting to inhale him, make his cells part of me.

I broke away. Took a breath. Put a hand on his shoulder and stared up at him. "This is rash. How can I work with you if we kiss like that?"

"It'll be fine," he said, and kissed me again. "Christ," he whispered. "I can't think when my head's been so crowded with thoughts of a woman."

"I know," I said. Snow was starting to fall. "Me, too."

"Shall we find you some supper?"

"That would be nice."

He drove into the city, and I drank it in like a giddy child, trying not to press my face too much against the windows. He was a sophisticate, a man of the world, one who'd seen everything. I didn't want to look like a hick.

In his warm cello voice, with that musical lilt, he said, "It is a magical place, isn't it?"

I smiled at him.

We had to walk up a street filled with tiny, narrow shops crowded together, their signs bright against the night. A jeweler, gold chains in the window, a dark man nodded at us as we passed; a shop with bright silk—turquoise and red and white—flowing against the walls. He took me to a tiny Italian restaurant where there were checkered cloths on the tables, and flowers in tiny white vases, and candles in wine bottles with the wax dripping down the side. I didn't think such places existed.

We drank Chianti, and talked about our pasts. Cowboys and Indians, that was the fare of his childhood. I chuckled. Mine had been castles and keeps.

He talked about his travels—he'd been everywhere. I'd been almost nowhere, and it made me feel as plain as the prairie. There was an air of adventure and exotica surrounding him, a scent of something foreign and far away, a cloak of excitement that might rub off on me.

"What was your favorite?" I asked.

The gray eyes stared off into the distance. "So many are beautiful, but I must say the place I miss most is home. Galway. It's the only place I care to travel to now, fortunately work requires it at times."

"Is it beautiful, Ireland?"

"It is. You would like it—it's so different from Colorado. Rolling hills and not many trees, and very very green." He took my hand across the table. "I have been talking too much. I do that when I'm nervous."

"Do I make you nervous?"

"Not you," he said, stroking the center of my palm. "This. It's not the usual, is it?"

I lowered my eyes. "I should tell you I don't get involved as a rule."

"That's all right. Neither do I."

"I'm not being coy," I said, lifting my eyes.

"I can see that." He tapped my palm, once, and straightened. "Check, please."

CHAPTER ELEVEN

India

We pause in Raton, so my mother can smoke. She doesn't stand and rush through it, either, like any thoughtful smoker would. No, she settles on a bench and crosses her legs, adjusts her glasses and holds the cigarette at the ready, smiling when a trucker—his belt stationed around his hips in order to accommodate his belly—halts to light it for her. She smiles happily, takes off her sunglasses, and he walks on. Jauntily.

The moment is so very Eldora, I have to share it with someone, and reach in my purse for my cell phone to call Hannah. The phone isn't there. It takes a minute to sink in, a minute during which I'm patting and probing through the whole bag, over and over, as if the phone is a penny stuck in a seam.

It's not there.

And with a flash of memory, I remember why: It's still lying on my kitchen counter, plugged in and ready to go.

Damn. It makes me feel panicky, thinking of those empty miles, the desert stretching all around us and me with no phone. Visions of banditos with bullets crisscrossing their chest rise in my imagination. I also think of things like flat tires and blown gaskets.

Then again, this is trucker alley, and there is my mother.

I lean on the car, watching her. She takes her time. Inhaling, dropping her hand to her knee, exhaling as her foot in its strappy shoe wiggles. From a distance of twenty feet, she doesn't look more than forty, and even up close, she doesn't look more than fifty.

The forgotten phone is annoying, but not a disaster. Perhaps I can rent one in Santa Fe or something, just for the sake of my own sense of safety.

Eldora finishes her cigarette, stands up and carries the butt to a nearby trash can, and takes her time walking toward the car. "All right, sweetie. I'm done. Thanks."

We stop again in Maxwell, in a little diner where I eat a hamburger because I'm starving. My mother smokes, drinks coffee, and picks the cherries out of a piece of pie. I think of my sister and smile. "Can you imagine how Gypsy would be shuddering over you doing that?"

"Lord! That used to drive me nuts—no round food. Everything is round, ever notice?"

"Was she always like that?"

Eldora spears a cherry, examines it, makes a weary noise. "From the time she was little tiny. Which says something about how they don't think children suffer from schizophrenia, doesn't it?"

"She was always a little different." I poke a french fry into a pool of heavily salted ketchup. "But a lot of kids have eccentric habits."

"And she wasn't all that weird, really, was she? Not when she was little. The round food, but that's like a kid who won't eat anything orange because he doesn't like carrots. Gypsy got the stomach flu right after she ate some grapes once and I always figured it came from that."

"Right." I laugh. "I've never been able to touch ramen soup after eating it just before I got sick." Even the idea of ramen noodles makes me feel a little green, and I push the thought of them away.

She lights a cigarette, blows the smoke away from me. Her vividly blue eyes focus on something distant through the plate glass window. "I remember the first time she ran away. Dear God, I nearly died every day, wondering what was happening to her, and there you were falling apart, and your daddy crying over both of his babies—that was the worst six months of my life."

"Mine, too."

"Well, at least until lately," she amends.

I touch her hand. "I know." She endures it for three seconds, then pulls away, touches the pad of her thumb to the side of her nose, smokes furiously.

"I miss her," I say. "Gypsy. When she takes off, it's always like a piece of me is gone, too. Even when she goes off her meds, it's like that."

"Well, she doesn't have much to do with me, so it's not like I notice a difference. I do always worry about her, though."

I nod.

The rest of the drive is dull. High desert, which means mountains on the horizon if you're lucky, but mostly open fields of dun-colored grass pinned by stands of walking stick cactus. Sometimes we see a rabbit dashing away from the road, sometimes an antelope.

I find myself remembering the first trip. Gypsy and me taking turns in the passenger seat. My mother smoking with the window down, playing the radio, her face so focused and grim we didn't dare push too much. At lunch in some town I don't remember, we'd picked up the extra place mats at the diner, a clear outline of the United States, and we used it to fill in the license plates we saw.

"Mom," I say, "what the heck were we doing in Tucumcari? The rest makes sense if we were headed for Las Vegas, but Tucumcari is really out of the way."

"India! That was your doing! You don't remember that you wanted to drive Route Sixty-Six?"

I frown. The memory of a paper doll—a magazine paper doll?— wisps over my mind again, and evaporates. "No."

"Lordy! When I suggested we take a vacation together, that's all you could talk about."

"I think you must be mixing me up with Gypsy, Mom. I didn't even know until I looked up our plan that Tucumcari was on Route Sixty-Six. Weren't we going to Las Vegas?"

She smiles. "Oh, it was you, all right. Besides, we weren't going to Las Vegas that time. We were just doing a little tourist thing. New Mexico was close and I sorta knew the road and I figured it would be a nice adventure for you."

There's something in her voice and I look at her. "There was more, wasn't there?" For the first time I realize the very obvious truth, and it goes through my body like cold water. "You were leaving Dad, weren't you?"

She looks out the window. "Maybe. Maybe not. I've never really figured that out." In her lap, she twists her hands together. She sighs. "I was young, India. Confused."

"Not that young!"

"Think about it, sweetie. It was thirty years ago."

In front of the car, the road dips under a vividly bright sun, making mirages in the fields in the distance. I set my jaw. "Thirty-three." Seven years younger than I am right now.

"And your daddy was fifty and getting older by the minute. I'm not saying I'm proud of it. I was just confused. It happens. We did go home, you know."

Indigestion burns against my esophagus. I rub it, thinking maybe too much fat is not a good thing just now. "Do you have any Tums or anything?"

"Sure." She digs in her all-purpose purse, with everything in the universe in it, and produces a roll of Rolaids.

We did go home. There are a thousand questions in my mind, but the indigestion burns higher every time I try to phrase them, and I decide to let it go for now. "It was a long time ago."

"Yes, it was."

~

It's midafternoon when we reach Tucumcari. It's a small town in the middle of nowhere with nothing but a main street and lots of old neon. Every year, a sign tells me, they commemorate the Mother Road with a Route 66 celebration.

Oh, goody.

Memories unexpectedly splash through me as I drive slowly down the main drag. Eldora grabs my arm, "Look! It's the motel we stayed in, all those years ago! Let's stay there again if we can." I reluctantly pull into the lot. The Blue Swallow has a blue neon bird on the sign, and a little garage attached to each room.

I stick my sunglasses on my head and stretch as we get out of the car. "I remember this!" The garages, especially. There is one for each room, making it look like an apartment complex in miniature, which completely thrilled me when I was a kid.

Turning in a circle, I get a mental picture of Gypsy and me at eleven, me in red cowboy boots and red bandanna, Gypsy in her fringed vest and moccasins, both of us agitated after being in the car all day. *Can we eat pie? Can we use the Magic Fingers later on if we behave? Can we have hamburgers for supper? Ooh, look! Can we go to the TeePee Curio shop and buy something?*

My mother has a pensive expression as she gets out of the car in the twenty-first century. She brushes imaginary lint from the front of her slacks, lights the cigarette already in her hand, and exhales in a gust. "Whew! I've been wanting this for miles and miles!"

She looks exactly right in her green blouse and headscarf and cat-eye glasses, standing in front of the fifties-style motel. "All the world's a stage, huh, Mom?"

"What?"

"Never mind. Let's get checked in."

The rooms are inexpensive, and I pay for two of them, so my mother can smoke herself sick if she wishes. She wants a nap, and I want to find the homeless center, so we split up. In my room, I carefully unpack my small bag, putting my underwear in the drawer, my makeup on the sink, hanging my clothes in the small closet area. When I'm finished, I neatly zip the suitcase and tuck it behind the door, and head out to see if I can discover anyone who remembers Gypsy.

The clerk who checked us in points me to a soup kitchen down the road. Glad for a chance to stretch, I head out on foot.

It's a lazy spring afternoon. I stroll past a diner and more motels and a tourist trap with red bandannas and fake silver and turquoise jewelry in the windows. I almost stop in, thinking that Jack would laugh over a postcard from here. I could get him a six-gun in a holster.

Then I remember.

Tucumcari is only a five-hour drive south of the Springs, but the climate is decidedly hotter. There are already lilacs in bloom in the yards and along alleys, the scent piercing and fresh in the late afternoon. Aside from the traffic on the road, it's quiet. I spy a lowrider in gleaming purple and green parked beside a neat, white clapboard house. A fat, very old dog waddles up to the fence as I walk by. If Jack were with me, he'd stop and talk to him.

"Hi, baby," I say. When the dog's tail starts to wag, I relent and hold my fingers up flat for him to sniff. He licks them, and I reach over to pet the soft, graying head. A small kindness—a concept that didn't have much space in my life until Jack came along. It's something good I'll take with me, I guess.

The back door of the soup kitchen is standing open to the breeze, and I hear women's voices spilling out. I knock on the threshold. "Hello?"

"We're not serving supper till six," says a voice.

"I'm not here to eat. Can I speak to you for a minute?"

A bright-eyed woman with a yellow scarf over her hair comes around the corner. She's Hispanic, slim, in her sixties. "Yes?"

"I'm looking for someone who might have eaten here over the past week or so. A woman, mentally ill, who would only have been here a week or two at most." We are identical twins, but Gypsy takes on personas when she's delusional, and she's very good at making them seem real to observers. I never know if she'll think she's Hispanic, and speak Spanish, or Native American and wear feathers and beads. "She has really amazing hair. Nearly to her knees."

"Oh! Yeah. She was here, every day for almost a week." She calls over her shoulder, "Sylvia? Remember that woman with the hair?"

Another woman, younger by a decade, comes out wiping her hands. "Spanish woman, kinda fat?"

I nod. Spanish this time. That helps, though I'm not sure how. It's just a way of knowing where she is in her mind, I guess. "Do you remember when she was here last?"

Sylvia sucks on her bottom lip. "Not exactly. Was she here the night Harry had to go to the hospital? 'Member? Yeah, she was. That was what, three days ago? Day before yesterday?"

"Monday, maybe." The older woman looks at me. "Haven't seen her since then."

"Did you notice if she was by herself or with others, anything else?"

"Is she in trouble or something?"

"Oh. No. Not at all. She's my sister—my twin, actually—and our father died and she went off her meds and she sent me a postcard from here." I notice I'm twisting my fingers together and force myself to drop my hands. "I'm just trying to find her so I can take her back home and take care of her."

"She's your twin?"

I nod.

Sylvia starts to form a commentary on that, then the other woman says, "She was with a guy. We see him off and on—I think he's a vet. An Indian from somewhere in the Midwest. Calls himself Loon." She grins.

I smile back. "Thanks." I take a breath. "Did she seem okay? I mean, I know she's delusional, but did she look healthy?"

"Yeah." It's emphatic. "Pretty clean, really, and I noticed because, well, people aren't usually. She talked in a weird language."

"Right."

"It was like Spanish, but not exactly, you know?"

"Really." I frown, pondering. Could the twin language be some variation of Spanish? But how? We didn't know any Spanish in those days, though both of us studied it later, in school. "Thanks." From my wallet, I take out my card. "If she comes through again, will you call this number and leave a message?"

"Sure, sweetie." Unexpectedly, the woman touches my arm and gives it a squeeze. "I'll say a prayer for her, too. God looks after those who can't look out for themselves."

"Thanks." Without knowing why I add, "She's a wonderful artist, you know. Well known. Beautiful things. I wish I could spare her—"

The sinewy hand squeezes my arm once more. "I know."

CHAPTER TWELVE

India

When I get back to the Blue Swallow, my mother is sitting outside of her motel room in a metal rocking chair. She's smoking, her eyes hidden behind her sunglasses, one foot wiggling a little bit. "Hey, sweetie," she says. "You find anything out?"

"Yeah." I sit down in the other chair and tell her the news. "Let's go get something to eat, huh? I'm starving."

She lifts a shoulder, draws on her cigarette, blows a plume of blue smoke into the still air. "Don't know that I'm all that hungry."

"Mom, all you had at lunch was pie cherries. You need to eat real food. Besides, I don't want to eat alone."

"I can keep you company, I reckon." She stands up, stabs out the cigarette in a big metal ashtray. "Let me get my bag."

As I sit there waiting for her, I admire another lowrider ambling by on the old Route 66. This one is an Impala, meticulously painted with a scene of desert and mountains and magenta flowers that might be geraniums. The driver, a man in his early thirties, sees me watching and makes the front end dance. I smile.

Eldora emerges. "Oh, that's a beauty, isn't it? I was watching the traffic and I saw a couple of others, too." Her breath smells of Juicy Fruit and cigarettes. She has fresh lipstick on. "C'mon, then, girly-girl. Let's go get you some supper."

My stomach is dead empty. Growling, rumbling. I don't mind being hungry—with the hippy body I was born with, you learn to go hungry or get bigger with each passing day—but this feels as if the very marrow of my bones has been consumed and I will fall any minute into a heap on the floor. The smell of onions and hamburgers on the grill makes me dizzy.

We're led to a booth by the windows, and as we sit down, a body memory weaves through me:

Gypsy in her braids and moccasins, sticking the wrapper from her straw to her top lip as a mustache. Me laughing so hard I nearly choke. Coke comes out of my nose, requiring my mother to intervene and clap me on the back.

"Look, look, look," my sister cried, pointing out the window to the license plate of a passing car. "Pennsylvania! We haven't got that one have we?"

The waitress today is a sloe-eyed girl wearing two stripes of eyeliner, one black, one shiny turquoise. Her silver hoop earrings nearly touch her shoulders. "Hi. Want something to drink?" She's wearing a polo shirt and black slacks and her name tag says Diane.

"Coffee," says Eldora.

"Coke," I say, recklessly. "And two straws, if you wouldn't mind."

She grins, pops her gum. "Sure."

Looking at the menu is only a formality. My empty bones require meat. Red meat and fat and heft. "I'm having the chicken-fried steak," I say, slapping the menu down on the Formica table.

"I've never seen you eat so much. You all right?"

"No lectures. I'm on vacation."

Her frown is quizzical. "Why're you so mean all the time, India? I wasn't about to lecture a forty-year-old woman on what to eat. You just don't usually have such an appetite."

There's a spot of heat at the tip of both of my ears. "Sorry. Maybe it's just spring."

"Or being in love." She winks and looks over the menu.

"I guess."

She orders a grilled cheese and a bowl of beef and barley soup. I order my chicken-fried steak with extra gravy. When the waitress gathers the menus and bustles off toward the kitchen, I take the paper off the straw and twist it in the middle and lick it, then stick it to my upper lip. I fold my arms in front of me, squinching up my lip to see if it will stick.

Eldora grins, takes the other straw and makes a V with it, sticking both ends to her chin for a goatee. She folds her arms, too. "You think she's okay?" The goatee wiggles.

"Sounds like she found somebody to look after her."

"A man." It's not a question.

I nod, and the mustache falls off. "She's good at that, at least. It makes me feel better."

"Me, too."

"You know what I wonder, though? How does she have such good judgment to pick out men—and these are homeless men with nothing to lose—who will be good to her when she's so crazy she thinks she's an Indian? Some of my friends have all their mental faculties and pick losers who beat them, steal from them, and sure can't commit."

Eldora shrugs. "Who knows, honey? I'm just grateful she got that gift to balance out the rest."

"Yeah. Me, too."

I stare out the window, remembering my bright, loving, curious eleven-year-old sister. Who might be under a bridge tonight, or camped down in some abandoned building. Or any number of other places I can't stand to think about.

"It makes me angry," I say to my mother. "I hate it that she's out there because there wasn't any room for her in the system. I hate it that she's one of the lucky ones and we're out here looking for her and she has good instincts and good care and she's still out wandering the streets. What kind of a society does that?"

"I know, honey."

"I mean, would you send a five-year-old out there to take care of herself? No. How can the people in power not understand that a person suffering a schizophrenic episode doesn't have the tools to cope with such a confusing world? How can we be so rich and so idiotically poor all at once?"

"I know," Eldora says again.

"How can we build another bomb and turn out old ladies who can't remember to take their meds?"

She pats my hand, and I realize she has heard this same soapbox speech from me at least a hundred times, from my father twenty thousand. He ranted and raved, wrote letters to his congressmen and his presidents, got involved in any organization that supported care for the mentally ill and their families. "I guess I channeled my dad for a minute there."

"It was nice to hear it." Her smile is clear and true. "He did some good, India. Maybe it would make you feel better to get involved."

I raise my eyebrows, drop them. I'm a lot more selfish than my father, and Eldora knows it. But she's not out there fighting, either, is she? "Maybe."

We're silent for a minute, and my mother stares out the window. She taps her cigarettes and I finally say, "Go ahead and smoke, Mom. It's not bothering me."

"No, no." She taps the case, draws a fingernail around the jeweled decoration. "I was just thinking."

"About?"

She's silent for a while, then looks at me. "I've been wanting to tell you some things." She bites her lip. "About when I was a girl."

I sip my Coke. "Okay."

"Well, it's kind of hard. Some of it is not very good. And I, uh, I might not have told the whole truth exactly."

"What do you mean?"

She takes a breath, lets it go. "Well, for example, I didn't grow up in Texas."

"What?"

"It was Oklahoma. Elk City, Oklahoma."

I give her a quizzical frown. "That's a weird lie. Such a big difference between Texas and Oklahoma, after all."

She chuckles nervously. Swallows. "Well, yeah. I also wasn't a dancer."

There is something about her manner that's so alien to the bold Eldora that I'm beginning to feel a little concerned. "And?"

She takes out a cigarette and taps the filter end on the table. "Um, well, the truth is, India, the whole childhood is something I made up. I didn't have a big old happy family in Dallas. I never had dance lessons or piano lessons or any other kind of lesson you can think of." She meets my eyes, and for one moment I'm struck by the extraordinary color of her irises, a blue as vivid and deep as the Mediterranean.

"So, what is true?" I ask it with a taste of copper in the back of my throat.

"My mother," she says, then clears her throat and starts again. "My mother was fifteen years old when I was born and she had six more children before she was twenty-one. She was pretty sick the whole time I was a little girl and we lost her when I was eleven. My daddy wasn't too much use after that."

I feel I'm meant to ask the question. "What happened to her?"

She taps the cigarette hard, puts it to her mouth. "I sort of let it sound like my mother died," she says. "She didn't. I mean, she's probably dead by now, but she wasn't then."

I put down my spoon. "Go on."

"I mean," Eldora says, and blows out a lungful of smoke, pretty as a picture of the wind, "that she might as well have been dead, but she was just very ill." She meets my eyes, and I know what she's going to say. "She was a paranoid schizophrenic. They locked her up when I was eleven."

On some level I have felt this coming, but it still slams into my chest like a medicine ball, knocking me backward into the red vinyl booth. My hands fly over my belly protectively, but how can I ever protect this child from something that might or might not go off within her own brain, like a time bomb, ticking away?

But the sudden sting of tears in my eyes are not for me or this child, but my mother. "Was she delusional when you were a child?"

She smokes fiercely, and I see her swallow, take a deep breath. "Not so much, really. She was really young, like I said, and we all kept her busy and maybe that helped, I don't know. Sometimes she wasn't there, like, you know, like it was with Gypsy." She pauses, looks hard at the coffeepot. "I knew about Gypsy a long, long time before I let myself see it. I just didn't want her . . ."

"I know."

"My mother," Eldora says, lifting her chin, "had one psychotic break that we know of. She heard voices that told her that my brothers were devils and they needed to die."

She is eerily calm, her cigarette curling smoke away from her long fingers. The sense of doom falls down around my shoulders. I want to stave it off. "Mom—"

"India," she says without looking at me. "I need one person on this planet to know the whole truth about me. Do you understand?"

"Yes."

"I came home from school and found her about to butcher the youngest one. I had no idea what to do. She scared the living hell out of me."

"What did you do?"

"I grabbed the knife out of her hand, picked up my brother, and ran. My other brothers were coming down the road and I told them we had to go find Daddy. 'It's Mama,' I told them, and we all looked at each other and ran like hell, all the way to the neighbor's house. They called the sheriff and they took a couple cars out there and that was that. We never saw her again. She was so clearly crazy that there wasn't even a trial. Not one that I knew about anyways. They just locked her up and threw away the key."

I can't think of a single thing to say. She's busy with her cigarette, the heavy lashes obscuring her eyes, and the world shifts the slightest bit—not out of alignment, but rather more into alignment. Her hick accent. Certain little mannerisms. "Why did you lie?"

She lets go of a little laugh, rolls her eyes as she blows cigarette smoke toward the ceiling. I notice the length of her throat. When she looks at me again, there's a slightly different Eldora sitting there, one a lot less soft than the mother I've always known. "Oh, who wants to be poor white trash, India?"

"It wasn't that bad, was it?"

"Yeah, honey," she says sadly. "It was."

The waitress brings our plates, and Eldora leans back. When the waitress has gone, my mother says, "Waitresses didn't used to be able to chew gum."

CHAPTER THIRTEEN

Eldora, 1953

It's been more than forty years, but I can close my eyes and be right back there, at Dina's café. It stood right on Main Street, which was Route 66 through town back before I-40 was built through Oklahoma and left the town behind.

I loved working there. Loved my pink nylon uniform with its white apron, which I kept sparkling clean. Everyone says redheads shouldn't wear pink, but I looked real nice in that dress. It fit just right, narrow at the waist, the skirt just to my knee. The only bad part was the white shoes, but they were required.

We couldn't chew gum, not like now, where I see a waitress popping her gum everywhere I go. And you had to leave your jewelry off, unless you were married and had a wedding ring, like Pricilla Mackey who wished she didn't and tucked hers into her pocket and pretended it was the soaps that gave her eczema on her fingers. She was always hoping to catch the eye of a trucker or somebody, anybody who'd carry her out of Elk City.

It was a nice-size place and prosperous. There were twelve booths around the windows and another dozen tables, plus the long counter with its stools. The food was real good—basic American fare, I guess, but it was fine in its way. We served hamburgers made fresh by hand,

and real malteds, which you made by adding malt powder to a regular shake. We had vanilla, chocolate, and strawberry of course, but we had some specialty flavors, too. Butterscotch and rocky road, which was my favorite. I used to drink a rocky road malt, with double malt powder, nearly every single day on my break.

We served sandwiches, all the usuals including grilled cheeses, BLTs, and open-faced turkey and roast beef on white toast; soups home-made every day, not out of cans like you get nowadays; all kinds of good dinners, too—roast beef, pork chops, real mashed potatoes and gravy, chicken-fried steak, liver and onions, hot corn bread. Pie, of course, and a full breakfast, hearty enough to hold you all the way into New Mexico if you were going that way.

I loved to eat there. My papa did what he could to keep us fed, but he was never much of a cook. Everyone knew my situation, of course, and they'd let me take leftovers home if it was something like potatoes or the last of a pot of green beans or the soup of the day. Whatever it was, my brothers were mighty happy to have it.

I started working there after school when I was just turned twelve. In those days, it wasn't such a big thing for a child to work early, and I expect Dina and Ned would've let me work there anyway. As I said, everyone knew the situation. My daddy never was worth much after Mama was gone, and while nobody much blamed him, considering, there were folks around town who hurt for us children, going to school in our raggedy clothes. Everybody was clean—I made sure of that—but I was no seamstress, and we'd got pretty threadbare by the time I started working at the café.

It was a good thing to be making money, and also having some-where to go nearly every day. I hated being at home with my brothers in that pit of a house. Nobody would ever do anything to help me, and my daddy sat around and stared out the window about twenty-three hours out of twenty-four. We had a little bit of money coming in from the government, and charity baskets now and again, but I loved making money for real.

I'd been pretty shy till then, but I caught on quick, and pretty soon was getting more requests from regulars than anybody else. I could make even the cranky folks fresh off the road feel better by the time they left, and it showed in my fat pocket of tips every day.

On slow afternoons, that dead time between two and five, us girls would play all our songs on the jukebox. All country at the time, of course, Patsy and Tennessee Ernie Ford and Jerry Lee Lewis.

I'd sit by the window and listen to them, and listen to the waitresses talk. We'd smoke cigarettes and look down that open road, watching cars go by to somewhere else, and I'd dream about faraway places that all seemed to be somewhere to the west of here, places where men were prone to falling head over heels with the wrong woman, and women were prone to mourn them. Our place mats had a map of Route 66 on them, with the place names in funny letters along the road, and sometimes a drawing of something to represent it—like a rattlesnake in Amarillo and an Indian in Gallup. I'd trace the names and say them to myself like a chant or a poem or something—Tucumcari, Albuquerque, Flagstaff. Like the yellow brick road, it ended in the most magical place of all: California.

Hollywood.

The other thing my job gave me was money for the movies. I had to steal it, more or less, out of the grocery money. Every once in a while, I'd take one of my brothers, in the open, even though it made my daddy mad and he'd sulk for a week after. I didn't have many girlfriends, which sometimes hurt my heart, and I didn't have a mother to tell me it was jealousy, plain and simple. Or so I tell myself now. Maybe I just wasn't that likable.

Anyway, I went to the movies every week, and I read the magazines at the drugstore, because Fred the pharmacist had once loved my mother and felt bad for me. I studied the actresses to see how they made themselves so beautiful, how they moved and what they wore and did their hair. Marilyn Monroe and Elizabeth Taylor were my favorites. Marilyn was sexy and earthy and I loved the way she wore her clothes, but there was something elegant about Liz. I mixed the two styles to come up with something of my own. Pretty silly on a flat-chested, skinny fourteen-year-old girl, but it gave me practice in wearing the lipstick that was right for me, and how to get my hair into some kind of shape I could manage.

And then, the spring I turned fifteen, Nature gave me a gift. I didn't see it that way at first, you understand. It was a pretty sudden change, and I didn't feel my usual self at all.

First thing that happened was that my breasts got bigger. A lot bigger, and they hurt every minute of every day. I bought one new bra, then had to buy another, and then another one two months later. It was embarrassing. None of my shirts would button anymore and I kept forgetting at first that the breasts were there, and I'd bump them into things, which made them hurt even more. A bump could bring tears to my eyes.

The worst thing was the boys at school. They stared right at my chest all the time. One even said, "You got tissues in your shirt, Eldora?" and grabbed me to see. I slapped him so hard he liked to fall down and he didn't do it again, but he made a real big point of staring right at them whenever he could.

And I thought the breasts were what was making me all emotional, too. It stressed me out, as we'd say now. All I knew then was that I was not happy. I started falling all apart for no reason at all, like leaving my best lipstick in the powder room at the movies, or when Betsy Patterson snickered at my scarf in fifth-period language class. My breasts ached all the time, and I had backaches, and one day, I started bleeding. I wasn't so ignorant I didn't know about menstrual cycles, you understand. I'd been hoping I might someday get my period, though I wasn't entirely sure what was involved. There wasn't anyone to tell me.

It happened in the worst possible way, too: in school. I'd had a backache all day and went to the bathroom after fourth hour, and there was all this blood. It didn't leak through, thank God, but there it was and I piled up a bunch of tissues and waited until it was only me in there and then rushed down to the gym teacher to get a pad. She didn't spare me hardly a glance, just handed over the flat little box and went back to her class.

I tucked it under my arm and hurried into the stall. It had safety pins with it and I figured out you were supposed to pin the thing to your panties, so I did, but all day long, I was pretty sure I'd done it wrong. It felt like I had to walk like a duck, like everyone would know.

After school, I walked right to the restaurant and went to Pricilla. "I got my period today, Pricilla," I said, "and it's the first time and I think I've got the Kotex on wrong and I don't know what I'm supposed to do."

And I burst into tears.

She said, "Oh, you poor dear." She took off her apron and told the other waitresses we'd be back after a while, and took me to the drugstore and showed me what to buy, and did it boldly to show I shouldn't be embarrassed. "It's natural, honey, and every woman bleeds every month, so don't let any man snicker over it. It's like them buying shaving supplies or something, all right?"

In the next few months, my body felt like it belonged to somebody else. They had to get me new uniforms at work to fit the changed shape, and I knew the first night I worked in it that something was going on. It was like I was wearing bright red neon in big fat circles on my chest. Men I'd known my whole life started acting different around me, nicer or a lot more distant, depending on the kind of man.

I remember this one day, I had gone to the JC Penney's to buy some new blouses that would close, and a new bra, too, since the breasts had finally slowed down a little and I needed to be able to wash one and wear the other. The woman who took care of me, Mrs. Pachek, had been working there a hundred years or something, and she took some measurements and fitted me. "You'll want to wear good support, honey, all the time. It's worth it to pay a little more for a good bra." She patted her own fallen bosom. "I know what it's like."

She helped me pick out some blouses, too, and I left the store wearing one, and my new bra with its good lift, and was swinging my bag along beside me, thinking maybe I'd head home and put it away and maybe watch television with my brothers for once, or read them a story, when two boys fell in beside me. They were a little bit older, and I knew one of them worked at the Phillips 66 where my daddy took his rattletrap truck for gas. They came into Dina's quite a bit and always asked for me, so I knew them that much. They tipped me good if I kept the coffee coming and joked around with them a little bit.

"Hey, Eldora," said the first one. His name was Earl.

"Hey." I was pleased. They were handsome boys, which wasn't so easy to come by in Elk City. Earl was blond, with a ducktail smoothed into a point on his neck. His friend, Derrick, was Indian, with slashes of cheekbone and hot black hair shining in the sunlight. He was always the quieter one, and even when he talked he had a nice husky voice I liked.

"Whatcha doing?" Earl said.

"Nothing much."

"You're looking mighty fine, sugar."

I smiled. "Thank you."

"You headed home? Want a ride?" Derrick pointed across the street. "I got my truck right over there."

Nobody had ever asked me to do anything before. I figured it would be okay because I knew them from the café, and it was a long walk home in that hot Oklahoma sunshine. "All right. That's nice of you."

"Who wouldn't be nice to a girl as pretty as you, Eldora?" said Earl. He had eyes as blue as morning, and they gave his face a kind-looking aspect.

I didn't think anything about it, getting in their truck. It wasn't but three miles down the road, on a Wednesday afternoon, broad daylight. It made me feel shy to sit in the middle, with the gear shift sort of right there, and Derrick's hand kept bumping my knees. Earl seemed to be sitting too close, but it was crowded, and I kept my arms over my chest.

But they didn't take me right home, as you probably suspected. Derrick took a turn I didn't expect, down a narrow road beneath a big lane of trees, far away from everything.

I said, "This isn't the way home."

"Why don't you come sit with us at the river for a little bit?"

"No, I don't think so. They're waiting for me at home."

"Oh, Eldora, you gonna lie to us now? We know what it's like for you at home. Why don't you just come and relax with us?"

I was getting a bad feeling about this. I looked at Derrick to see if he would be more help, and said, "Derrick, will you drive me home, please? I'll give you some coconut cream pie next time you come in."

Earl snickered. "Yeah, Derrick, you want some pie?"

I lost my temper a little bit. "Now you're just being ugly, Earl."

"Aw, honey, I'm sorry." He took my hand. "Here's the truth. I've been dreaming of you every night. I just wanted to go somewhere quiet where we could kiss a little bit." He touched my face, brushed a little hair away from my cheek, looked at my lips real hard. "Wouldn't you like that?"

I had good instincts, even then. "Maybe another day," I said, and pulled my hand away. "Today, they need me at home."

"Just one kiss? We don't even have to go nowhere. Derrick, stop the truck and let me kiss this beautiful girl."

"No!" I said. But Derrick was stopping already and I had a bad feeling, and it turned out I was right. Earl half-climbed up on me and started kissing me, sticking his tongue in my mouth, putting his hands right on my breasts, his grimy, clutchy hands, and it made me so angry, I bit his lip. "Let me go!"

He only laughed. "All right, sweetheart."

They drove me home after all. I knew better than to go anywhere with two boys or men ever again. I got lucky. It could have been a lot worse, and I learned from it.

CHAPTER FOURTEEN

India

I leave my mother with a pint of bourbon, two Cokes in cans, and her cigarettes, sitting in front of her room in the rocking metal motel chair in the mild night, thinking her thoughts, drinking her cocktail. I kiss her cheek. "Thanks for telling me, Mom," I say.

She squeezes my hand. For a minute, I pause, feeling something thick in the air between us, something unspoken. Then she takes a cigarette out of her case and puts it in her mouth.

I get the message. "'Night."

Back in my room, I sit down and reorganize my purse. Cosmetics—check. Wallet—check. Zippered pocket with tampons—check, though I sure haven't needed any of them.

When my purse is in order, I head for the tiny bathroom and close the door. I wash off the day in the shower, thinking about my mother as a fifteen-year-old girl with nothing to her name but wits and beauty. I find myself smiling as the Dallas majorette version of my mother drops away, plastic and hollow, and is replaced by this more substantial Eldora. It's so much easier to see her in a pink nylon waitress uniform and red lipstick than white boots and a flouncy skirt.

Smoothing lotion on my hands, I wonder about her brothers. It seems unreal, a television movie I saw a long time ago. I wonder if she ever wants to see them now that everyone has grown old.

The fact of my grandmother's schizophrenia, added to my sister's, increases the chances that my baby will eventually fall prey to the disease. It's so depressing, I can hardly bear to think of it, and I skitter away from a baby to thoughts of my mother as a girl. I wonder what damage such a terrible scene left on my mother's little-girl heart.

Although, really, she seems just fine, doesn't she? Maybe it just made her tough.

When I wander back into the bedroom, drying my hair, there is a sound of highway traffic and nothing else. I suddenly feel very far away from everything I care about—no Jack, no Gypsy, no Dad. I think about calling Hannah, but the whole thing seems so bizarre that I don't know what I'd say. And she'll sense that I'm hiding something—the pregnancy—and I don't want to talk about it with anyone yet.

I'm not really a talker, have always been accused of being too private, but I'm not sure how other people find it in themselves to tell you everything. It makes my skin crawl with horror to imagine it. Maybe it's being a twin. Maybe it's being my mother's daughter. Whatever. I can't stand it.

I poke my nose through the curtains, and wish I was looking at the burly shoulders of my mountains, of Pikes Peak. Instead, there is only the neon sign, glowing thinly against the dark.

I wonder again where Gypsy is tonight. Is she sleeping under a bridge with the Indian veteran to keep her warm, or has she found a place with a cot, a place to wash her face and hands? She's faithful about carrying a battered army backpack, and I have often loaded it with things she might need under these circumstances. Hand sanitizer, tampons, and Kleenex; pens and colored pencils, file cards, Carmex; phone numbers in case she forgets or gets hurt.

It's something, anyway.

To avert my creeping depression, I turn the clock radio on to a local station playing Top 40 hits, then turn off the light and open the curtains so I can see the road and the blue neon swallow on the sign. I remember, so clearly, being here with Gypsy. The two of us curled up in the chair together, our bodies tangled like a pair of kittens. There was no space where mine began and hers ended, not until quite a bit later. We slept in a double bed at home. Her smell was as familiar to me as my own.

That night in 1973, we were waiting for my mother. She'd been gone a little less than an hour, and we had strict instructions not to go anywhere at all, not even outside. Eldora went next door to the café, and we could go get her if there was an emergency. She'd written the number on a pad of paper beside the phone.

We rolled our eyes. "Mom," Gypsy said. "We aren't babies."

I didn't like it, though, being left alone in a strange place with no familiar smells or sounds. I wanted my father's pipe smoke, the sound of him turning the pages of his newspaper. I wanted my mother to be scrubbing dishes in the kitchen and humming a show tune under her breath. At the very least, I wanted her in the room with us, smoking by the open window and tapping her nails on the table.

But Gypsy was always much braver than I. She was the aloof one, bold and sturdy, heeding only the directives of her own heart. I was the scared one, the worried one, the one who watched out for the bad things that might happen. I knew how to get out of the house in case of a fire, how to call the police in an emergency, what to do in case a rattlesnake came out of the brush. That night, waiting for my mother to come back from the diner, I checked my mental lists for what to do in case of a fire (out the front door if it started in the back, out the back window if it started in the front), or if a bad man came to kidnap us (kick him in the ankle and run really fast).

I was entertaining the horrible possibility that a truck could lose control, careen off the highway, and smash into our room, killing us both instantly, when Gypsy turned to me and said, "They told me crosses are signals to other worlds."

"What?" I said. At first I thought she meant something to do with trucks.

"Crosses. Like all the ones we saw today? They're message stations to other planets."

"Like *The Forgotten Door*?" It was a book we'd both read in a gulp recently.

"No." Her voice was disgusted. "That's made up. This is real. There is a little thing inside the crosses that sends information into space."

I tugged on the end of my sock. "Who told you that?"

"I just know."

"That's stupid, Gypsy."

"It's true, India. There's a thing inside of them that sends out messages, and the other planets get them and send them across the galaxies to others, so everybody knows what's happening on Earth, which is the center of everything." She chewed on her fingernail, and I didn't do anything about it, even though I was supposed to remind her not to do it. She gnawed her nails down to skin and then some, even when my mother put pepper stuff on them. "I didn't know until today that the crosses were how they did it, though."

I looked through the window at the stars. "Do they ever come here?"

"Sure. They're Indians, silly. You knew that."

We spied my mother coming across the parking lot then, hurrying in her high heels—she always wore high heels. Her hips shifted side to side in a way that made me want to look away, and I wondered if she knew her breasts bounced a lot when she hurried. How embarrassing.

But she brought in pieces of pie for us. "You are such good girls," she said. Her cheeks were flushed and damp-looking. "Gypsy, I got you pecan, and India, yours is cherry. How's that?"

"Yum!" We dug into the pie. "Can we call Daddy now?" I asked. My heart was hollow with being so far away from him. He missed us, I knew. I could think of him sitting in the living room all by himself, and it made me want to cry.

"Not right now, honey," my mother said. "He went to the Elk's Dinner tonight."

I licked my fork and thought of him in his funny hat, with his friends from the Elk's Club. At least he wasn't alone. He was probably having a good time. Which didn't make me feel any less lonely. I carried my pie over to the corner and stared out the window, wishing I could be in my own room, my own bed.

Thirty years later, I'm sitting in a chair with bare feet, a towel around my head, watching eighteen-wheelers and lowriders and ordinary Tauruses whiz by on the road time bypassed, and I'm feeling just as hollow. I wish I had my cell phone.

In the odd, weaving way of grief, tonight I miss my father, his calm wisdom, his easy humor. He had a big nose that seemed to get bigger every year, and bright blue eyes and long ears. He taught me to cook and how to tell jokes and change spark plugs in my car. I am grateful that he didn't have to suffer, that he died as he lived, but I still miss him.

And I miss the sense of my sister's presence in the world. It's a hard thing to explain to a nontwin, that sense of being able to just reach out and touch her mind, or spirit. Essence, maybe. We do it as a matter of course when she's stabilized, but I can't find her when she's delusional, and it makes the world too empty. One of my greatest fears is that she'll die and I'll never be able to feel her again.

I eye my laptop. I miss Jack most of all. I'm aching to sign on to email to see if he's left a note, but I'm terrified I won't find one.

It irks me that I'm feeling so stirred up about it. About him. All these years, I've been so good about keeping myself safe from people, making sure I never got too tangled. It was the art form at which I excelled.

How is it that Jack slipped under my defenses?

~

That first night in Manhattan, Jack took me back to his apartment, a prewar building in Hell's Kitchen that was, I would discover, incredibly spacious by New York standards, with good long windows that let in plenty of light. In the living room, he turned on a lamp and took my coat and asked me if I wanted a drink. I folded my hands. "Sure."

"Guinness?"

It warmed me that he remembered. "I hear it doesn't travel well."

He remembered, too. "But you're being served by an Irishman, so it'll be fine."

He headed for the fridge and I made a circle of the room. It was more cozy and cluttered than neat. A long sofa piled with pillows and a cast-off throw and a book sat against one wall. Papers and magazines and books were stacked hither and yon. Bookcases overflowed, double stacked, triple stacked. Framed photos crowded every surface and lined the walls, along with magazine covers from many many travel publications, some in English, others not. "Are these all yours?" I asked.

He handed me a heavy pint glass, filled to frothy fullness with dark stout, and nodded. He pointed to several photos, "Portugal, Madagascar, South Dakota. Oregon."

"Madagascar! Is that the island off Africa?"

He sipped his drink. Nodded. "This is Galway," he said, pointing to a strip of houses and a slice of sea. The sky was low and dark over them, threatening rain. A lone girl with an umbrella walked in the street.

"They're lonely, your photos."

"Are they?" He frowned in surprise, looked at them. "Not really. The idea of a photo for a magazine is to show the scenery, right?"

"But you don't just show the scenes, do you?" I pointed. "There's either an empty chair or a lone person in most of them."

He was quiet for a long moment. I wondered if I'd said something wrong, and moved a little away, feeling awkward. He caught my hand. "Wait. Let me look at them a moment more."

I stood there and looked again, seeing if I'd perhaps been too quick to comment, but each one showed the same thing, over and over: an empty chair or bed or bench, sometimes in the foreground, sometimes only a spot in the far distance, or a single human.

Jack looked down at me. "You're right," he said, and did not sound happy about it. He took my glass from my hand, set it on the table. He put his down, too, and took his time turning to face me. A quiet pull moved along the lower end of my spine as I anticipated him coming closer, the smell of him, the taste. He put his hands on my face, touched my cheeks, looked intently in my eyes. "I am going to make love to you unless you stop me," he said, and I liked him for plainly saying it.

"I'm not stopping you," I said quietly, and put my hands around his wrists, then his back as he bent in and settled that hot mouth on mine.

It's so hard to put into words the difference I felt in kissing him. It wasn't so much that the actions were so different. We did the same things as any new couple. Our lips touched, our tongues danced; his hands moved down my back, pulled me tighter to him, and I wrapped him closer to me to feel his body, my breasts tight against his chest, our hips crushing closer. But it felt to me like I'd always kissed some other entirely different species before this: cats, say, or antelopes.

And it was the same as we moved to his bedroom and shed our clothes, and moved our skin into full contact. It seemed new, different, strange, magical. The sight of his white skin, the dark hair over it, his sex, his thighs, his long shins, his beautiful hands that knew exactly how to touch me. His mouth, and the heat of his tongue on my breasts. His hips, which fit my hands just right.

All newly made.

I barely remember the meetings the next day, but I remember every instant of that night, the first one we spent together. It snowed. We drank Guinness naked. We lit candles and talked. We kissed until we'd chapped our lips. We slept, tangled together.

~

In my room at the Blue Swallow, in Tucumcari, New Mexico, I wrap my arms around my middle and prop my feet on the windowsill.

All these years, I worked so hard to keep everyone at a distance. I built my life into something out of a book, maybe, all the pieces glittering and lovely. Pretty dishes, pretty rooms, pretty clothes. A cool job. Cool friends. A cool address. Even a cool boyfriend—is anything more cool than an Irishman these days?

And I liked it that way. Nothing too serious, too involved, too dark. I was not one of the women I knew who ached for a baby and a husband. I shuddered when I walked by fields of five-year-old soccer players and the mothers with their sweaters and tennis shoes. I would rather die than need to drive a minivan or mini-wagon or even a four-door, for that matter. The idea of living in the suburbs, where the topic of discussion was property taxes or the best buy on kid's coats, made me feel claustrophobic.

One of my girlfriends, who married happily at thirty-four and had three toddlers by the time she was forty laughed at me. She said I couldn't pretend to be twenty-something forever.

And I guess that's how it appears—that I don't want to give up my youth—but that's not it. I am perfectly all right with getting older, with being a sixty-something single, trotting the globe with my aging lover. What I can't stand thinking of is being sixty and sitting with a man who has told me everything in his entire head, a man who has lost interest in my thoughts, so we sit on that beautiful cruise with nothing to say to each other. I can't stand the idea of being a wife, instead of a lover.

Which is weird, considering my father flat-out adored my mother every minute of my life.

With a sigh, I get up and open a bottle of red cream soda I brought to the room with me. There are modems in the room, and I plug in my computer, fire it up, and wait for the machine to bring up the screen.

While I'm waiting, I call my voice mail at home to make sure there is nothing from Gypsy.

Jack.

The electronic voice says, "You have no messages." There is a cruel emphasis on the "no" part. With a scowl, I hang up the receiver. I dial the voice mail on the cell phone. Still nothing.

I want to be angry, but I'm just bereft. It's possible he's been very busy all day, so I plug the phone line into my computer, dial in to my service. The connection is slow, and the laptop is ancient, so the combination means a long, long wait.

I lean against my pillows and sip the cold, unbelievably sweet cream soda. The taste takes me back to summers in childhood, when my dad would bring home six-packs of flavored pop for Gypsy and me. I loved red cream soda and root beer. Her favorites were, ironically, orange and grape.

The screen times out, and with exasperation, I try it again. While it crawls to life, I find my hand resting on my lower belly. A weird sense of shifting reality steals over me. Below my hand, beneath my skin, cradled in a sac of fluid and flesh, is a new life.

No, that keeps the distance. New life could be a seed pod, a fern, a star, bursting to life in the heavens.

This is an embryo. A human child. I close my eyes and try to sense it, the shape and presence of it. Arms, legs—or is it still at the tadpole stage?—a too-big head and eyes sealed shut. What color, I wonder? Blue like my mother's sapphire? Dark like mine and Gypsy's?

Gray like Jack's?

In my imagination, I can suddenly see Jack's face clearly. His forehead, slightly creased with puzzlement, his dark, thick lashes. I think of his white belly, hear his voice in my ear, murmuring something wicked down the phone lines as we sit in the dark, thousands of miles apart. With a shiver of heat, I see his face, his eyes closed as he bends over my breast and touches his lips to the tip. Slow and delicious. Such a rich and decadent imagination.

I think of the dark things he's told me of his childhood, the bully who waylaid him and beat him up in a lane on the way home from school one day. He had pretended to his mother that he'd fallen, and plotted revenge for two years. When it came, Jack nearly killed the bully, and would have if someone hadn't pulled him off. I think of how hard he is working with the Galway tourism commission to build the tourist trade in the town.

I think of our fantasy house on the sea, and my Jack and a dog and a cat.

But he's never wanted children. Doesn't particularly like them, so I'll be doing it on my own. Unless I have an abortion.

In which case, he'll be disapproving, too.

Bastard, I think. How dare he? I didn't get pregnant by myself, and I've never wanted children, either, but I sure as hell don't want to raise a child on my own!

Panic rises, and I take a deep, long, slow breath. Just breathe, I think. It'll be fine.

Maybe it's the vision of the house on the sea, but I feel suddenly tender toward the developing child within me. Protective. How terrible could it be, really, to be a single parent? So I'll give some things up— that fancy apartment in Denver, the late-night parties. I'll trade silk for cotton blouses that won't get ruined by spit-up.

Drowsily I imagine the floppy-soft weight of a warm baby against my neck and shoulder, the milk-sweetness of untainted baby-breath. The silkiness of baby hair. The unbearable smoothness of baby skin.

When I start awake, the laptop is too hot on my legs. I glance at the clock and realize I've been soundly asleep for more than forty-five minutes. The connection timed out. Rousing myself, I click the button to sign on, and realize I'll just fall asleep again. Instead, I turn it off, click off the light, and surrender to the ocean of sleep.

I dream of a baby girl with black ringlets, dancing on a rocky coastline, of a border collie, and a man in the distance, walking in the wind with his hands in his pockets.

CHAPTER FIFTEEN

Eldora, 1973

After India goes off to bed, I make a second cocktail—bourbon and Coke—and sit in the chair right outside my room. It's a pleasant evening, with a nice breeze blowing off the desert. It smells of something spicy and clean. I light a Salem and lean back, tucking my sweater closer around me, to blow the smoke in a thick line into the air. Cars whiz by along the street, and the blue neon swallow on the motel sign buzzes faintly. I stare at it for a long time. I wonder if that damned bird is a curse for me.

Or maybe I'm my own curse, which is more likely. My own luck, all the way around, bad and good.

Wonder, wonder where my baby girl is tonight. At least it isn't cold. That kills me, when she's gone missing and it's wintertime and she might have sandals on in the snow, or not have any place to sleep.

India doesn't remember why Gypsy comes here, but I have my suspicions.

I hadn't intended on stopping in Tucumcari that time with my girls. What was it, 1972? Must have been 1973. The girls had just had their eleventh birthday. Don and I bought them new bikes, with banana seats and tinselly plastic ribbons that fluttered off the grips.

It was India who loved Route 66. She'd seen something about it somewhere, and just went into collection mode, which she always did. She'd just get a passion for something and go crazy with it. Route 66 had been the thing that whole winter, and she'd been nagging Don and me to take them on a vacation down the highway.

Don didn't go. I took them by myself, and I was planning to stop that first night farther along the road—maybe in Albuquerque or something—but the girls were so restless and bored and getting on each other's nerves and I was afraid they'd kill each other, so I decided to just pull over. We'd only gone a little ways down the main drag when India started hollering about the motel.

"The Blue Swallow!" she crowed in my ear. "Stop! Stop there!" Like it was the Taj Mahal. She read about it in *Life* magazine or something. She was such a fiend for Route 66 that it's weird she doesn't even remember now that she had begged for months to go down the highway. Like she doesn't remember the language now, either, and she and Gypsy were driving me crazy with it that trip, chattering in secret to each other whenever we stopped in a restaurant.

Truth is, too, I had a headache like a hammer was banging on my skull, probably from smoking too many cigarettes and thinking too much. All I know is that when I wanted to reach out and slap both my girls for doing nothing more than just being little girls, I knew we had to get out of that car.

We pulled into the Blue Swallow, India screaming and jumping up and down in the seat in her little cowboy outfit. She even had plastic spurs on her boots, and a six-gun holster around her skinny hips, and sometimes she'd say her name wasn't India, and I should call her Tex. It made her daddy laugh and laugh, and he'd say, "C'mon over here, Tex, and help me rustle up some biscuits." He encouraged her, because he was plumb crazy for westerns. That's where they both got it, India being the cowboy, Gypsy being the Indian, when it plainly should have been the other way around.

Gypsy was in one of her moods. Dull, sleepy, grumpy when she didn't get her way. She'd taken her turn between the seats and had a mark on her cheek where her face rested against the seam of the leather. Her hair stuck out, and I made her come over and let me smooth it down before we went into the motel lobby. "We need a room, please," I said to the woman behind the counter.

"You got your hands full, don't cha?" She grinned down at the girls. "You two twins?"

Gypsy ignored her, going over to finger the brochures lined up in a container against the wall. India nodded, but turned around and rolled her eyes at me. I couldn't help but smile, but I pushed her over toward her sister so I could get up to the counter. My heart was racing as I pulled out my driver's license and let her write the number down. When she saw what I'd written for the model of my car, she whistled. "Fifty-seven Thunderbird? Mind if I take a look?"

"Go ahead." It wasn't as pretty then as it had been, but it was still a beauty. Don saw to the upkeep, and even though it was nearly sixteen years old and covered with dust from the road, it was a fine sight in front of that motel.

Standing out there, I got a memory that shoved right through all the things I had in place to keep it where it belonged. It was the bird, turning itself on in the late day, the neon buzzing to life. I thought about how staring at the blue bird all one long night, clear until dawn made it fade into nothing. My heart started racing again and I took out a cigarette.

The woman from the motel walked clear around the car. She was a little older than me, but dowdy in the way of so many small-town women. I could see her hunger when she looked at the inside, at the leather seats. "How long you had it?"

I took a drag of my cigarette and smoothed down my avocado-green skirt. "Drove it off the lot, brand new."

India, who'd trailed us out in a clatter of spurs, said, "My mama used to be a showgirl in Las Vegas!"

The woman gave me a look, up and down, to see if it could be true, I suppose. "Isn't that something!"

"Mama, can we have pie for supper?" India asked.

Gypsy had come out behind her. "I want to play with the Magic Fingers!"

"Me, too! Can we, if we're really really good, Mama? Please?"

"We'll see, girls." I smiled at the woman, who said, "Let me get your key."

We got all settled into the room, which thankfully wasn't the same one I remembered from when I was sixteen, then the girls were bouncing off the walls and we walked down the street to a little café. It made me smile, walking in there. Country music was playing on the jukebox, and there was a wagon wheel on the wall, and the lights were wagon-wheel chandeliers. The air smelled like biscuits and chicken-fried steak. "Can we have a booth by the window?" I asked the young girl who came up to us with a smile on her face.

"Right this way," she said, the syllables as twangy as Elk City.

I ordered a Coke and lit an L&M and started to feel better. The girls had root beer floats, and grilled cheeses since Gypsy wouldn't eat a cheeseburger, but I nixed the pie. They'd be crazy all night long as it was. I wanted to have a martini and sit with my book for a while before I went to sleep, and the sooner they were in bed, the better I'd be.

Which made me think of a phone call I needed to make. Couldn't do it right now, and I couldn't do it from the room. "Did you girls bring your books?"

"Course!" India said. Like me, she couldn't imagine going anywhere without a steady supply. "I have four: *A Wrinkle in Time*, a Trixie Belden, a Cherry Ames, and *Mistress of Mellyn*."

I smiled. "Good for you. And what about you, Gypsy? What did you bring with you?"

She twitched her shoulders in a shrug. Reading wasn't something she loved. "I brought my notebook and crayons. And *The Forgotten Door*."

"Well, that's real good. In a little while," I said, "I'm gonna look around a bit here in town. You girls are big enough to stay on your own, aren't you? Just for a few minutes or so?"

India tried to keep her face steady, but I could see she didn't much like it. "What if—" She looked at her sister.

"What if the bad guys come?" Gypsy said for her. She stuck her straw paper to her upper lip and wiggled her nose, deepened her voice. "You can just shoot 'em with your six-gun."

India giggled, and said something in their language, which made Gypsy snort and then they were back and forth, putting the mustaches on, then beards. I looked out the window for a while, wondering what they were saying. I tapped my cigarette pack on the table, round and round, watching the green L&M menthol triangle turn up, then down, like an arrow.

India started laughing so hard she choked. I banged her on the back and she stopped. Then our food came and they were back with me, chattering about jackrabbits.

~

I got out of the room easy by promising we'd go to the TeePee Curio shop the next morning, which India found a flyer for. She made me cross my heart and hope to die and stick a needle in my eye. Nothing would do but that. She had to be there, stand inside, after seeing the big cement tepee shape of it on the street.

I promised. So I could get out for twenty minutes and make my phone call. I felt jittery and nervous as I did it, like I was lying or something, and I wasn't.

It half broke my heart to look at her face as I was leaving, those big old eyes like her daddy's all soft and sad. She always seemed practically certain something terrible would happen. I kissed her head. "You're a big girl, and I won't be but a minute, baby." I pulled out quarters for the Magic Fingers, and she finally let go of me.

Who I had to call was their daddy. I walked back to the diner and waved at the girl behind the counter and went over to the pay phone on the wall and put in my quarters. Don answered and accepted the reverse charges. "Eldora," he said, real mean, "what the hell are you doing?"

Hearing his voice made me feel kinda seasick. It was so normal, so real. I leaned my head on the wall. "I just need some time to think."

"Are you meetin' him somewhere?"

"What are you talking about?"

"Eldora, I'm no fool." His voice sounded tired, and that made it worse than if he'd been mad. "I know you've been seeing someone the past few months."

I didn't know what to say. I try not to lie directly unless there's no way around it. "Don, I—"

"I know you've been unhappy, Eldora, but there's gotta be something we can do, some way to work it out." His voice got all rough around the edges. "Without you and my girls, I'll die. I swear it."

Something hot bubbled around my chest then, like acid. It made me feel crazy and mean. "Don't be so dramatic, Don. People don't die of broken hearts." Just saying it made me see how bad I'd become, and I banged my head against the wall, once, to remind myself to stop it. "I'm sorry. That's not what I meant. I just don't know what to do or think anymore. I'm going crazy. I can't breathe." What I couldn't say was, *I don't want to end up like my mama.*

"I know, sweetheart. But this isn't the answer. We'll take a trip somewhere. How's that? We could go to Bermuda or Hawaii or even to Europe. You could see castles. We'll go alone, a second honeymoon."

I thought of us, walking on some beach, me in my bikini, him with his pot belly and plaid shorts, his hair going all gray and wispy now that he was fifty. He looked old. He smelled old. I couldn't breathe around him anymore.

"No," I said. "I have to think. Just give me some time to think, Don, all right? Can you just do that?"

"Take all the time you need," he said. "I haven't much of a choice, have I?" He sighed. "Just don't drag the girls into all of it, Eldora. I have a right to ask you to take care of my daughters properly."

"That's true. And I promise you this, Don Redding. I'm taking good care of them."

"Are you? Put them on the phone, then, let me talk to them."

I thought of them next door in the motel, India looking all worried and tense and big-eyed, and wanted to slam the black receiver against the wall until it shattered. "I couldn't talk in front of them, could I? They're right next door. I can see them through the window."

"Eldora, don't ruin your life, baby. You're just confused right now. That man doesn't care about you or your children."

"You don't even know him."

"Don't I?" he said quietly and hung up.

I rested there in the corner for a long minute, trying to find my breath. I lit another cigarette and tapped my foot on the floor. Maybe I was trying not to make the next phone call, but I did it anyway. This voice was deeper, more liquid. The sound of it melted my hips, just like his tongue melted my spine.

"What am I doing, Glenn?" I asked him, my voice thin with terror.

"You're living your life, Dora. You'll rot out there in suburbia, you know you will."

I could see him. next to me on that imaginary beach, all right. Tall and lean, his belly firm as a dolphin's body, his skin tanned like cinnamon. He was thirty-five, two years older than me, and he made love like he had five hundred years to touch every inch of me. I let go of a breath. "That's right. I miss you. This is hard."

"I'd be glad to meet you anywhere you like, sweetheart. Stay there and I'll come get you."

"No. I don't know. My girls . . ."

"They'll get used to it. Las Vegas is a land of opportunity."

"I know." It had been, once upon a time, for me. It was for him, now.

We met on a dance floor, Glenn and me, at The Hogan nightclub in Colorado Springs. I'd gone there with one of my girlfriends, and Glenn was in town visiting his mother. I saw him the minute I came in, and he saw me.

Which led to this, with my girls in the other room, and Don's heart back home breaking, and me doing this stupid thing. "I'll call you tomorrow," I said.

"Dora, darling," he said. "Let me meet you tomorrow. Santa Fe? How would that be? You don't have to do anything else or decide anything. We'll just talk. How's that?"

"This is just crazy. I can't . . . they're . . . I just can't do this."

"You're a good woman, Dora. I respect you for that. At least let me say goodbye, all right? Will you let me do that?"

I took a breath. "All right. But I'm going home. You hear?"

"Dora." His voice was rough. "I love you. I don't want you to do anything that isn't right for you."

"Thank you," I whispered.

"How about I pay for a nice room for you and the girls tomorrow night, huh? You can even stay there a few days if you want to. La Fonda, right on the plaza. The girls will love it. It's on the way home, and, well, at least we can say goodbye properly."

"You don't have to do that."

"I want to."

I couldn't think. Squeezing my eyes shut against all the pictures flowing through my mind, I sighed hard. I knew I shouldn't. I knew I should hang this phone up and drive right back to Colorado Springs first thing in the morning. Instead, I said, "All right. I'll see you tomorrow."

"Dora, I do love you," he said, and the damnable thing about it was, I knew he really meant it.

"I know." I went to the ladies' and blotted my face, and lit another cigarette and stood there smoking it, staring at myself in the dinged mirror. A lot of other faces floated around me in the air. Glenn's, Don's, India's, and Gypsy's. Others, too. My chest felt tight with them all.

"God," I said aloud. "What am I doing?"

And it seemed perfectly idiotic, now that I was standing here by myself in a public restroom with my little girls alone in a room next door. I was leaving a perfectly good home where they set up a lemonade stand outside on the lawn, where their daddy took them to movies and I cooked them oatmeal and cream of wheat every morning. I was leaving the kindest, best man I ever met, and even if I didn't have that passion for him and never really had, I did care about him. He'd given up a lot to be with me. I owed him.

Determined, I dropped the cigarette in the toilet and flushed it and went out to the restaurant to buy some pie for my girls. We'd head to Santa Fe tomorrow and I'd meet Glenn and tell him my decision. The girls and I could go right home from there. Everything would be all right.

~

In the spring darkness thirty years later, I breathe out a lungful of smoke and stare at the clear, dark sky. Stars sparkle, thousands and thousands of them, and the sight makes me lonely. My glass is empty and I stand up, feeling the long day of riding in the small of my back. I pour a very, very small measure of bourbon into the glass and add lots of Coke. This'll be my last for the evening. Only three, and one of them very small. India won't know that I've been good, but I will.

She's bound to be asleep by now. I open my suitcase and unzip the top layer—it's such a fancy suitcase! Don bought it for me when we went on a cruise the first time—and lay out the dresses I brought with me. There are four of them.

Tonight, I take out a cream-colored silk with threads of turquoise around the hem and neckline. It looks Moroccan or Egyptian or something. A man bought it for me to wear to the Sands—he always did have a silly sense of humor—for an anniversary we were celebrating. It had a sweetheart neckline that showed off my bosom in a fine way, and I'd had it in my bag that night with my girls.

Gypsy makes her *descansos* all over the place, and it gave me an idea when India said she'd take me on this trip. I decided to make my own.

But now I'm standing here with the dress, and all I feel is stupid. What difference can it make? Only I'm going to know I did it.

My friend Candace and I do a lot of craftwork, and lately we've been painting with glass paints. I have tubes of it in my bag, in a special plastic container so they won't ruin my other stuff, and I figure, what the hell? I'll just do it.

I cut the dress and stain it. I almost can't do it. Mess up something so pretty. But I do, and I place it in the bathtub. Afterward I take a lipstick out of my purse and take it to the bathroom. On the tiles that witnessed my grief, I write only ELDORA WAS HERE. Then I'm embarrassed. How foolish! How small!

But then I think, oh, who'll ever see it but the maid who cleans the bathroom? Let it just be there. I take a sip of my watery drink and admire my handiwork, and think about it some more. What if I'd just gone home to Don, all those years ago? How would our lives all have been different? It makes my stomach hurt.

What if, even before then, I hadn't run out of Elk City with nothing but the shirt on my back? I think of my poor aching legs, that deep, fiery pain, and the damned blue neon swallow burning through the window all night long.

CHAPTER SIXTEEN

India

In the half twilight of almost awake, I hallucinate that Jack is beside me. I can smell his skin, feel his smooth soft belly hot beneath the covers. In my fantasy he nuzzles closer, loops an arm around me, pulls me close. His hand settles over me.

When I start awake to the reality, the empty bed, the motel room with the sound of the road beyond, I feel like someone scooped my heart out of my chest with a shovel.

Damn.

Here I am, lonely and lost, and what can I do but let it all come flooding in? I was probably lost that first night, when I walked into that pub and saw him in his leather jacket, his hair unruly on the collar.

Your picture does you no justice, he'd said, and pathetically charmed, I'd swooned at the sound of those lilting syllables. If foreign men knew what accents could do for their love lives, America would be crowded shore to shore with plain, lumpy, oatmeal-colored guys whispering in the ears of lovely women.

But Jack. Ah, Jack. He had the most wonderful laugh, the chuckle soft and ironic somehow, coming from low in his lungs. An ex-smoker who missed it, he often took a cigarette from someone and pretended he was going to light it, and in the gesture, I could see the serious smoker he'd once been. He had a way of glancing at me beneath one arched eyebrow, the gray of his eye glinting in an intimate inclusion.

Oh, just stop it!

I roll off the bed in a pique with myself—if there's one thing I hate, it's a woman moaning over a man!—and look for my robe. The quick move is a mistake first thing. Nausea slams me so hard I have to race to the toilet and throw up. Impressively. It leaves me shaky and cold, and I sink down on the edge of the bathtub. My forehead is damp. My bare legs are freezing.

What am I going to do about this? I press my hands to my mouth, trying to breathe through a second wave of nausea, but it doesn't work and I have to throw up again.

Ugh.

After a few minutes, I can stand up and wash my face, brush my teeth, but I'm going to need a cup of tea and some food immediately. I pull my hair into a scrunchy letting the twisty curls just be, and put my jeans on. Later, I'll shower and pull myself together. My mother wouldn't go out in public without her full makeup, but nobody I know is going to see me in Tucumcari, New Mexico.

The light outside is luminous and soft, the color of a little girl's hair. The air smells of growing things, lilac and fresh grass and new shoots on the yucca plants nestled into corners of xeriscaped lots. The smell enchants me and I feel something like tears in my throat. I wish, fiercely, for the counsel of my father. I want to sit him down and say, "Daddy, I have a problem and I don't know what to do. I need your advice."

In the foyer of the busy diner, I wait for someone to come seat me, wondering if I would have done it if he was still alive. He was nearly eighty, after all, and more or less Catholic. He wouldn't have approved of abortion.

"One?" the hostess asks. I nod and she leads me to a small table on the aisle. I sit so I can look through the window. "Hot tea, please," I say. "Milk on the side."

My father would not have approved of abortions under most circumstances. But his heart had been as shattered as any of ours by Gypsy's illness, maybe even more so. He hated the toll her nightmares took on her, even before she had her first psychotic break. He was the one who'd come running when she screamed in the middle of the night, the one who rocked her and held her while she babbled about monsters and devils coming through the floor and out of the walls. It took her forever to calm down sometimes, and Daddy would hold her and rock her as long as she needed him. My mother couldn't cope. She didn't know what to do. The nightmares scared her even more than they did me.

Daddy, I would say to him now. What do I do? With or without this man, how do I know what the right action is? How can I bring a child into this world knowing it might be cursed with schizophrenia down the line somewhere? What do I do?

Again the protective sorrow makes me put my hand over my belly. How can I bring her into the world knowing the monsters she might face? But how can I let her go, knowing she might have Jack's eyes, his merry chuckle, his hands?

I eat a hearty meal of eggs, potatoes, toast, and coffee. The orange juice tastes strange, so I order grapefruit, and the smell of bacon is absolutely impossible. I can't begin to gag it down.

But the food does make me feel better. It's oddly freeing to be able to eat for a change. Really eat, instead of picking through the dangerous items on a menu. I can't even remember the last time I did that.

After breakfast, I walk some of it off by checking with the soup kitchen women again. No sign of Gypsy—I hadn't really expected one. The morning is smooth and cool, and instead of rushing, I take my time, stopping now and then to really look at things. A yard full of tulips and budding irises; a mural painted in bright pinks and greens; a graveyard lying in tatters behind a fence.

At a junction of the highway a *descanso* is planted in the earth where someone died. I have read a lot about them since Gypsy is so fascinated. They're protected by the state in New Mexico, and there are literally thousands of them, everywhere. This one is small, a wooden cross with a woman's name, Pam Esquivel, carved into it. A black-and-white picture, showing a young woman with teased eighties-style hair, is laminated and glued to the center. She must be local, because the site is well tended. Pink silk daisies bloom in a white vase, and there is a loop of blue plastic rosary beads over the cross. I step back and look toward the road, and as always, imagine the accident in pure detail: the car, maybe a Galaxy, coming down that angled ramp too fast, late at night, and slamming into the bridge supports. I can see the lights, hear the crash, imagine the horrible silence of the aftermath.

There are stretches of road in New Mexico that can give me nightmares for weeks. I've never understood why Gypsy loves these memorials so much.

I glance at my watch and see that I should be on my way. The TeePee Curio shop is open and I duck inside. A lot of my memories of that early road trip are irritatingly blurry, but the inside of the shop is instantly familiar. There are copper bracelets and fake plastic turquoise and Route 66 signs, books, maps, everything you can think of. The small Indian drums covered with plastic hides and fluffy, dyed ostrich feathers are pretty cute. I bang on one lightly.

"Oh, Mama!" Gypsy cried. "This one! This one!"

"All right, but no playing it while we're driving."

There are coloring books and key chains and postcards. I look away from the kachina dolls carefully—they've always frightened me. I had nightmares about them after seeing them throughout New Mexico on that long-ago vacation. Not nightmares like Gypsy's, of course, but bad enough. They were always coming after me with their skinny arms upraised, their wooden legs clunking on the ground, their horrifying masks leering in the darkness.

Gypsy seems to take pleasure in the images that frighten me, and always did. Her nightmares were—are—a unified life, a world of outer space invaders and demons, a world of good and evil, pitched in an eternal fight. There's a very Catholic tone to them, I suppose, medieval

Catholicism. Eldora absolutely flat-out refused to come, but our father took Gypsy and me to Mass sometimes. It was years before I understood why he didn't go up for Communion or get involved in any other way—because he was divorced, and his ex was Catholic, devoutly so.

It all seemed odd to me. Give me something I can put my hands on.

Unlike Jack, who attended church every week as a child, and still says prayers to various saints. Under his breath, it's true, and with some abashment in my presence, I've noticed. I linger over some postcards of famous churches—the Santurario de Chimayo, the Rancho de Taos—and I think about taking him some holy relic. We'll be going through Chimayo. I could bring him some dirt. The thought makes me smile.

Instead, I choose a cartoony postcard showing Route 66 with armadillos and six-guns and tepees drawn along the dun-colored land, and pay for it. Outside, I scribble a note on the back, along with Jack's New York City address, and stop at the post office. There are Love stamps, and I buy one, stick it on, and drop the postcard in the mail slot on the way out.

It's bad this morning, my missing him. It feels like a lost thumb. As I head back to the motel, his face floats with me—the little lines fanning out from around his eyes, the slight softening of his jaw that worries him so much these days, the hard line of his cheekbones. His black, black hair, as thick as a pelt. He loves it when I stroke the hair back from his temples and forehead. Sometimes I sing folk songs I remember from childhood, and he likes that even more.

The pain goes through my solar plexus again. I haven't ever met anyone I liked as much as Jack Shea, and there really isn't anyone who ever let me just be myself in the same way. It's been a strange pocket of relief to discover that as a possibility, that someone would still find my company desirable if I let down my guard. If I snored. If I sang songs. If I had a cold and a red nose.

Thinking of these things makes me believe again—my gut says this connection was not a mistake or a joke or something false. It was real, even if it did take place on long weekends once a month. They were really great weekends. I don't know how the current situation will work out, but whatever thing it is that blooms between people sometimes was true between us. I hurry back to the motel.

I still can't sign on to email. The connection keeps timing out. It's frustrating for more than missing Jack. I really shouldn't leave email untended for days on end. I do a lot of business that way, and clients get touchy if I don't get back to them swiftly. I once lost an account when I didn't return a woman's email in twenty-four hours. She was high strung and difficult, and I knew better. Maybe you'd say she wasn't worth it, but, well, let's just say you'd know her name if I told you what it was. It was a big-money account.

I've been lucky in that way, falling into charmed connections that lead influential people to seeing my work and wanting me to design their pages. I'm not sure why. I'm not my sister—or even my mother, who has a color sense that's just astonishing—but I do have a sense of balance and breadth and a very strong idea of how to get a client's vision into the world for them.

I try three times to get the connection to work, and finally give up. I call voice mail on my home phone and the cell phone, and there's nothing. Without seeing the caller IDs, I can't know if anyone has called and hung up. Wishful thinking.

For a minute, I sit with the phone in my lap, wondering if I should call Jack. After all, we haven't been out of touch like this since the second month we were dating. Every day, one way or another, we talk. Email, phone. Something. I glance at the clock. It's 11:30 New York time. He'd be in the office.

It's stupid to sit here and vacillate. I'm forty years old. If I want to pick up the phone and call my lover, I have a right to do that.

His secretary answers. "Shea Publications, Jack Shea's office. May I help you?"

"Hi, Penny. It's India. Is Jack around?"

"Hi, India." She murmurs something to a woman in the background. "I'm sorry, but he's in a meeting. Do you want me to have him call you when he gets out?"

My heart squeezes. Why am I so sure she's lying? "No, that's all right. I'm on the road and don't know where I'll be. You can tell him I called."

"I sure will."

I hang up the phone.

That's that.

~

By the time I've showered and dressed, and gone down to find my mother, Eldora is outside her room, her hair gleaming with that coppery sheen, her lipstick fresh and perfect. This morning, she's wearing a turquoise sundress and espadrilles with ties that go up her ankles. There's a sweater tucked neatly over the crook of her arm. "You look terrific, Mom."

"Thank you, sweetheart." She unwraps a piece of Juicy Fruit. "Did you eat already?"

"Just a little," I lie, because I want her to eat. "I woke up very early and was pretty hungry." I don't look at her. "Why don't we put the cases in the car and then get you some breakfast?"

"Oh, I'm not hungry. A little coffee would do me, and then maybe we can have an early lunch."

"You need to eat breakfast."

She waves a hand. "You fuss too much, India."

"And you don't eat right. But that's the deal this time. When I say eat, you have to."

"All right, all right. I'm sure I can eat something or another. I bet a place like this has great cinnamon rolls."

I laugh. "A cinnamon roll doesn't count as good nutrition."

"It's food!"

"It's fine. Let's get your stuff in the car." I open the motel room door and the room looks as if no one has slept there at all. The bed is made pristinely, the towels folded. "You don't have to clean a motel room, Mom. That's what the maids are for."

"I don't like them to think I'm a slob." She minutely adjusts the directory on the dresser, picks up her purse. "Let's eat, then, shall we?"

"I need to use the restroom first, if you don't mind."

"The restaurant is right next door, India!" She nudges my arm a little. "I'm ready for some coffee."

"It will only take a second."

She stands her ground. "I'd rather you didn't."

I narrow my eyes. If it were anyone else, I might think they were embarrassed about an odor or something, but my mother isn't embarrassed about anything, and I'm sure the bathroom is as pristine as the rest of the room. "What's going on?"

"It's none of your business. Let's go."

For a minute, I'm so curious I'm burning to see what she's done in that bathroom. It's not like her to be so private, so protective. Then I meet her blue, blue eyes. "Okay," I say. "Let's go."

She grabs her rolling suitcase and tugs open the door. "Beauty before age, sweetheart."

It's not until we're seated in the restaurant and she's ordered eggs and toast that she lights a cigarette and leans forward, a glitter in her eyes. She really is so beautiful still, it's just amazing. The light coming in through the window strikes her irises so that the pupils shrink to tiny dots, leaving a blue like a pearly marble I once had. Like a Siamese cat. Like . . . I don't even know. Her lipstick is always good, always even, her eyebrows perfect. The turquoise dress she's wearing has a square neckline that shows off just the right amount of cleavage.

"So," she says, wrapping her gum in a little piece of napkin, "you want to know what I left in the bathroom?"

"It's up to you, Mom. I don't want to pry."

"It's a dress. I made it into a *descanso* and put it in the bathtub, because I was in that room a long time ago."

"I was with you, remember?"

"Before that, sweetheart." She inclines her head, looks the tiniest bit shy, and whispers, "I lost my virginity in that room."

My mouth opens. "Tell me."

CHAPTER SEVENTEEN

Eldora, 1955

I'm not gonna tell India every little detail, only the highlights, but as I spin it out, it all comes back like a movie.

I learned a lot over that next year, between fifteen and sixteen. Truth is, life was getting harder all the time at home, and I spent most of it at work, trying to get away from my daddy's drinking. Not like he was mean to us or anything, just filthy. I kept my little corner neat as I could, but three little brothers and my daddy drinking, only bringing in what he could shoot or catch—squirrels and catfish and trout—'cause he plain just couldn't hold down a job anymore. Well, it just wasn't tidy, that's for sure.

Understand, I don't blame him. He was a drunk, that's true, but he was hanging on the best way he could. You know how you sometimes see people who've just shattered, just broken into a thousand pieces when something happens to them? They never get over it. One minute of their lives stops them dead and all they are the rest of their lives is an echo. That was my daddy.

But he didn't leave us. Didn't beat us or neglect us, at least not on purpose. Tried his best to keep some food in the house when he could. He didn't have much to say, and those blue eyes, which forever after had a stricken look to them, were too hard to look at anyway.

Don't ask me why we didn't shatter, my brothers and me, but we didn't. We were strong. I worked there at Dina's. When he got old enough, my brother Perry got on a road crew, which took him out of town a lot. He got strong and muscular fast, though, and every few months he'd bring home a big envelope of money he'd saved for us. After a while we didn't see him too much anymore. That left the little ones and me.

Can't talk about them too much, really. It sticks in my throat, that one thing. The boys. I know what I did to them was wrong.

Wish I could explain to India what it was like there in that little house. The air was gray, stained with the disaster that had fallen on us. There wasn't a spot of color or a tiny bit of song. Just the grim silence, the echoes of all that had been lost. I did my best, but there wasn't a way to keep it really clean or nice or cheer it up any.

Through that year, there was a man who used to come to the café. Always asked for my section, which wasn't unusual. There were probably a half dozen traveling types who stopped in on a regular basis, every month or every couple of months. Truck drivers with a regular route, salesmen of various sorts. The truck drivers tended to be earthy and funny and I didn't mind their half-serious come-ons. Mostly, I got the idea that they'd run like hell if I ever took one of them up on it.

The salesmen were cleaner but a little more threatening. Too slick, too polished. Like they had women in every truck stop on the route, the landlocked version of a girl in every port.

Cliff was different. I liked him right away, the first time he stopped in. He was in insurance, and I could tell by his jewelry—simple, but all gold—that he did pretty well. His suits fit him right, across nice wide shoulders and a slim waist. He was a lot older, of course, in his early forties, I reckon, though he never did tell me exactly how old. He had some sun lines around his eyes, that was all, and he was married. Showed me pictures of his kids—a girl and a boy—on a vacation somewhere by an ocean.

Now you might say that a man past forty who wanted a sixteen-year-old girl wasn't a good guy on any level, but you'd be wrong. Cliff was kind. I saw him once stop his big fancy Lincoln and fetch a loose dog off the highway. It was ragged and scared and covered with mud, but Cliff talked him into the back seat, onto a blanket, and drove him into the next town and took him to the dog shelter, just so he wouldn't get hit by a car and suffer a terrible death.

From that first time he sat in my section, I saw something else, something I'd see in men's eyes a lot more. I didn't know what it was then. It just made me want to touch his hand, give him a smile. See if I could get the light back into eyes that looked so sad I can't even tell you. Sad like there wasn't anything anymore, and never would be.

He came through once every two weeks, going and coming, for three or four months before the first time he waited for me after work and took me to have some coffee. And then that went on a long time more.

I knew he wanted me. It came off him in sweet-smelling waves. It made his hand shake sometimes when he helped me back into the car. It gave me the headiest sense of power, too. A man like this could want me. It might be the only way out I ever had.

One night he kissed me, and to my complete surprise, I liked it. My whole body liked it. His lips were firm and he smelled of aftershave, and I could tell he'd shaved before he'd come to see me because his chin was smooth as a porcelain pie plate.

Since the summer, I'd had plenty of dates, with plenty of boys. They kissed like their tongues were swords, and I was always having to keep a cigarette lit between us so I could keep their hands in place. I wasn't about to get myself pregnant and stuck in Elk City, I can tell you, and I didn't let boys get to second base, though once in a while, one would get a hand on a breast over my sweater. I never saw him again if he did.

Cliff's lips and tongue were silky, more like a drink than a stab. He went about it slowly, even though I could tell by his breathing that he wanted to do the same things those boys did. His hand stayed on my neck, touching my ear. He kissed down my face, up to my eyes, and that hand never moved.

Then he stopped. Apologized. Took me home, and I didn't see him again until two weeks later.

For those two weeks, I studied all the men I saw. I studied the happy ones, who came in with a wife they'd loved for sixty years. I studied the sad ones who seemed to do nothing but smoke over coffee at Dina's or go down the road and smoke over beers at the bar, and only go home reluctantly at the very very end of a day. I looked at the young ones, who seemed so lost. I looked at my daddy and remembered how he used to be with my mama.

And I looked at my life. What I could do with it. Where I'd be in five years. I didn't want to be the wife some man avoided. I didn't want to be the worn and weary mothers coming in on Saturday afternoons. I didn't want to be stuck in Elk City for the rest of my life, either, waiting for the chance that would take me out of town, like my friend Pricilla, the waitress who left off her wedding ring. She was the one who gave me the idea, really, that you could leave.

When Cliff came back, I was ready. We left Elk City in April of 1955, driving down Route 66. We arrived in Tucumcari at dusk. Cliff rented a room at the Blue Swallow and bought me some supper. There we made our bargain: He would not ever leave his wife. He loved her and his family. They would never know about me. I would never make any trouble for him, and if I did, it would be over. In return, he would take me to Hollywood, and establish an apartment for me. I could pursue my dreams of acting.

Now, a girl who'd more or less said straight out what she wanted and what she was willing to trade has no right to feel hollow or sad about it when somebody takes her up on it. But I reckon I'd had some romantic dream about him being in love with me, some dream of romance. Star-crossed lovers or some such thing. Maybe that's how I made it okay in my mind to do what I did, taking off like that and leaving my two little brothers behind.

But in the end, what are you gonna do? There wasn't anything back there for me. I didn't have any money and no way to get an education. What I had was myself. My face and breasts and the longing they stirred up.

We walked back to the motel room. Inside, he pulled the curtains and started taking off his clothes. I just stood there in the musty-smelling dark, hearing cars drive by, not knowing exactly what I should do. He took off all his clothes and stretched out on the bed with his hands behind his head. His penis, red and rubbery-looking, fell on his thigh. I hadn't expected him to be so hairy, either, I have to admit. In the movies, men without their shirts always had just a plain triangle of hair over their chests, not all this black fur from head to toe. His arms were hairy, not just the bottoms, but the tops, and his shoulders. His legs looked like a gorilla's.

He said, "Take off your clothes. Real slow."

I know, I know. I didn't have any right to be, but I was pretty humiliated. In that minute, I'd have given a lot to just be back at the diner, dreaming about Hollywood, rather than trying to get it this way.

And it says something about me, I reckon, that I didn't stomp right out of there and get a bus right back to Elk City. Instead, I raised my hands and unbuttoned my blouse, one button at a time, and let it fall on the floor.

"That's right," he said, and he touched himself, just a little bit. "Now your skirt."

I dropped that, too, and stood there in my plain cotton panties and white bra while he moved his hand up and down. I was trying not to watch, but in fact, it was pretty interesting.

"Now your bra, sweetheart," he said, and when I undid it, he made a noise and said, "Come here."

So I went. And I can't say I enjoyed what came next. He wasn't a gentle man, and it all went too fast for me to work up any enthusiasm. Fact is, some men are just pure clumsiness when it comes to pleasing a woman, and I never learned a thing about my own pleasure with Cliff. But he wasn't awful, either, which is about the best I can say.

His fantasies never included anything like a soft and tender session of love-making. They were all about the things he couldn't do with his wife, because she was a good girl.

But that was later. That night, after he finally went to sleep, I crept out of bed and went to the bathroom and ran me a big tub of hot water, and while the water thundered in, I rubbed my sore thighs and tried to forget the ache between my legs and cried.

Sitting there in the hot water, I wondered about all kinds of things.

How to make it work better. If I should just go on back to Elk City and find some man to marry me and live the way everybody else did.

And it came to me that it wasn't gonna be any better there. Men were men, weren't they? They'd all want pretty much the same thing. At least in Hollywood, I'd have a chance to do something, be somebody.

In Elk City all I'd ever be was Nobody on the Highway to Nowhere.

PART THREE

RANCHO DEL LLANO BED AND BREAKFAST

You will enjoy Kiva fireplaces, viga ceilings, Mexican-tile floors, private baths, flower-filled patios, and extensive gardens. The village of Truchas is located within a 15,000-acre Spanish land grant established in 1754. In the heart of the Sangre de Cristo mountain range, the population of the village is approximately 1,000 and the elevation is 8,400 feet.

CHAPTER EIGHTEEN

India

It's a grueling day of driving, east down I-40 alongside the old Route 66 to just beyond Santa Rosa. I once had an aching desire to visit Santa Rosa when I was a kid—there was a famous Fat Man restaurant there. Even now, the eleven-year-old inside of me jumps up and down and wants to stop, but I keep driving. Twenty miles beyond Santa Rosa is State 84, and we turn north toward Las Vegas. New Mexico, not Nevada.

It's a slightly longer route than heading directly to Santa Fe from Tucumcari, but I chose it for two reasons: It avoids repeating the landscape we saw the day before, and at least I drive the interstate for sixty miles.

After Las Vegas, we head into the mountains. As if to lend drama to the shifting landscape, the sunny spring day turns softly moody, with low clouds sliding over the tops of the peaks. The road is quiet. We listen to music on the CD player, Neil Diamond's *Tap Root Manuscript*, the African side. "Remember when we decorated pillowcases listening to this?" I say to my mother.

"Oh, I forgot about that! You were such a creative little girl—one craft idea after another."

"You showed us how. With some kind of paint in a tube."

"Tri-Chem! I forgot about that. And the next year it was decoup-age, remember? You made that pretty plaque I have in my kitchen now."

It was a wedding picture, she and my father, along with a notice from the newspaper and little bells and flowers. "I can't believe you still keep it hanging up. It's so corny."

"It is not!" She slaps my arm. "It's beautiful, and the colors are very sophisticated for a girl so young. You were always good at things like that."

"Not like Gypsy, though." While I'd been slapping decoupage together, my sister had already started on her crosses and graveyards. While I laboriously practiced my calligraphy so I could write little poems on pillowcases in a beautiful hand, she was smearing blue and purple Tri-Chem into mountain landscapes scattered with crosses. They were too pretty—and too rough—to sleep on. I hung one in my bed-room, in a frame my mother had made for it.

"Your talents are different, that's all."

"No. Hers is huge and mine is small." I hold up a hand to keep her from arguing with me. "I'm not trying to get strokes. It's just true."

She shakes her head, but doesn't argue.

A young girl's voice comes on the CD, singing a sweet little song about lions, and I'm transported with almost physical force to that summer so long ago. Why did that summer make such a difference?

We started counting *descansos* and I find myself repeating the count now. There are a lot of them. I'm up to twelve before I realize they're starting to give me the creeps.

"You're quiet this morning," my mother says.

"Nothing much to say."

"Did I shock you?"

I give her a quick look, realizing that is how it would seem. "No, not at all." My heart squeezes a little and I think about touching her hand, but I don't. "I hate the man who did that to you," I say quietly. "You were a child."

"I was," she agrees. "But I wasn't blameless. I wanted to get out of there, and he was my ticket. You do what you have to do."

It still breaks my heart. I can see her in my imagination, in her pink nylon uniform, nubile and perfect, breathtakingly beautiful, and innocent. "What happened to him?"

She lifts a shoulder, fiddles with her purse straps in that way that lets me know she'd love to take out a cigarette and light it. "I think I'm tired of that story for right now, if you don't mind." She clears her throat. "How's that man of yours doing?"

I shrug. "I haven't talked to him. I'm sure he's fine."

"I sure hope you're—" She halts when I glare at her. "Fine. Never mind." She wiggles into the seat. "Can we stop for a cigarette break sometime soon?"

"Maybe in Mora. I'll need some gas."

She stares out the window for about five minutes, then tries again. "Something on your mind, baby?"

"No. Why do you ask?"

"I am your mother, you know. I've known you your whole life."

"Yeah?"

"You just have a way about you when you're fretting. Are you having problems with Jack?"

"Mom, not everything is about men! Especially not in my life. They're not exactly my biggest priority."

"Well, I have noticed, and I have to say I've wondered about it. You had a good relationship with your daddy. That's usually what puts a woman off men, not having that right."

"I just don't want to get tied down to all of that."

"To what, India?" Her voice is softer. "I'm curious."

I roll my shoulders slightly. "Just the whole business of marriage and the little trade-offs you make. It's like cutting off a little piece of your own flesh, and another, and another."

"It's not always like that. A good partnership helps each person become more of themselves, don't you think?"

"Yeah, probably a good one does. It's just that most of them don't."

"A good man, a good relationship is a sweetness in life, India."

I really do not want to talk about this right now. I tighten my hands on the steering wheel and don't say anything. I'd honestly been thinking along those lines with Jack, and here it is again, the letdown.

Again. The word has a curious weight in my mind, and I frown. What other time did a man let me down?

"You're so stubborn. You always were."

"Mmm." What I want to say is, I'm not stubborn. I just don't have any faith.

A voice in my head says that I never tell my mother the truth about anything I think, and I don't even know why. So I say "I'm not stubborn. I just don't believe in romance and eternal love and all that." She looks at me, waiting, and I straighten in my seat, slow for a curve. "I'd like to, you know. I'd like to believe life was like a movie, and there could be happily ever after somehow, but all I feel when I go to romantic comedies is pissed off."

"Why?"

"What do you mean?" I snap. "Why? Just because it's stupid and banal and idiotic. Love doesn't conquer all. People fall in love for a half hour, then spend the next forty years being annoyed with each other's bad habits."

"Is that what you think will happen if you settle down with Jack?"

"Settling down with him has never come up, Mom. I don't know why you keep wanting to take it there."

"You've been dating for more than a year."

"Yeah, so?"

She just looks at me. "So, usually that means, at this age, that you're getting serious."

"Well, we haven't ever discussed it." That much is true, at least. "I don't want it to suddenly become boring, and everyone taking each other for granted."

"I didn't feel that way about your father."

"Mom, you barely acknowledged his existence! He waited on you hand and foot and you brushed by him like a ghost most of the time."

"Oh, India. Did I?"

Too late, I realize that I'm the mean one. I glance at her stricken face and there's a pain like the Grand Canyon in my chest. Why do I keep slapping out at her? Why can't I just be kind and nice to my mother like other people are? I'm not mean to anyone else. Only her. Hannah keeps telling me that I have unresolved anger toward my mother, an issue, according to her, that I'll have to address.

And maybe she's right. Maybe I am angry with my mother. Otherwise, why would I feel this petty need to wound her in little ways all the time?

"I'm sorry, Mom," I say now. "No." The word is too small. "No, you didn't." There's a roadside stand ahead, closed for the season, and I pull into it. "This is a good place for a cigarette, huh?"

"It's all right. I don't need one just this minute." She's staring out the window in such a focused way I know she's trying not to cry.

I touch her shoulder. "I really didn't mean that, Mom. C'mon. Let's get out and stretch our legs."

"Give me a minute."

I nod and get out, slamming the door behind me. It's utterly silent, only the sound of wind blowing over the vast high landscape. There are pines in the distance, but just here the mountain is covered with open, grassy fields. The roadside stand is substantial, red-painted wood with solid tables in front of closed, boarded windows. The sign says "Montoya Chiles," and has a painted list of items: Chimayo, Poblano, Sun-dried, Powdered, Pueblo-roasted whole. After each word is a space for next season's price to be entered in.

It's crisp enough outside that I want a sweater, and fold my arms around my torso. In the air is a scent of a storm. Even in April, it will more likely be snow than rain up this high.

I wonder where Gypsy is, if she has a good coat. She left Colorado on a cold February night, so she probably does. With a futile but ingrained gesture, I find myself reaching out for her essence, that twin-ness, that other part of me. I think of her curled up in some doorway, cloaked in her yards and yards of springy, thick hair, a blanket she can carry with her like an animal carries its pelt. Sometimes when she comes home, I have to go through it and cut out little burrs and bits of whatever that have become tangled in the long strands. I'm careful doing it, combing out whatever I can, only resorting to scissors when I've loosened all but a few threads. I never suggest she should cut it off.

Behind me, the car door opens and closes. I give Eldora space to light her cigarette, smoke a few drags, then I turn around. It strikes me that I've never seen my mother really cry hard, not even at my father's funeral. It's funny because you think she'd be the kind of woman who'd be good at it. Tempers and dramas and tears.

Instead, she smokes them away, her tears. She's doing it now, exhaling that verbal slap.

"He worshiped the ground you walked on, Mom, you know that, don't you?"

She doesn't look at me. Nods. Takes a long draw on her cigarette and brushes the hair away from her face. "I didn't deserve it, you're right. I took it for granted until he was gone."

"No, you didn't."

"Oh, India, don't try to make me feel better. What do you think I've been trying to make peace with since he died? I know I wasn't good enough to him! I know it."

I step closer. "Who cooked his meals, Mama? Who lined up his pills every morning, right beside his plate so he wouldn't forget them? Who bought him special socks for walking and taped western movies for him?"

She swallows. Smokes. Stares hard at the line of mountains to the east. A wind ruffles her glossy hair, swirls through an earring and makes it swing and shimmer against her neck.

When she doesn't say anything else, I put my hands in the pock-ets of my jeans. "One of the things that makes it hard for me to get involved with anyone is the way my dad loved my mother. Most men don't look at their wives like that, you know? But once you've seen it, how can you settle for anything less?"

"You should look at the glass the other way, sweetheart. At least you know it's possible." She drops her cigarette, grinds the butt to smithereens with the heel of her shoe. "It's cold out here. Let's get moving."

~

We ride in silence for a long time, passing the odd house, a tiny village hidden in the hills, a skinny dog, the rare car, usually an older version of something, or a pickup. The mountains surround us, purply blue and mysterious against dark skies. The emptiness feels lonely. We round a turn, and the only thing standing on the hill is a cross with bright-yellow ribbons flying in the wind.

"God, this is lonely country," I comment. "Why did we come this way back then?"

"It was an accident."

"An accident?"

She shrugs. "Yeah. A big pile-up closed I-25, and this was the only way to go. I'm glad now, even though it took so long. It's like another country up here, you have to admit."

"And everything Gypsy does artistically comes out of this road. Isn't that odd? How one day all those years ago should have made such an impression?"

She's quiet for a little while. "I don't understand anything about her mind. Not one single thing. I've read and read and listened and listened and"—a shrug—"it's just not in me, I guess. I just don't understand."

"I don't think anybody does."

"Your daddy seemed to."

I shake my head. "No, he was just more patient." Then I add, "Than either one of us."

"I'm afraid you inherited my attitudes toward illness, baby." She touches my wrist, lets me go. "It's hard to know what to do for a person who's sick."

"Especially someone—" I halt. "When she would be so afraid. So afraid."

My mother nods. Then she leans forward, pointing. "Oh, look! It's the graveyard! Stop, stop!"

It's the graveyard from my dream, spread out on the top of a hill, far from anything. We get out, and both of us shiver in the brisk wind coming up from the valley. I take out a red sweater that Jack brought me from Ireland the last time he went. Its cottony warmth is the perfect weight. My mother needs me to open the trunk so she can get her coat out, and she shimmies into it with a "Brr!"

"Do you think we should go in?" I ask. It's fenced to keep cows out, but there are two of them inside anyway peacefully munching grass between headstones.

"I like cows," my mother says. "They're so cute. I like their eyes."

"They're stupid, though."

"Not too stupid. They outsmarted the fence." She strikes out through the long dry grass toward the gate, and I follow, thinking if anyone yells at us, it will be her fault.

Within, she pauses and looks around. "I know why she paints it."

"Me, too." We walk along a line of graves for children, every single one of them piled high with pinwheels and plastic flowers and dolls and toys. They're vividly bright in the dark day—pinks and purples and yellows and oranges celebrating the fact that this child once walked the earth and lived here and was loved and is remembered. "It's so joyful."

My mother reaches out to set a pinwheel spinning, silver and red and turquoise. "I don't know how anyone bears to lose a child."

"I know."

She shakes her head. "No, you really don't. Not until you have a child of your own."

"I can imagine, though."

"Maybe." Her smile is meant to be kind, but it irks me anyway. It's so all-knowing, so superciliously sure.

"A person doesn't have to live through something to know what it's like or how it feels."

Reaching into her pocket, she takes out a cigarette and lights it. "There are some things you can probably understand without going through them." She walks on through the graves, and is so sure I'll trail along behind that I almost don't. Her cigarette annoys me, and I circle to the other side. "This is probably not one of them."

She pauses by a short iron fence enclosing three graves. Sisters, I can see by the headstones. The birth dates are not there, leaving me to wonder if they were maybe triplets born too soon or lost in some epidemic or a car accident. I find myself crossing my arms across my belly.

My imagination fills in a picture of a family in an adobe house, on the day these three died. The sun shining too hot, flies buzzing on in their lazy way as if there was nothing changed, and a mother—

"You go along in your life," Eldora says, "thinking everything is like so." She spreads her hands, palms up, to show an expectation. "Then you see your baby's eyes for the first time, and everything is different." She flips her hands over, cups them to hold something precious. "Right then, forever."

It was Gypsy my mother saw first. She was born before I was, six minutes ahead. My mother didn't even know she was having twins until, while holding her daughter and cooing to her (or so I've always imagined), the nurse said, "Hold on! There's another baby!"

"And there were two of you at once," she says now. "My arms were overflowing and there was absolutely nothing bigger in the world. Nothing."

My heart lurches and I nearly spill it out to her, my secret. Nearly say, *Mom, I'm pregnant, what do I do?* But then I think of her reaction, of her excitement, of her way of taking everything over, and I don't. It makes me angry again, that I don't have the sort of mother who would be wise and calm and easy. I move away from her, walking hard, a wash of absurd tears in my eyes.

I can be so cruel to my mother sometimes, but in a lot of ways she deserves it. She really does suck up all the available oxygen in a room. She's self-centered, the star of every stage, every set, every everything, always. She'll make it about her somehow, this baby, and I won't be able to stand it.

While we're on the subject, what kind of mother would I be, anyway, with an example like that to follow? I'm just as selfish and self-centered as she is.

Only I'll be even worse; I'll be controlling. I'll see to it that things are taken care of, by golly. I know this because other parents tease me about it. When the newspapers or television report something terrible that happened to a child, my answer is always, "Why didn't the parents take better care of him?"

Not just in terms of kids getting snatched out of a front yard (Why don't they make them play in the back?) or a baby getting killed in a car accident (use a freaking car seat!), either. It's things like choking (Don't give them grapes and peanuts, for heaven's sake!) or poisonings. Watch them, watch out for them, keep them safe. Get credentials from the day care, don't let strange teenagers walk away with them.

And I can see how I'll take this into further life—battling with teachers and walking her to school and warning her about strangers.

God! How can I possibly face such a huge task? How can I keep her safe in such a dangerous world?

My mother comes up behind me and puts her hand on my back. "Something really is bothering you, isn't it, India?"

"I can't talk about it yet."

"All right."

A single puffy snowflake catches in her hair, and I look up to see its brothers and sisters. Not so much snow, but enough that I'm worried about the rest of the drive through the mountains. "We should get going."

My mother nods, but she doesn't move immediately. "Listen."

I raise my head, looking toward a line of dark pines arrowing into the sky at the edge of the graveyard. There is the distant caw of a raven, but nothing else. "What?"

"The quiet."

There is that. It's utterly still, only the softness of a wind now and then, the faint clatter of a pinwheel spinning. I turn, looking around me, and think of Gypsy in my dream, dancing through these graves. It's so beautiful!

I wonder if one of the reasons she likes it so much up here is because of the quiet. Maybe it's easier to sort out the real sounds from the not-real sounds. Maybe if it's this quiet, she knows there's no one talking to her, that it's just her voices and she can ignore them.

There is, in me, a sudden shift. I am myself and not, Gypsy and not. She is me and I am her, and I can see through her eyes. It's a ripple up through my abdomen, then my neck. A noise comes out of my throat, and I find my hands over my middle, and I'm turning, looking at the tumble of colors—the oranges and pinks of the flowers piled on the graves, the purple and blue of the mountains, the dark blacks and greens of the pines along the edges. Mostly, I see the exuberance of the piles and piles and piles of flowers and toys and pictures on the graves—it's extravagant and excessive; it's love and dancing and laughing. I close my eyes, breathing through my tears, and finally feel my sister.

"She's okay," I whisper. I touch my chest. "She's okay."

CHAPTER NINETEEN

India

When I come back to me, to now, I look at my mother. She's waiting, looking at me. "How I wish I could feel her the way you do."

"I always tell you."

"I know." She shakes her head, smiles the faintest bit. "It's all right. It's what twins do. It's good that you can."

Back in the car, I say, "When did you know that there was something really wrong with Gypsy?"

"A long time ago. How 'bout you?"

"I started thinking there was something wrong on that trip."

"Her nightmares were terrible that time."

"Yeah, but it wasn't that. She was odd that whole trip, just thinking strange things. Like Indians were aliens from outer space, and the crosses were their method of communication."

Eldora says nothing. Her fingernails pluck at her skirt.

"Did you notice it, too?"

"I had other things on my mind. Unfortunately." She opens her purse and takes out her Juicy Fruit. "Want some?"

"Sure." The snow is starting to fly a little thicker through the trees, and I frown. "God, I hope we don't get stuck in a blizzard up here."

"How far is it to Santa Fe?"

"Check the map." I point to the glove box with my yellow gum wrapper. "It's around eighty from Las Vegas to Espanola as far as I can make out. We're more than halfway."

"It'll be all right." She folds the map. "She was afraid of me, you know. When she started getting delusional."

I nod.

"It broke my heart. She was sure I was poisoning her food or setting traps for her."

"I didn't know that. When was it?"

"Right before she ran away. I'd been trying to get her to a doctor for a couple of months, but your daddy wouldn't hear of it. He kept saying she was just different and he didn't want her labeled and—"

"I thought it was the drugs, making her so weird."

"That's what he thought, too."

I think back to those miserable days with Gypsy before she ran away. It was like something out of *Go Ask Alice*—she was drinking and drugging all the time, sleeping around, never coming home on time. She barely held on at school, passing with D's and the odd C. A's in Art, which was the only reason she kept going, I think. Art class was the one place, she told me later, where she felt the voices weren't totally trying to take her over. Even then, so young—fifteen, sixteen—she was winning awards and prizes for her work, her crosses and graveyards and neon signs and cactuses and sad-faced people.

And it wasn't like Gypsy was the only drinking, drugging, out-of-control teenager on the block. It was an epidemic, but this was the late seventies, and there wasn't much in place yet to get kids sobered up and back on track.

"How did you know it wasn't the drugs, Mom?"

She lifts a shoulder. "I didn't know, exactly. Just had my suspicions. Gypsy used to do little things that reminded me of my mother."

"Like what?"

"Little things, really. Like sometimes when she'd shake her head like a horse snorting? Remember that? And the hand-wringing. It's so nervous."

I sigh. "It wouldn't have made much difference, anyway."

"Maybe it would have," Eldora almost whispers. "I sometimes think about that. What if they'd gotten her on something when she was younger? Fourteen or fifteen? Maybe she wouldn't've ever had a psychotic episode and maybe now her life would be different. People sometimes do get well, you know."

"But you didn't know when she was fourteen or fifteen."

"I knew," she says. "I guess I didn't want to look at it." She turns the wedding ring on her finger. "I didn't want to tell your daddy about my mother."

"He never knew?"

She smiles, and it's somehow enormously sad. "No. He didn't know a lot of things."

It's selfish, but I say it anyway. "From my angle, I'm glad you waited. I lived in mortal terror for years and years, waiting for it."

"I never really thought it would show up with you, India. That's the truth. I know the doctors scared you, talking about twins and mental illness and they watched you like hawks, but there was never the slightest worry in my mind."

That was one of the more brutal aspects of my sister's illness—the twin of a person diagnosed with schizophrenia is far more likely to fall to the disease as other relatives, and since it most often doesn't arrive until early adulthood, how would I know if I was to be lucky or unlucky?

I think of those years when I'd been so afraid, all through college and beyond. I kept to myself a lot, watching myself for signs of voices or obsessive behaviors, and believe me, once you start questioning normality, it's easy to find evidence of mental illness. If I found myself walking along, reciting my to-do list on my way to class, I worried, even though it was something I'd always done. If I had a terrible nightmare, I worried. If I double-checked something, even the answers from a test, I worried.

And I was so isolated, too. I'd lost Gypsy, my sister, my heart, and I was afraid of anyone new, so I kept to myself. It was how I got into computers so early. They gave me something to do.

I think of the baby inside of me, think of how miserable I was, how much misery is still Gypsy's portion. How can I subject a child to that? How monstrously selfish of me to even consider it! I lean forward, resettle my hands on the wheel.

This is the reason I've kept men at arm's length, kept myself from falling in love. I never wanted to make this choice, and the safest way to avoid it was by never getting too attached to anyone.

And now I know my grandmother was also virulently ill with schizophrenia. How can I possibly curse a child with such a history?

I'll have to have an abortion. It's the only answer. I can't bear to go through it again, and I surely can't bear to sentence someone else to the worry. I will have to find some way to explain to Jack how terrible it is.

I feel nauseous for a minute, and my mother hands me another piece of Juicy Fruit.

"Thanks."

~

We drive into Espanola under cover of light snow. The town makes me think of a hostile middle-aged man, eyes narrowed, signs meanly placed, a sense of deafness when you want to ask a question. But the homeless shelter is one that draws Gypsy—she's turned up three or four times here, and she loves to go to Chimayo, a few miles to the east.

There are a lot of *descansos* along that road. Maybe more than any other place. I count thirty-five on the way down from Truchas.

In front of the shelter, there is a little knot of ragged men, smoking. Their hair and the elbows of their coats are greasy, and most of them carry either that almost amiable hopelessness of a longtime alcoholic, or the too-focused gaze of a schizophrenic. They shift toward us as the car draws their attention, their shoulders hunched against the cold, their eyes following the sleek fins of the Thunderbird.

These, I think, are Gypsy's compatriots. They terrify me.

"We'll go together," my mother says, grabbing her purse from the floor. She shoves her sunglasses on top of her head and tucks in her blouse as she slams the door. "Good afternoon, gentlemen," she says, as if they are bankers at a meeting. *"Buenas tardes,"* she adds, and I see the small Mexican in the corner, his collar once a bright yellow. Several lift their chins, measure us through the smoke of their cigarettes. Eldora takes out her own cigarettes and lights one, then holds the pack in her hand.

"We're looking for someone," Eldora says, and points to me. "Her name is Gypsy."

A youngish one says to an older one, "She means Gitana."

Spanish for Gypsy. I nod.

He grins at me. "She's your sister, huh?"

"Yeah."

"She was here last night."

"Really. Was she with anyone?"

"Nah, man." He snickers, looks at us, then thinks better of his joke, and an ache goes through me. I don't want to think of what she does to get by when she's out here. How they treat her, what men like these think about her. It makes my knees hurt.

He drags on his cigarette hard and blows out the smoke. "She was drinking. They made her go."

Eldora hands the half-full pack of cigarettes to the guys. "Thank you. If you see her, you tell her that her mama was looking for her, all right?"

"Is there any point in going in?" I say.

"Might as well." She drops her cigarette to the ground. "You never know what they'll have to say."

I guess. But I hate this place. The odor of despair. The stench of urine inside. The hunched, shivering shoulders of a woman on a cot in what looks to be an infirmary. There is so little meat on her bones that I can clearly make out the joint of her wrist, each knuckle on her hand.

"Can I help you folks?" A man with a white apron comes out. He's in his fifties, his black hair slicked back from a hard-lived face. Acne scars give him a particularly rough expression, and his arms are heavily tattooed.

"Yes," my mother says. "I'm Eldora Redding, and this is my daughter India, and we're looking for India's sister. She's mentally ill and she's gone missing, and we're worried about her. She shows up around here pretty often, really long hair?"

He looks at me for a long moment. "I know her," he says, but his voice is gruff. "She's drinking, so I can't have her in here."

"I know," I say, and take out a card and a pen from my wallet. "But if I give you my phone number, will you call if she shows up?"

He lifts a shoulder. "I guess."

"I'm sorry, I didn't get your name," Eldora says, leaning closer to extend her hand, her whispery Marilyn-tones suddenly penetrating his hard-case expression.

"Ramón Medina," he says, a little less harshly, and accepts her handshake.

"You look so familiar," Eldora comments. "I wonder if she's painted you. Did you know she's an artist, that her paintings are famous?"

"She's always drawing," he says. "Famous, though, huh? I didn't know that."

"She's had shows all over the country. Even in New York."

"Yeah?" He looks perplexed. "She must have money, then. Why doesn't she hire a nurse or something, somebody to make sure she gets her meds on time?"

My mother gives him a look. Sad and real. "She does," Eldora says simply. "When she's thinking right. Her daddy died and—" The sigh isn't theatrical this time, just heavy.

His gaze flickers down to the card I've just handed him. He nods. "If I see her, I'll give you a call," he says to me.

"I don't have the phone with me, but I'm checking messages every evening."

"She doesn't usually hang around more than a day or two," Ramón says. "I don't think she likes it here much. Not sure why she comes."

I notice the scars on his wrists, and look again at the chain around his neck. It's a silver cross, shaped to look like it's made of thorny branches. His face clicks in. Like a director who casts the same actor over and over, Gypsy often reuses faces, and this is one she uses a lot. I smile. Despite his scars and gruff manner, he is always an angel. "You must have been kind to her," I say, and touch his arm. "Thank you."

"Let me know if she turns up, huh? And why don't you give me her whole name, so I can find her paintings somewheres." He takes the stub of a pencil from his back pocket. "Where could I look for 'em?"

"It's Gypsy," I say. "That's all. Just Gypsy. You can get prints from a website, if you email me at that address on my card." I think of him seeing his own face in her vivid work and wonder how he will feel about it.

Eldora asks, "Ramón, was she with anybody? They told us in Tucumcari that she was with a man."

He finishes scribbling Gypsy's name on the back of my card, which makes me feel better because it increases the likelihood that he'll hang on to it and actually call me if Gypsy shows up. "Yeah. I didn't know him, though."

"They said outside she wasn't with anybody."

Ramón snorts. "That's because Danny wants her and she won't give him the time of day." He calls over his shoulder to an invisible person, "Allen, who was Gitana with last night? You knew him from Albuquerque, right?"

A white guy with a shock of red springy hair comes out of the back. "Loon. He's Lakota, early fifties. Good guy, mainly." His face twitches a little.

My mother says, "Mainly?"

"Well, he's a Vietnam vet, and when he gets delusional, sometimes he's behind the lines." His blue eyes meet mine, and I see in them the harsh reality.

"Thanks." My heart races a little. For a minute, I feel another flutter, as if another heart, the baby's or my sister's, is racing along with mine.

God, let us find her, I pray. Soon.

PART FOUR

LA FONDA HOTEL

When Santa Fe was founded in 1607, official records show an inn, or *fonda*, was among the first businesses established. The current La Fonda was built in 1922 on the site of the previous inns. Spring special: stay the second night free!

CHAPTER TWENTY

Eldora, 1973

There's a drag against my sinuses as I open the curtains in my room at the La Fonda Hotel in Santa Fe. India doesn't know what she's doing, bringing us here. She thinks she's being kind, treating me, or maybe she's treating herself, I don't know.

I light a cigarette and look down at the plaza, watching snowflakes as big as my palm float out of the gray sky. I can see my girls, aged eleven, as clearly as if they're really out there. Gypsy in her braids and India in her bandanna, venturing out into the wilds of the square, using each other as a foil against danger. It's true, what I told India at the graveyard, that you just have no idea what love means until a child swells your heart up like that.

Love doesn't necessarily mean you're a good parent, however.

Across the square in 1973, a man arrives. He's tall and broad-shouldered, a substantial man with thick black hair and a tailored suit. He looks clean and elegant, and I see women noticing him. My body goes soft at the sight of him, and by the time he's at my door, all he has to do is come in, take me in his arms, kiss me, and I'm ready. We both are. It's a wild lust, this one, and we don't even get all of our clothes off. Even as I want him, take him, devour him, I'm hating myself for it, a cut and tangle as sharp as any I've ever known.

I understood early on that sex was a dangerous thing, a weapon that could turn against you in a second. Only twice did I let it turn my head, and each time, it was a disaster. The first time was in Las Vegas. The second time it was Glenn, who waltzed into Hogan's nightclub in the spring of 1973 and melted my bones. I took one look at him and thought, *Oh no oh no oh no.*

He was a big man. I like big men in general, but especially men with some substance to them—shoulders, hips, solidity. Dark men. Italian, Spanish, Arab, Indian—American or Eastern version. One of my favorite flings was with an Arab prince who had more money than just about anybody on earth. He kept me in fine fashion for a time. Until I met Alex.

But that's another story. Or maybe it's part of the same one, since with both Alex and Glenn I let sex turn my head, let the boiling juices in my body bubble up until they poured right through me and tried to burn away everything good in my life. Alex was first, in Las Vegas. I wasn't even twenty years old—a girl that age is inclined to passions, and I think I can be forgiven that one.

The second time, though . . . there's just really no excuse. I'd been married a decade. I'd put my past behind me. Mostly, life was good, but there would be pockets of restlessness that welled up in me every now and then. I'd go dancing or throw a party and it would all be okay . . . for a while.

The night I met Glenn I was sitting with my friend Juanita in Hogan's. Juanita was married, too, and her husband was a soldier, so sometimes he was gone down-range or whatever, and we'd head down to the bar, where we'd smoke cigarettes and drink a little too much and dance, then go home to our husbands and families.

Glenn walked into The Hogan that night wearing a white suit, his dark hair long and wavy on his neck, and those high dark cheekbones. I just thought, "Oh, shit." I didn't, as I should have, tell him no when he came over five minutes later and asked me to dance. I looked up into those brown eyes and put my small hand in his big one, and that was that. I could smell it on him, the desire, and he smelled it on me.

There's just something about that first moment of knowing. It blooms all through a person, toes to eyebrows, all of it swelling and aching, until you feel as crazy as a drunk. He had long eyelashes and a beautiful mouth with big white teeth. He held me a little too close, but not obnoxiously, and whispered, "I have never seen a woman so beautiful in all my life. I can't even believe you're real."

I'd always had a strong sense of destiny, you understand. I knew something would carry me away from that awful world in Elk City, and it did. I knew I'd have a great love someday, and I did. He died and I made do, but remember, I was only thirty-three when I met Glenn. Old enough to know better, but young enough to hope for some passion in my life. Glenn's eyes, his hands, the genuine ardor I saw in him, made me think it was destiny that had come knocking again.

When I got back to the table, my friend Juanita, who was good and smart and knew me pretty well, said, "Eldora, you don't want to mess up your life. You've got it good. I hope you remember that."

And she didn't know the half of it, really. Didn't know how much Don had given up, what he'd done, to give me and the girls the life we had. I forced myself to light a cigarette, order a martini, and forget about the man across the room who looked like a cross between Dean Martin and Tom Jones. I made myself think about Don, and especially about India and Gypsy and how much they loved their daddy. He was babysitting tonight so I could be here, sitting there with his daughters, probably eating Jiffy-Pop and watching the Movie of the Week. While I sat here dressed up in a miniskirt and a low-cut blouse, my innards aching for something I couldn't even really name.

In those days I had no idea why Don let me go out with my girl-friends, knowing that I took off my wedding ring and danced with other men and flirted all night long and usually came home fairly drunk. It's not like I did it all the time—maybe once or twice a season.

It would build up in me, the need to be something besides a mommy and a wife who did things like remembered to go to the dry cleaners. Honestly, sometimes I'd sit there in my pretty little car, with the smell of dry cleaning in bags and five pounds of hamburger in the trunk, and I'd want to laugh and laugh. Better than screaming.

It just seemed, sometimes, like I went to sleep in one movie and woke up in another one.

Don knew it. That's what I can see now. It had to kill him, but if he didn't let me blow off steam once in a while, there was no telling what I'd do. So he'd kiss me on the head, tuck another ten-dollar bill in my cleavage, and wink at me. "Don't run off with anybody tonight, sweetheart," he'd say.

I'd say, "Not as long as you're in the world, Don Redding," and kiss him full on the lips.

It was April when I met Glenn. The spring had been making me crazy, and I was haunted by memories that sometimes felt like they'd kill me. I'd just wake up in the middle of the night, out of breath, reliving the worst moments as if they'd just happened. Never screaming. I didn't scream when it all happened, and I didn't scream in my dreams, but I'd be shaking and shivering so hard Don would crawl out of bed and get me a brandy when even his big, burly arms couldn't get me to stop.

See what I mean when I say . . . oh, never mind. You just can't see diddly when you're young, and that's the truth. All the things you think are so important, things you think you'll just die without—none of 'em add up to a dime's worth of happiness in the end.

A man who will get up out of a warm bed to bring his wife a brandy because she has nightmares, and he doesn't even know what those nightmares are because she won't tell him, well now, that's a man worth having.

The nightmare is always the same, about a very bad night not long before I met my husband. I still get it sometimes. Right after Don died, I had it about three times a week, and on the off nights, I'd dream about Bea.

Anyway, Glenn. Like I said, I met him at The Hogan and it might never have gone any further except, by a sheer stroke of luck, three days later I stopped at the liquor store to get some vodka—those were the vodka tonic years—for a dinner party we were having for some of Don's business associates, and there he was.

Glenn. Dressed this time in a pale-champagne linen shirt that was open like he was too hot, so I could see just a tiny hint of hair on his chest. Don't get the wrong idea. He wasn't some Lothario-looking man. He was just damned good-looking and well dressed. I was going to turn around and go right back out, but the clerk saw me and said, "Hey, Eldora. A fifth of Smirnoff?"

Glenn's head snapped up at the sound of my name, and those big brown eyes were on me. I could tell he remembered my name, and when he saw it was me, there was a flash of nerves and hope that's very hard to resist in a man. Confident, but pretty sure you are way out of his league. When a man like that gives you that look, I can tell you it's a pretty heady feeling.

"So we meet again," he said.

"Guess so," I said, taking money out of my wallet to pay for the vodka. It was easier to be sensible in the bright light of day. "How are you?"

"Better," he said. "Now."

I mocked rolling my eyes to the woman behind the counter, who knew Don, knew I was married.

"Men," she said, shaking her head.

He waited for me to pay, then held open the door and I ducked under his arm, ignoring the heady smell of his skin. "I'm married," I said outside, fitting my key into the lock of my car door.

"This is your car?"

"Yes."

"Whew." He admired it with the kind of full attention that let me know it wasn't a put-on. "I once had this very model, back in Arkansas when I was a teenager. It wasn't in this shape, but it was still a hell of a car."

"What happened to it?"

He looked up, pinned me with those brilliant eyes. "I totaled it one night after a lot of beer."

I couldn't think of anything to say. There was liquid lust burning through my knees, like I'd drunk antifreeze and was about to die. And it was just about that stupid, which I also knew.

He came around the car. "Let me help you with that bag," he said, and took it before I could say anything. When he was right in front of me, he looked at my mouth. "I don't care if you're married."

"Well, I do," I said. And I took the bag back.

"Let me buy you a cup of coffee. What would it hurt to drink coffee?"

I looked back up at him, and there was a lock of black hair on his forehead that reminded me so much of someone else that it caused a sharp pain in my middle.

That was the trouble, of course. It wasn't so much that I wanted Glenn, but that he reminded me so very much of Alex, my lover, the one lost to me forever one night in 1962.

"All right," I said.

Which led to the affair, which led to the road trip with my girls, which led to us having wild sex in this very hotel.

Thirty years later, I stand at the window of the La Fonda Hotel, smoking a Salem, and look down at the snowy plaza and wish with all I am that I could have made some different choices. Not all of them, just the really ugly ones. The ones that hurt so many people. I wish there could be some clean snow falling on my soul, making it look new and fresh.

Trouble is, though, you can't go back in time no matter how much you might want to. All you can do is see if you can find ways to live with yourself.

Or make amends. I wish I could, but all the folks I wounded so badly with my selfishness and confusion are dead. Or crazy.

Except India.

CHAPTER
TWENTY-ONE

India

After I settle my mother into her room, I carefully unpack my things, tidy my room, then head out to check the homeless shelter in Santa Fe. It's a busy place this afternoon, but the woman I speak with remembers Gypsy and knows she has not been around. I give her my card, ask her to call. She promises she will.

As I leave, I realize I'm absolutely bone dead weary. Tired of driving, tired of looking in shelters for my sister, tired of thinking about my mother, tired of everything. I need some time on my own. Instead of going back to the hotel, I wander into the streets of Santa Fe. The spring snow has followed us down the road, and as I walk toward the plaza from the chic La Fonda Hotel—I've sprung for two rooms in the upscale hotel as a treat for her—the snow lends a lovely hush.

Here is another New Mexico: well-tended adobe and wide wooden planks for sidewalks; vigas sticking out of the roofs, elegant paintings, and exquisite handmade goods in boutique windows. The shops are trendy and pricey, and I know what a coup it is to land in one of the upmarket galleries along the narrow streets because it took Gypsy a long time to break in. With a sense of soft pleasure, I follow one lane down a hill and around the corner, and pause. Across the street from a very famous restaurant is the Turquoise Hare.

I peer in the window and see two well-dressed women in boots and skirts, one with long hair, one with very short. They have their heads together, admiring a painting, and to one side I notice the proprietor obviously not looking their way, giving them room to decide.

It is one of my sister's paintings these two are admiring. It isn't the first time I've seen strangers looking at her work, but it's rare to come across it in such a way. This one is part of her purple series—purple skies, purple ground, purple graves and crosses. Smoky purples splashed with a little orange or whispers of blue or white or red. They're somehow moody and serene at once, threatening and promising.

They make me miss her. I want to feel her beside me, hold her hand, brush her pelt of hair.

I walk on, stop in a drugstore for some snacks for later, then carry my bag to Plaza Café on the square. It's an old landmark, and justifiably so—the homey smell of hamburgers sizzling and coffee brewing hits my nostrils as I enter. It's midafternoon and quiet, so I take a seat by the window, order a cup of tea, and look out at the plaza. The waiters and waitresses chat behind the long counter, a cozy, Spanish-inflected sound. I cross my arms on the table and gaze out at the square, quiet and beautiful beneath the falling snow. Across the way, in front of the Palace of the Governors, lines of Indians, draped in jean jackets and parkas, sit in lawn chairs, their silver and turquoise spread before them on multicolored blankets. I'm transported to another day.

Our mother had a headache and asked us to go find something to do for a little while. With a five-dollar bill tucked in each of our hands, we rushed out to the plaza to see what we could see, buy some souvenirs and maybe a soda or candy.

And it was a thrilling place. The sun cut downward in thick yellow curtains, and the buildings were all soft, low adobe with balconies and features like wooden windowsills. It dazzled me.

"Look!" Gypsy cried, squeezing my arm. "Indians! Real Indians!"

We crossed the square, holding hands, and peeked around the wooden pillars holding up the porch roof of a long gallery. There was a woman, round as a pear, sitting cross-legged before her blanket of shining goods, her hair woven into braids that fell over her breasts to the ground. "Come on," I said, "let's go look at her stuff!"

But Gypsy could not move. She shook her head and held on to the pillar, just staring.

"I want to look."

She gave me a glare. "Go ahead. I'm not the scaredy-cat."

"Don't go anywhere!"

"I won't."

Drawn by beaded barrettes a little farther down, I wandered away, kneeling to finger the bright red-and-yellow columns. "You have pretty hair," said the young woman weaving more beads into order as she waited for tourists. "The butterfly would be nice."

"I don't have enough money of my own right now," I said. "My mom is in that hotel over there." I pointed to the La Fonda. "She's taking a nap, but she might come out later with us."

"You can look without buying," she said. "Take your time."

"How did you learn to do that?" I asked her.

"My mother taught me." Her lean, long athletic fingers gestured me forward. "It is not hard. You see?" She dipped a needle thinner than most thread I'd ever seen into beads no larger than a mustard seed, and looped it into line with the next one.

"Wow." My fingers ached to try it, handle the circle of cool bead, the tensile length of the needle. "Can you buy beads like that here?"

"You can buy them, better by mail. Do you have a good memory?"

"Very good," I said. "My teachers say I'm really smart, though I'm not as smart as my sister." I pointed. Gypsy was still hugging the post, her attention fixed on the blanket of goods in front of her. "She's kinda shy."

"Twins, huh?" The woman put down her beads and picked up a pencil. "I can tell you the place you can write to for a catalog of beads if you want them, but I'll write it down instead. It's in Albuquerque."

"*Thank you.*" *I tucked the paper in my pocket.* "*Is it okay if I keep watching you do it?*"

"*Sure. Sometimes I have to take care of customers.*"

"*I know. That's your job.*"

She smiled and made a place for me to sit beside her. I don't know how long I sat there, watching her nimble fingers weave tubes of perfectly straight, neat beads. She told me she lived with her husband and children in a pueblo, not far away, and they grew corn and beans, and lettuce in the spring.

I finally noticed my mother across the street, sitting on a bench by herself, smoking. Her hair was piled up on her head because it was so hot, and she wore a sundress with wide blue-green straps over her shoulders. Her legs were crossed and she swung one foot lazily.

I waved at her. "*That's my mom.*"

"*She's a pretty lady. Is that your dad with her?*"

A man in a white suit carried Cokes purchased from a nearby vendor and sat down next to her. I didn't like the way my mother laughed up at him, like a flower turning petals toward the sun. "*No. I don't know who he is. My dad is at home.*"

"*Hmm.*"

I suddenly remembered Gypsy and looked around for her. She was no longer standing by the pillar, but had stretched out on a bench and had fallen asleep. Why hadn't my mom gone to her?

"*I have to go wake up my sister,*" *I said.* "*Maybe my mom will let me buy some barrettes.*"

The woman nodded, her mouth serious. "*Thank you for sitting with me today. It made the time go faster.*"

~

Back in the present day, the skies are dark and the snow is heavy, but I smile anyway at the little girl I was. It was the first time I'd ever done something purely because I was curious. Mostly I held back, observed, made all those little plans.

I did learn to bead. There was something about the symmetry and order of the patterns that appealed to me mightily. I loved taking the tiny masses of beads and turning them into a thing of orderliness and color. I learned freehand beading on my own from a book, then a neighbor taught me how to use a loom and I made belts and bigger pieces. As time went on, I amassed a huge collection, sorted by color and size into egg cartons I kept in a special box my mother bought me. One year, when we were fourteen, I spent the best part of the summer and fall hand-beading a pair of doeskin moccasins for Gypsy. They were her prized possession.

It was the beadwork that led, indirectly, to the web design work. My degree was in graphic design, but because computers were just emerging and I had so much time on my hands, I spent a lot of time on them, learning languages and admiring the ordered world. Computer programming was, in its way, much like beadwork—exacting, orderly, beautiful. As the internet developed, web design brought both of my loves into combination. What is a pixel but a bead of design?

But one does need inspiration. I find, as I sit there in the Plaza Café on a snowy day in New Mexico, that my mind is springing in new directions, flavored by new colors, shapes, relationships of one thing to the next. The café itself is fantastic—the quiet yellow light over the counter in the restaurant, the angles of the waitress's eyebrows and cheekbones, the softness and whiteness of snow in comparison to the dark branches of trees.

I will never be the artist my sister is, but art has woven the backdrop of my life, too. My mother had been right: I am filling the well on this trip, gathering up images to put in a basket and carry home with me. Souvenirs of color and light.

And my mother, who birthed and tended two artists into being, what was her art? The question has never presented itself to me before. With it came another, this one a little deeper: If my mother had been mothered herself, what sort of life might she have had? Would she have painted, written, designed clothing?

A pair of young women comes in, wearing knitted sweaters, stamping feet clad in hiking boots. One is ruddy and curly-headed, the other darkly beautiful, her hair sleek as a seal's. Both have an air of Europe about them. I wonder why I think so, and sip my tea as I try to pick it out: They are both less polished and more—their clothes not quite so up to the moment, but solidly classic. A kind of freshness of skin, a different sort of body language than American girls.

"Do we wait or go sit down?" one asks the other quietly.

"Well, you could read the sign, which says, right there, 'Please wait to be seated.'"

Hearing their accents, I grin—I'd been correct in my assumption. They were European. Irish. Acting on impulse I say, "Would you like to join me? I won't be here long and the view is spectacular."

"Us, you mean?" The dark-haired girl smiles at me, and tugs her friend's sleeve. "That's very nice," she says, and they settle across from me, disentangling from backpacks and coats. "I'm Orla, this is Kate."

"I'm India." At the slight cock of her eyebrow, I add, "Odd name, I know. My mother said she wanted us to have adventures."

"Well, that's a good thought. Have you?"

"A few. And how about the two of you? How long are you here? What have you seen?"

"Oh, God!" Kate, with hair as springy as wool, widens her eyes as she leans on the table. "It's been seven—"

"Eight."

"Eight weeks. We've been all over. Started in New York City and we're working our way to Los Angeles."

"Are you going to stay there?"

"No, no. Not I, anyway," said Orla. She rubs chapped hands together. "I've a boyfriend waiting."

"She's being polite," her friend says with a quirk of her lips. "America doesn't suit her."

"Kate!" Orla rolls her eyes. "She's rude. I can't take her anywhere."

"It's all right." The waitress comes over with big menus. The girls order tea and dither over the choices.

"What should we eat here?" Kate asks me. "D'you live here?"

"No. I'm traveling, too. My mother and I are driving to Las Vegas."

"Ah! We're going there. Is it nice?"

"I've never been. My mother spent a lot of time there when she was young."

"It's nice you're going with her."

I smile. "Thanks." The sound of their accent is weaving through me like a twining vine, growing up green through my chest. "What part of Ireland are you from?"

"Cork. Do you know it?"

"No, I haven't been there. To the southwest, right?"

"Yeah. I'm a nurse," Kate said. "Orla's a teacher—or she will be."

They have the same eyes, I realize. Long, slightly tilted upward at the outside corner, vividly blue. "Are you sisters?"

"We are! No one ever guesses."

I nod, pleased. "All right, so you want some help ordering something authentic and delicious?"

"That would be kind of you."

We work out an order, so they can pick and choose through things they might enjoy, and have something bland and ordinary in case they find chiles not to their liking. "It's not that we're not adventurous," Orla says. "It's just that we haven't got much in the way of this sort of food in Ireland. It's hard to know."

"Right." I've been trying not to say it, but it comes out of my mouth. "I have a friend who is Irish."

"From Ireland?"

I nod, smiling at the faint emphasis on *from*. "Galway. He misses it, I think."

Orla's eyes glitter as she leans over her hands. "And you miss him."

I bow my head, a little abashed. "I suppose I do. I want to sit here and listen to you talk so I can hear him in my head."

They laugh. "Well, talking is something we do pretty well."

Their meal comes and we chat about travel—theirs and mine. I'd spent seven months in Europe at twenty-three, just wandering and exploring. They were shocked I'd not made it to Ireland, and I explained that there'd been a Greek who'd captured my attention for a bit.

In turn they told me what they'd discovered. Both of them had fallen in love with Krispy Kreme doughnuts, hamburgers, and Starbucks. They were bewildered by what they felt was a sparsity of news on American television, intensely disliked pickup trucks, and were appalled at the paucity of public transportation.

They give a thumbs up to tamales and stuffed sopapillas, and a thumbs down to the green chile stew, which they find too hot.

The light is beginning to fade and I realize I'd better get moving if I'm to check my email before going back to the hotel. "Do you girls know if there's an internet café anywhere close?"

"Not three blocks," Orla says. "We just came from there."

I put on my coat and shake their hands, and head out into the close, dark day. Snow is still swirling down, starting to stick in corners, though I'm not worried. The flurries are not unusual this time of year, and it will melt the moment the sun comes out. For now, I like the pinkish wash it gives the sky, the slight sense of hush and expectation.

At the internet café, there's a computer free in the corner. I sign in with a boy who has on a shirt with a collar and a striped tie, and pointy metal studs the size of bullets through his earlobes. There's a heady scent of coffee underlaid with something else, something vaguely unpleasant I can't quite pinpoint, and the music is alternative hip, as opposed to alternative heavy or alternative girl.

When I sit down at the long row of machines, there is a sound of click, click, clicking all through the room, and a dozen conversations, many of them on cell phones, conducted while the talkee types away on a keyboard. On one side of me is a businessman in his mid-twenties, balding, with shoes that somehow scream East Coast to me, talking into his cell, and flipping between a game screen, a chat screen, and an email list. It makes me dizzy.

I sign on to my email server through the web. There are 122 messages waiting for me. That's the downside of having most of your life on the internet. Without my usual software, I can only open the mailbox and check the headers one at a time, twenty per page. The connection is fairly slow, and each page takes a solid forty seconds to open.

There are a handful of notes from friends and some from business partners, but the address I'm seeking is particular, of course: jshea@sheaenterprises.com. It is not on the first page, though I have to delete five spam messages. None on the second page, and I delete three spams.

On page four I find what I'm looking for. Jack. It was sent this morning at twelve minutes after ten. After I called his secretary.

Before I open it, I click through the rest of the list to see if there are others from him. With a sense of unreasoning relief, I count five.

Five.

One email would be cursory. Three would show concern. Five . . . five might mean that he really does have strong feelings for me. If they're strong enough, maybe we'll figure out how to survive all this.

I open them in the order they arrived. The first is from Tuesday, the day we left, at noon.

TO: India@indiaredding.com
FROM: jshea@sheaenterprises.com
Subject: Tuesday lunchtime

India, I apologize. I was rude. You surprised me, that's all. Call me and we'll talk.

Jack

I feel tenseness return. There is no "love, Jack." Which may or may not mean anything. I click on the next one, time-stamped a few hours after the first one.

> TO: India@indiaredding.com
> FROM: jshea@sheaenterprises.com
> Subject: Tuesday afternoon
>
> I suspect you have left for Las Vegas and not taken your phone.
>
> Please call me when you get this message.
>
> Jack

Still no "love." The next one is late the night before. One a.m., his time.

> TO: India@indiaredding.com
> FROM: jshea@sheaenterprises.com
> Subject: Weds night
>
> Dear India,
>
> I was a bastard and I admit it. I am worried about you and what you're thinking. Let's talk. Phone me anytime, day or night.
>
> Jack

> TO: India@indiaredding.com
> FROM: jshea@sheaenterprises.com

Subject:

This is not fair, to drop the news and run.

Finally, I open the one he sent after my phone call this morning:

TO: India@indiaredding.com
FROM: jshea@sheaenterprises.com
Subject: Thursday morning

Penny said you phoned. I should have instructed
her to interrupt me.

I will be home this evening. Please phone at your
convenience.

Jack

Please phone at your convenience. As if I'm a client he needs to speak
with. My gut feels like I swallowed acid.

Maybe he's just angry, which I suppose I can understand. Or maybe
his feelings are hurt, which I can also understand.

Don't get your hopes up, says a little voice in my head.

I scan the rest of the mail, most of it business, and answer two that
seem urgent. Then I pay for the minutes I've used, and hurry back to
the hotel in the dark, surprised so much time has gone by. I glance at
my watch and discover it's almost seven p.m., which makes it nearly
nine in New York. A good time to catch Jack.

My mother is sitting in the lobby. "There you are! I'm starving."

"Sorry! The time got away from me." I'm quite hungry myself all of
a sudden, and I realize it's been many hours since breakfast.

I glance at my watch, thinking with an ache of Jack's voice, the sound of Ireland in those girls' voices. It's like a physical pain, the hunger to just hear him.

Eldora says, "The concierge says the Blue Corn Café is very close and very good. Shall we eat there tonight? My treat."

I'm not sure if it's the light casting shadows, or just my recognition of a truth, but she looks quite fragile all of a sudden. She's not only Eldora, Bigger Than Life. She's my mother, who is aging, and has lost her husband and a daughter in the past six months. The lines around her mouth are deep, exaggerated. "That sounds good, Mom."

She stands and smoothes her sweater down over her hips. "Will you have a margarita with me?"

"I don't know. I'm not feeling that well, to tell you the truth. My stomach has been a little off all day." Though I don't know what difference it will make if I drink since I've made up my mind to have an abortion. "We'll see."

She gives me a long look, then loops her arm through mine. "You don't have to be shy with me, sugar-girl."

I laugh. "Believe me, Mother, I do know that." I glance at my watch. I'll call Jack when we get back to the hotel. "Let's eat."

CHAPTER TWENTY-TWO

India

The Blue Corn Café is a touristy spot near the plaza, but it's pleasant inside, with low lights and attractively tall booths and lots of Southwestern touches on the walls. The smell of chiles is promising as we settle in and my mother orders a margarita. "Do you want one, India?"

In fact, I would kill for one tonight. Something tells me they'd be very good here. "I think I just want iced tea."

The waitress notes my hesitation with a smile. "Sure?" she coaxes. "We have a lot of varieties of tequila."

"Oh, I'm sure." I pat my tummy with a regretful shrug. "They give me indigestion."

The girl hurries away, taking a pencil from behind her ear, and my mother dips a chip into chunky salsa. "Since when?"

"I don't know. Lately. Lots of things have been bothering me." I dip a chip, too, and widen my eyes. "Hot!"

"Margaritas bother you, but salsa doesn't?"

"Weird, huh?" I bend over the menu eagerly. "Oooh, it's going to be hard to choose." In the air, again, is a faint scent I can't quite identify, a whisper of vaguely unpleasant something. "What is that smell?"

Eldora inhales. "It smells like a Mexican restaurant to me. Meat and onions and spices. Yum. I think I'm having the rellenos. I'll work them off when we get back home."

"Sounds wonderful." I nibble on another chip—buttery blue corn. "You can't get blue corn enchiladas anywhere else. Maybe I should have enchiladas. With beef and cheese. And sour cream." I slap the menu closed. "All right."

"Good choice." She looks around happily. "This is nice. Your daddy would have loved it, but I would have had to fight—nicely of course— about him not eating anything too hot."

I smile. "He would have liked the whole trip, probably."

"He did discover a love of travel at the end there. It was that cruise that did it, when we went to Mexico for our thirtieth anniversary. We had such a good time! Slot machines and dancing, and lots of chances to dress up."

"Maybe you'd enjoy another cruise, Mom. There's nothing to stop you."

Her gaze flickers away. "I've given it some thought. It felt disloyal at first, to think about going without your dad, but—" She lifts a pretty shoulder, meets my eyes. "I am only sixty-three. I could live a long time yet, and I guess I have to figure out what my life is gonna look like."

"Good for you."

"I'd like to get a little healthier. Walk, maybe, or something."

"You'd have a better chance if you'd give up those damned cigarettes."

"Well, now," she says smoothly, tapping the table with a long fingernail, "believe it or not, I have also been thinking about that, too. It's getting to be pretty hard to smoke freely these days and I really would rather smell like perfume. Not to mention, I've got enough wrinkles. Smoking gives you more."

I chuckle. "Leave it to you, Mom, to make it an issue of vanity." When she starts to protest, I wave a hand. "That's fine. If it makes you quit, I'm all for it."

"I didn't say I was going to, you understand. Just that I'm thinking about it."

The waitress brings our drinks—a big frosty, salt-rimmed glass for my mother. "Oh, look at that. How beautiful!"

The girl smiles. "Can I take your order now?"

We tell her what we want. When she leaves, my mother pulls the margarita toward her, admiring the salt, touching the pad of a finger to a perfect crystal. "This is when I'd like a cigarette." There is no smoking indoors in Santa Fe. "But it's funny that you don't die of the wanting. It can be pleasant anyway."

"Right." You don't die of the wanting. To distract myself, I say, "So you've been thinking about what you want your life to look like now that Dad's gone? Any ideas beyond travel?"

"Not many," she says, but there's no worry in it. She puts her elbows on the table, her graceful white hands one over the other, and leans forward intently. "I don't *need* to work, but maybe I want to. I've been thinking I'd like to work in a bookstore. I love books. I think it would be fun."

"That's a great idea."

"Too often, you see a woman just get old real fast after her husband dies, and I don't want to do that." She meets my eyes. "I also know you don't want to stay in Colorado Springs, that you're dying to get back to Denver."

"There's no rush," I say. In fact, if—

No. I'm not having the baby. Cannot take the chance. Made up my mind earlier and I'm sticking to it.

But if I did, it wouldn't be so bad to be here in the Springs, where I could call on my mother and her friends for guidance. What do any of my single friends know about babies?

This would be the perfect time to lean over the table and say, *Mom? I have this problem, and I need your advice.*

Instead, I say, "I'm fine in my apartment for now, Mom. Take your time figuring it out. It's a big change, and I do understand that."

"You're a sweetheart, you know." She nibbles the edge of a chip. "I hope you know how much I appreciate your support, and how much I'm enjoying this trip."

"Me, too," I say, and to my surprise, it's true.

"I'm dreading Gallup, I have to admit. Lot of bad memories there."

Gypsy ran away in Gallup. "Yeah."

"Do you remember?" my mother says with surprise.

"That Gypsy ran away? Of course."

She takes a breath, puts down her chip, and takes a sip of margarita. Carefully she says, "Do you remember your father's first wife at all?"

I frown, thinking about it. A picture comes up of a woman in an old-fashioned shirtwaist, heavy-bosomed and graying, staring with hot black eyes at me and my sister in the car. "I think I only saw her a couple of times. Dad did things for her around the house, right?"

"He took good care of her." Eldora clears her throat, an uncharacteristic gesture of hesitation. "She didn't handle the divorce very well."

"She had a bitter mouth," I say, remembering the tight lips. "It's hard to imagine anyone more different from you."

"I had an unfair advantage, India. I was a lot younger. And in those days, people of her generation seemed to get old faster, you know what I mean? Even in the seventies, forty was time to get out the tie-up shoes."

Laughingly, I shudder and toss a weight of wild, curly hair over my forty-year-old shoulder. "Thank God we don't have to now."

"She never gave up on your father 'coming to his senses' as she used to put it. Not until the bloody end."

"Really." I say it as an invitation, hearing my mother's storytelling voice, slower and richer than her normal voice, fill the small, enclosed area of our booth.

Eldora takes a sip of her margarita and looks off into the distance. Candlelight dances on her irises, and as she begins to tell me the next chapter in her tale, I imagine her at thirty-three, hanging out clothes on the line in a pair of neat shorts and a short shirt tied under her prodigious breasts.

CHAPTER
TWENTY-THREE

Eldora, June 1973

It was one of those still, hot, sunny days in June when nothing's moving between noon and five. The girls were at the swimming pool with their friends. I dropped them off right after lunch and they stayed all afternoon at least two or three times a week. It turned them brown as pinto beans, and sometimes it was hard to believe they were my children, these two dark-haired, dark-eyed girls. They looked Mexican or Indian or something. Pretty. I didn't tan as well as they did, but I was thinking about pouring a nice glass of iced tea and taking my book to a lawn chair for an hour or so once I got the clothes hung up. Get a little tan on my tummy.

I had a dryer, you know, but there was something nice about hanging clothes on the line, especially the sheets. It made me happy to smell the sunshine and wind in them when we crawled into bed at night. Don liked it, too, and he would curl up next to me, his big hands on my tummy, and cuddle close. "So nice," he'd say, and fall asleep.

It had surprised me to find out I didn't mind those little chores, hanging sheets on the line and going to the supermarket and planning meals. I liked my big modern kitchen and the pretty furniture Don bought for us, and having things looking tidy and beautiful. Everyone told me I ought to be an interior designer. There was more than one living room in Pleasant Valley that I'd made improvements on, let me tell you. Some of those poor women couldn't match a green to save their lives.

I clipped a clothespin to India's blue sheet. Over the top of the line I could see Pikes Peak, gone pale and gray in the bright sunlight, as if it were a fading painting. To the north of me, I could just make out the tops of the red rocks at Garden of the Gods, which is where Don walked every evening when he got home from work. The sky was that piercing blue of a postcard photo, so different from the skies I knew in Oklahoma, and there wasn't a sound in the world except the lazy drone of a faraway plane.

What I was thinking, standing there, is how lucky I was, and how foolish for risking it all with Glenn, who wouldn't've turned my head if he'd come in the summer. It was only wintertime with the early dark and the dismal routine of waking up and doing chores and reading endlessly that made me feel trapped. Stupid Tupperware parties and Mary Kay demonstrations and all the other idiotic things women did to see themselves through the dullness of winter. It bored me to tears. Ditto the room mother business. I did it for one year and was so sick of those other mothers by the end of the year that I would happily have taken a meat cleaver to their heads. Their whinnying laughs, their panic at the loss of themselves in their families. The petty struggles over brownies that took the place of the struggles they really wanted to fight for.

All around us the world was going crazy—Vietnam and hippies and women's lib and race riots—and what were we doing? These were smart women, some of them with good educations, but there wasn't much room for them to do anything with their good brains, so they turned petty and nasty. A lot of them, as time went by, dumped their straitjackets and found some new meaning in their lives, but that was a ways off just then, that winter of 1972–1973. We all knew Tupperware was about as important as watching grass grow, but what else was there?

By the time spring rolled around, I was stretched to breaking, and Glenn brought something that felt like meaning. Believe me, I hadn't missed the fact that he looked a whole lot like another man, the one man I never could get over in my heart, the one who could still come into my dreams after all these years, and make me hurt for days.

And Glenn was from Las Vegas. It seemed like a sign to my foolish brain.

What I wish now is that I'd gone to work sooner. I kept wanting to, but Don was against it. He wanted me home with the girls, home to fix his supper. I think he was afraid I might fall in love out there, that I'd leave him, and it was safer keeping me in the house.

But I never wanted anybody else. I really didn't. Don was good to me. Getting together with me had cost him, and I'd made a promise to myself that I'd see it through to the very end. It's true I didn't love him the way he loved me, but he never knew that. I made sure.

Work would have, and eventually did, give me a way to use my brain. That's the thing I never really knew about myself, that I was so smart. I'm a whiz at all kinds of things, but mainly people. I understand how people fit together, what makes them tick, and work gave me a chance to see that, use it, do something with myself every day.

Anyway, that afternoon, hanging up clothes, half dreaming about Glenn's smooth dark legs, and feeling guilty about it, I had an unexpected visitor.

Bea, Don's ex-wife.

She just appeared, like a ghost or something, not there one second and there the next. I made a screeching noise and grabbed the sheet to my heart. She stood in front of me, silent as a chunk of granite and just about as appealing. Everything about her had gone hard and gray over the years. Once she was an ordinary housewife, a little plump, wearing glasses that didn't do a thing for her face, but cheerful enough. She was a pillar-of-the-community type of woman: busy in her parish and in the neighborhood, visiting shut-ins, and planning the Fourth of July picnic.

That makes her sound stodgy. She wasn't. Don used to say the thing he'd liked most about her when they met was that she had a giant, wild laugh. I asked him, too, if she liked sex, and he said she'd been afraid at first, but came around.

When she was a girl, I'm sure she was pretty in an ordinary kind of way, smooth skin and clear eyes, and a nice figure. I've seen the wedding pictures. She had a good sweep of glossy blonde hair and wore red lipstick, and her wedding gown was white lace. They got married in 1943, since Don was 4-F and didn't have to serve in World War II.

At the time they were saying their vows, I was three years old.

And if you're judging me now as a harlot and a homewrecker, you go right ahead. I deserve it. I flat out stole that woman's husband, with foresight and intent as they say. There were extenuating circumstances, but I reckon they're not enough to make that okay, especially considering what happened.

Which is that divorce ruined Bea Redding's life.

That sounds dramatic in this day and age—though if you look around, I'll bet you'll see a whole lot more of it than you think—but in those days, what was there for Bea to do? She was forty, ordinary, trained to be a wife and mother and not much else. She got a job as a secretary, but I'm pretty sure she never went on a date or got another kiss or slept with a man's arms around her again the rest of her life.

Part of that was stubbornness. I'm sorry, but there comes a point where you just have to move on, instead of standing there howling and nursing your wounds. Everybody gets body-slammed by life once in a while, and how you get through it is what shows your character. I'm not saying I didn't feel some pity for her, and a whole lot of guilt, but she could have looked around at church for a nice widower or something. She didn't have to keep her eyes fastened on Don the entire rest of her life.

Now, before this June afternoon when I was hanging out clothes, we had not ever had a conversation. I didn't reckon she'd much care to have a chat with me, after all, the woman who stole her husband right out from under her nose. A younger woman, one who gave him twins after she'd been trying for twenty years and hadn't had any babies at all. It was bitter to her. Once she came after me with a shoe, but I don't blame her. She was hysterical at the time.

"Bea!" I said. "You liked to scare the life out of me." I was nervous, not really knowing what she was all about, and I made a joke. "Not that you would probably mind that, would you?"

She blinked. It looked reptilian, I must admit. "I saw you, Eldora, with a man, at the Red Wing Motel in Manitou Springs last Thursday afternoon."

Slowly, I straightened. Met her eyes. "And?"

"He was a good-looking man. If you like the flashy type."

I waited, though I was pretty sure I knew what was coming. "And?" I said again when she didn't say anything.

"I want my husband back."

"Don't be ridiculous."

"You have two choices," she said. "You can run off quietly in the night, or I'll tell him and you can be disgraced in front of everybody."

Both fear and amazement welled up in my voice. "Are you threatening me?"

"You better believe it."

"It would break his heart if you told him. And what makes you think he'd be with you anyway?"

"He loved me before you came along and ruined it."

"That may be true, Bea, and I am sorry for what happened."

"Save it," she said fiercely. Little bits of spit came flying out of her mouth. "You're a slut and you don't deserve that man or those children."

I met her eyes and spoke the truth. "You know what? You're right. I haven't done one damned thing right my whole life, and I don't deserve him or the love of those babies, but I'll be damned if I'm going to let some bitter old bag tell me what to do with my life."

Ducking under the sheets, I faced her head-on. "What do you know about it anyway? There you were, all spoiled little princess in your sweet little world, where nothing bad ever happened to you. You had a mama and daddy who loved you, and a nice house and a nice church and people to look out for you, and you even found one of the five men not in the war to marry you." She was glaring at me, her nostrils flaring, and I went on. "Not everybody gets it that easy, Bea. You had some bad breaks, I'll give you that. It wasn't fair, but it was ten years ago and you need to find something else to think about."

"I'll tell him. I swear I will."

Hot fear washed through me. Not fear for my safety but fear for Don, for what it might do to him. "Please," I whispered. "Don't."

"Then leave him."

"How can I do that? The girls love him."

"I'll watch over the girls for you. They're good girls."

"No." I lifted my chin. "You know, blackmail won't work. I know I've made a mistake, and I can fix it. I'll tell him myself, ask his forgiveness, and you know he'll give it to me."

She came after me then, screeching and yelling and clawing. She tried to scratch my eyes out, and succeeded in tearing my shirt practically off me. It made me think of another time in my life when a woman went crazy and came after me, and believe me, I wasn't going to let Bea hurt me. I was a lot taller, younger, stronger, and I managed to get hold of her and wrestle her down to the ground.

"Bea," I said when her face was in the grass, "you do whatever you think is right, but you're not going to come into my house and threaten me, do you understand? I'll break your neck if you come near my girls."

She said, "I . . . hate . . . you."

"I know." I stood up and let her go. "You've got every right to." I brushed grass off my knees, and there was a thud in my chest that told me I had to get my head on straight, start taking care of business properly, because she couldn't possibly hate me any more than I hated myself right then. I made up my mind to end it with Glenn. We'd only been together a few times, though he called me twice a week when Don was at work and we had long, lovely conversations.

It had been crazy, letting him in, and I knew it when I did it. I wondered, as Bea stormed off, how it was I'd become so corrupted. I wondered how to fix it.

And I just didn't know.

One thing I could do was some damage control. I lit a cigarette and called Don. "Honey," I said, exhaling all my adrenaline into the receiver, "Bea was just here, and I think she's losing it. She was talking crazy. I think you need to go see her on your way home."

"Are you okay?" he asked me.

I looked up at the sky so the tears flowing down my face wouldn't ruin my makeup, and took a drag off my cigarette. "I'm fine, sweetheart. I love you, you know that?"

"I love you, too."

CHAPTER TWENTY-FOUR

India

After telling her story, my mother looks pale and drained. I can hardly think of what to say. *You're a good woman anyway?* She wouldn't appreciate it.

We wander through the narrow streets back to the hotel, window shopping. There is hardly anyone out. Although the snow has stopped, it's very cold, the damp whisper of winter blowing back toward Canada for the season. I pause in front of a jewelry display, a cluster of inlays with fire opals and sugilite. "These are different," I comment. "Those earrings would look good with that purple angora sweater you have."

She smokes, peers into the case. Light from the showroom shines on the crown of her head. "They're pretty. I like that bracelet a lot."

We move along slowly, admiring upscale and ever-so-hip western wear—leather and conches and long fringes; lots of turquoise and red and silver, with splashes of black.

"I sometimes think I'd like to live here," my mother says. "Somewhere it feels different."

"Really? I find it hard to imagine you anywhere but in that house in Pleasant Valley."

She waves the hand that holds her cigarette. "What's there for me now, India?"

"Well, me, for one." I think of the baby inside of me. I wonder how she'd feel about a grandchild, if she would like it or not like it. "Gypsy." That would be three.

"Oh, you've got your own life now, India. I can see that. I know you're chomping at the bit to get back to Denver."

"Nobody ever made me do anything I didn't want to do, Mother." She chuckles. "True."

We part ways in the elevator—her room is on a smoking floor. Mine is one floor higher. "Take it easy," I say as she gets off the elevator.

Her blue eyes have a sorrow in them when she looks at me. She only nods, waves a hand. I do wish she'd just give up the drinking entirely.

Back in my room, I glance at my watch. Nine p.m., which is eleven New York time. I want to call, but there are two things stopping me. If he doesn't answer, I'll worry about where he is and who he's with. If he does answer, I'm afraid he is going to be terribly unhappy with me and I'll feel even worse than I do right now.

In the end, though, there is only one honorable thing to do: return his phone call. I pick up the phone, dial the first five numbers, and realize I really need to use the toilet. Hanging up the phone, I rush into the bathroom and close the door, wash my hands, and stare at myself in the mirror for a few minutes. My eyes are bloodshot, probably from driving. Any makeup I'd put on this morning has long since worn away. My skin is the color of the pale adobe walls—a nice color for deserts and houses, not so great for a face. And when did my jawline start looking so soft?

I dry my hands, smooth back the corkscrew curls poking up out of my scrunchy, head back into the bedroom. Pick up the phone again. Dial the numbers fast enough I'm not tempted to hang up. It rings. Once. Twice. Three times.

I'm almost ready to hang up when he answers. "Hello."

"Hi, Jack. It's me."

"Jesus, Mary, and Joseph! I've been worried sick about you. Are you on the road?"

"Yes. I'm sorry I was so rude."

"Where are you now?"

"We're in Santa Fe." I settle on the edge of the bed, look around. "It's a gorgeous room, at the La Fonda Hotel. You'd like it—first class all the way."

"Good bathroom?"

I smile. "The best. Ceramic tiles, and vigas, and I even have a little kiva fireplace with a sand painting over it."

"Sounds lovely."

I don't know what to say next, and the silence stretches, echoey and pressing into my chest. Suddenly, I blurt out, "Jack, I'm so—"

At that exact instant, he says, "India, I'm—"

"You first," I say.

"No, please. Go ahead."

"Oh, I insist."

A touch of humor in his voice. "Ladies first, of course."

I take a breath. "I'm sorry I took off like that. It was rude."

"And I apologize for not calling the very next morning. I was surprised, that's all."

"We don't have to talk about it tonight."

"All right." I can't tell what this agreement means. "How is it all going? Any sign of your sister?"

"Not yet." The stunning weight of the past two days comes rushing back over me. "It's quite amazing, this trip," I say, and scoot up the bed until I'm leaning against the wall. "We've been right on Gypsy's tail, and I'm hoping she might show up here in Santa Fe overnight. She might have gone on to Gallup—she doesn't seem to stop here as often, but my mother loves it, so I thought it would be nice for her to have a day of enjoyment."

"That's good."

"Yeah. I've heard some stories from my mother that are a little bit of a shock, but it's good that she's telling me." I curl the cord around my finger, watch it bounce. "You were right about that one thing, that time goes too fast. Tonight, over supper, I was thinking that she's a lot older than I realize. I mean, her health is good, but she smokes like a fiend."

"Ach, don't discount her health. My grandfather smoked till he died, and he was eighty-seven." A pause. "He was kicked by a mule, so it wasn't even smoking that took him."

"And I suppose he drank six pints of Guinness a day, too."

"Sure." He chuckles.

I missed his voice so much! I'm feeling the color yellow in me, pouring, gilding, flowing. No, not yellow, exactly. The amber shade of alfalfa honey. "How are you?" I ask. "Finish up your meetings?"

"It's all finished, thank God. Signed papers yesterday."

"Very good. I know it's been driving you crazy."

"Well, that's that. What sort of things did your mother tell you? Or would you rather not share?"

"No, I don't mind. It's just . . . . odd. She's lied about a lot of things, but I'm not quite sure why."

"Such as?"

"She grew up poor, for one thing. Her mother had a psychotic breakdown when she was eleven or twelve and she had to help raise all these brothers. She was a waitress. It sounds like her father lost it and my mother was stuck holding things together." I frown. "I mean, I guess I can understand being ashamed of poverty and maybe the business with her mother was painful, but she also lied about where she grew up—in Oklahoma, not Texas. Why lie about something like that, especially when there isn't that much difference between them?"

"Because none of the rest is true, perhaps?"

"You mean she made up the whole life, so she had to set it in a different place?"

"Right."

"That makes sense."

"Or she committed a terrible crime and was running from the law." He chuckles to let me know he's kidding, but it scares me.

"You know, Jack, all of a sudden I realize I don't know her at all. Maybe she did kill somebody back there." I sit up on the bed. "You know, she ducked a question today about what happened to the man she ran out of town with. Maybe she killed him!"

His laughter is low and soft. "Perhaps. I somehow do not see your mother as a murderess."

"No, me neither. Unless she tried to charm someone to death." I think of her at the shelter in Espanola. "She gave a pack of cigarettes to a group of homeless men this afternoon."

"It sounds like you're enjoying yourself, India. I'm glad."

"She gets on my nerves, but I do love her. There's really no one like her on the planet." A spear of something goes through my heart. "It's just that . . ."

"What is it?"

"Did I ever tell you that she and Gypsy and I made this trip when I was a kid?"

"You mentioned it."

"Well, what I didn't know is that she was leaving my father. Or maybe I did know it," I say, thinking of my memories this afternoon of the man in the white suit bringing my mother a Coke in the plaza. I sigh and rub the place between my eyebrows. "I guess I did, more or less. A man showed up."

"No one is perfect, India. And you don't know what was happening in their marriage."

"That's true. My father was quite a lot older than her. And she did go back to him."

"Right." He pauses a moment. "It's hard to remember that our parents are only human."

I think of the baby, wonder if he's thinking of it, too. The silence stretches between us, thickening as the time goes on. I think of Eldora's mother, trying to kill her children. It makes it impossible to breathe.

He begins, "India—"

Interrupting, I say brightly, "I met some Irish girls this afternoon. From Cork."

"Did you." Is that disappointment I hear, or relief? "India, I truly am sorry I did not call sooner. We've always said there'd be no talk of the future."

"I know. I don't want to talk about it now, either."

"We'll have to."

"It's not your problem, Jack. I just wanted to tell you. It seemed fair."

"It seemed fair to tell me but you'll not listen?"

Pressure builds in my chest. "It will wait for a few days. I had plenty of time to think about it. You haven't."

"I have now."

"Jack, please. Let's not tonight, okay?"

A short pause. Then I hear him sigh. "All right. Perhaps then you should get to your bed."

"It's much later where you are."

"That it is. And I admit I am quite tired tonight. When do you plan to get to Las Vegas?"

"I'm not quite sure. We'll stop in Gallup tomorrow, but maybe we won't stay overnight. It's a pretty depressing little town, in my opinion. We'll see. Then Las Vegas for a couple of days and we'll come back home."

"To sleep with you, then."

"All right. You, too. I'll call you tomorrow night."

"India, you know that I think of you all the time, don't you?"

A welter of quick tears came to my eyes. "Me, too, Jack," I whispered. "Good night."

CHAPTER
TWENTY-FIVE

Eldora

In my pretty, Southwestern-style room, I settle the freshly filled ice bucket on the dresser, kick off my shoes, and pour myself a hefty bourbon and Coke. There are long doors leading to a tiny balcony. I open them up and light a cigarette, blowing an easing breath of nicotine into the cold night. A new scent of snow is hovering. I have to wrap a sweater around my shoulders.

I look north, as if it is possible to see across the night and the miles and the geography of mountains between us; as if I can see my girl out there, as if all it takes is me looking hard enough at the dark to see her revealed.

I try to see her in a shelter, warm beneath a blanket, or failing that, in the arms of her Indian. There's a backpack she's good about carrying with her, even when she's delusional, and I tuck in packs of cigarettes when I think about it. Since they go so fast, I also put in rolling papers and bags of Red Man tobacco so she can roll her own if she needs to.

"Ah, Gypsy-girl," I say to the night. "Where are you?"

From the deck that makes up my collection of shames, a card detaches itself and flutters to the floor of my memory. The last night in

Santa Fe, back when I was running away from my good husband and my good home to chase . . . what? I take a sip of my bourbon and Coke. Can't go there right now.

I also can't stop thinking of Gypsy. There's a sense of dread or worry in me, and I don't know if it's the weather or the men we saw today—oh, God, they'd break your heart, the whole lot of them—or visiting graveyards. It might be that I'm just remembering too many depressing things.

What I'm really worried about is a sense of something bad that might be happening to my girl tonight. I take a long swallow of my drink, trying to ease the heat of it, wash away the pictures that come to me of my daughter's body broken and bleeding, or too cold and frozen. I used to like those crime shows on TV, but I just can't stand to see the morgue shots anymore. Too many things could happen to my baby.

"Keep her safe," I pray to whoever might be listening. I try a visualization Candace gave me once: praying an army of angels in white around her, a wall of safety and protection.

The first time she ran away, we all nearly died of frantic worry. For weeks, Gypsy had not been herself. Not that she was an ideal teenager, you understand. Me and Don had been at our wit's end about her for quite a while—she showed up at school when she felt like it, and took up smoking cigarettes and other things; she stayed out all night with boys drinking, and no matter what we did, it wasn't enough to stop her for very long.

It's easy to see in retrospect that she was self-medicating, as they say, trying to find some relief. Nowadays, the schools or the courts or some other official would have seen the pattern and slapped her into a teen rehab program, and likely someone there would have recognized that she was mentally ill.

But this was the seventies. The world had been turned upside down, and nobody hardly knew what to do about it. Things didn't settle down again for a long time. Gypsy was hardly the only drinking-drugging teen on the block.

Just after Christmas when the girls were seventeen, I noticed she was getting a little odder and a little odder and a little odder. It was a lot of little things that didn't seem too strange until you added them all together. She'd always been particular about her food, so it took me a while to notice that she was not only avoiding all round food, but also anything green. Not only vegetables, which she used to eat pretty well, but green Jell-O and green Kool-Aid and green hard candies. Not that there are that many that aren't round.

She wouldn't eat meat or cereal of any kind. She lived on milk she drank out of a particular glass she liked, made of carnival glass, with a blue rim, and saltine crackers spread with peanut butter.

She was also afraid of me. She tried to hide it, but I could tell. She'd shrink down into herself if I came into the room. If I accidentally brushed her body in some way, she'd actually shudder down to the bottom of her shins. When I asked her what was wrong, she only looked at me with her flat, emotionless eyes.

It was something small that tipped me off finally, related to something my mama used to do, a little ritual of lining up her fork, knife, and spoon, just so with the edge of the table. The bottom of the plate had to be in line with the edge, too, and the napkin. And only then could she allow food to be put on her plate.

Now, as I said, Gypsy had always been a little bit weird. That's a terrible thing to say about your own child, maybe, but it's true. She was fussy and peculiar and eccentric. This habit of lining things up didn't seem so strange, considering she wore a line of safety pins attached to the top layer of the skin of her wrist. Most children discover this trick at one point or another, and teenagers are notoriously strange, but a whole row of safety pins, all lined up with the edge of her palm? Weird.

Don brushed me off several times when I tried to bring it up to him. Her grades had never been as good as India's, especially as regarded anything to do with reading. She was a terrible reader from the git-go, and we tried to avoid ever making her feel bad about it, and she was truly gifted at artistic things, so we tried to keep the focus on the good things. Don was busting with pride over the personal interest Gypsy's art teacher had taken in her. The pair were working to put together a portfolio of her work, and the teacher had managed to get Gypsy invited to an exhibition. It all looked promising.

And I wanted to believe it would be okay. That she'd come out of the dark period of adolescence and we'd all chuckle over the horrors of that period. In my own defense, I didn't know much about mental illness. I thought you were born crazy or not. I didn't know that schizophrenia doesn't show up until later.

So I kept letting it go, and letting it go. And for that, I do blame myself.

One night I realized that she'd been wearing the exact same clothes for more than a week, sneaking them out of the laundry and back into her room every night. At supper, her nails were grimy.

I decided to make Don listen. He was watering the early tulips in the softness of twilight when I carried a fresh bottle of RC cola for him to drink. "Don, honey," I said, lighting a cigarette. "We need to talk about Gypsy."

He gave me a quick look, one that showed he'd been worried about her, too. "She's all right, Eldora. Just eccentric. A lot of artists are a little odd, don't you think?"

"It's more than that, honey."

"What do you mean?"

I glanced over my shoulders at the blank windows of the back of the house. "She needs a doctor."

"No," he said, and wiggled his nose, stuck his hand in his pocket. "She's fine." He said it loudly, as if that would make it more true.

"Don—"

He shook his head stubbornly. "We both know what crazy looks like, and it's not Gypsy."

I knew better than he did, but didn't say it. He was referring to poor Bea, his ex, who probably wasn't crazy until I came along, and I just plain couldn't stand to think of her. "What would it hurt to just take her in, honey? Make sure she's okay?"

"She'll get labeled, that's what." He moved the hose back and forth, back and forth, over the thick sturdy leaves of the tulips. "And what difference will it make if she's a little bit crazy all her life as long as she has us to look after her? I don't want her to start thinking of herself as different."

I lost my temper. Moved in close and said, hard and quiet, "Don, the only food she can eat is saltine crackers. The only fluid she can drink is milk and whatever alcohol she can get her hands on. She's terrified of me and keeps asking me what's wrong with my voice." I narrowed my eyes. "I think she's afraid of water. She is not showering. She goes in there and turns on the tap so we'll think so, but there's grime on her skin that hasn't had water on it in a long time."

"That's silly. Why would she pretend?"

"She's afraid of the shower, sweetheart. Just like she's afraid of my voice and the color green and round food."

He could be the most stubborn man on the planet, and this time, he couldn't stand to think that Gypsy might really be sick. He took a long pull of his soda, and cleared his throat. "Let's give it two or three weeks, huh? I'll really pay attention, I promise. If she seems bad, still, we'll take her in."

I took the last drag off my cigarette and stubbed it out in the ashtray on the picnic table. I thought of my mother and my brothers and how much misery could come out of it all, not just for us, but for poor Gypsy. "Don—"

"One week, then. Please?"

I touched his arm. Nodded. Went back inside.

It was too late anyway. Gypsy was gone. We heard nothing from her for nearly seven months; when she surfaced in a homeless shelter in Tucumcari, New Mexico, she was completely delusional. They only knew to call us because we'd put her on a network of runaway children.

It was the first time we lost her, but not the last.

Not by a long shot.

CHAPTER
TWENTY-SIX

India

I wake up in the dark of my hotel room with a sense of abject terror weighing on my chest. For a minute, coming out of the nightmare, I'm disoriented, dry-mouthed with unuttered screams, and I don't know where I am—the windows are not those of my apartment in Colorado Springs or the condo in Denver or the spare bedroom in my mother's house in Pleasant Valley. For a moment, I think I feel Jack's warm body next to mine, but when I fling out a hand, the illusion of body warmth bursts like a soap bubble.

Finally, it comes to me: I'm in Santa Fe, in the La Fonda Hotel, and I am forty, not eleven. The dark presses into me, malevolent and impenetrable, and I reach over to turn on the lamp. My nightmare retreats.

My body has a fine trembling beneath the skin, even when I pull the covers tightly around me. I fervently wish for someone to be with me, to pull me close, pet my hair, tell me everything will be okay. I've been pretty much alone for the past twenty-three years, since Gypsy took off the first time. There are times I'm heartily weary of it. Punching the pillows into a better shape, I try to make a nest, covers and pillows piled up to protect me and keep me safe, all alone.

Like all nightmares, this one abates the minute there is light and reason on it. It was Gypsy, beneath a bridge, shivering and screaming, fighting off—I curl my knees closer to my chest—what? It was never clear what she was fighting, what was after her. Nothing real.

It's no mystery why I dreamed of her and her nightmares, either, in this room, in this hotel. This was where she had the first of her very, very, very bad dreams. We were eleven.

She woke me up, thrashing and screaming with such horror it scared me half to death. I put my arms around her, but that seemed to scare her even more, and she started babbling in some unknown language and I couldn't make out what she was saying.

What I know now is that it was probably the first of her psychotic breaks, the first sign of the twisted synapses in her brain. It became quite common over the next few years. We thought she was sleepwalking, and were very careful with her. Maybe she was, in a way. Maybe all of schizophrenia is a sort of sleepwalking in an alternate reality.

But that night, as I struggled to ease Gypsy's terror, I cried out for my mother, and she didn't come. She was sleeping in the double bed next to ours, and I didn't understand how she couldn't hear Gypsy's noises. It's a sound that's hard to describe—a keening terror that went on and on, as if she were being tortured.

"Mom!" I cried, and climbed out of bed to shake her awake.

The bed was empty. I stared at it, Gypsy's stuttering sobs breaking the air behind me.

It didn't sink in for a minute: My mother wasn't there.

I turned on the light and she was still gone. My heart exploded with dire imaginings: She'd been kidnapped. Or . . . killed. There was a man with a big knife in the bathroom, waiting to attack us and kill us next. I whirled around to look at Gypsy, suddenly certain I would see that her screaming was because she had been cut to ribbons and left for dead.

She moaned and put her hands in front of her face, as if something was indeed coming at her, but her skin showed no damage. Her nightgown was twisted and her hair was damp with sweat, but she wasn't hurt.

The room was empty. And I noticed, suddenly, that my mother's purse was gone.

She'd left on purpose!

Gypsy screamed and started thrashing around on the bed, making so much noise I was afraid somebody would come and find out my mother wasn't here, and then what would happen to us?—so I put my hand on her, whispering, "Shhhh, Gyps. I'm here. It's okay."

It didn't help. The instant my hand touched her, she reared away, banging her head on the nightstand. Her eyes were open and wild, but I could tell she couldn't see me. A little blood showed up in a cut on her forehead and she pulled pillows around her.

At least it was something I could offer. Whirling around, I yanked the pillows from my mother's bed, and the covers, and pushed them onto our bed, and covered Gypsy up, put a pillow behind her so she wouldn't bang the nightstand again. Then, shivering, I pulled the sheet off my mother's bed and wrapped up in it and settled at the foot of our bed. I cried myself to sleep, wishing for my daddy.

The woman I am now, the woman carrying a baby in her own belly, thinks of those two girls alone in that hotel room so long ago, and I'm furious. What was my mother thinking? How could she have been so casual?

I'm sleepy and cold, and pull the covers more closely around me. The nest comforts me, and I imagine, as I did when I was a preadolescent, that the bed is a solid raft afloat upon the sea, a perfectly safe and comfortable cradle to keep me from the dangers of the deep. I hug a pillow and wish I could call Jack. It's four a.m. in New York, and I'd never disturb him, but some part of me knows that I could if it were bad enough, that he'd be bewildered and sleepy and not particularly talkative, but he'd pick up the phone. He'd stay on the other end as long as I needed him.

For some reason, this makes me want to cry.

God, I'm tired of being alone! The cold depth of my loneliness tonight makes me even think of my mother, close by, just one flight of stairs away. I could crawl into bed with her, put my face against her shoulder and let her sing to me. Sleepily, I imagine myself in an oversize flannel nightgown, dragging a teddy bear up those stairs and knocking on her door. The imaginary smell of Tabu wafts over me and I fall asleep.

~

When I awaken at seven-thirty, I am very ill. It's morning sickness to the twelfth power, repetitive waves of nausea that roll over me with the monotony of the sea. Lying there in my pile of pillows and covers, trying to breathe slowly I think I shouldn't have imagined my bed was a raft on the ocean.

It takes me a half hour to even get to the shower, another half hour to keep down a cup of tea. From somewhere floats a smell of sizzling meat, and it sends me to the toilet again. I'm absolutely certain I can't face a café this morning. I call my mother's room and tell her to get some room service breakfast. "I'm just going to take my time."

Her voice has the particular raggedness that comes of smoking dozens of cigarettes. "Anything you need, sweetheart?"

"No." I pause. Then again, "No, I'm fine. It's just a headache."

I order breakfast for myself, breads and tea only, nothing with an odor that might send me back to the toilet. And finally, it's better. An apricot Danish stays down. Another cup of tea. The top of my stomach feels bruised, and I do wonder how people get through a whole pregnancy like this. I wish I could ask my mother. I can't remember if she ever said she was sick when she was pregnant with us. Probably not. She probably smoked and drank and danced like normal. In the old days, pregnant women were not quite under the hostage situation that I will face in public, as if my belly does not belong to me, but the world in general.

Creepy.

I'm finally able to dress and get downstairs, but it's wobbly all the way. Everything seems off-kilter. Smells, sights, sounds. I feel like I'm underwater, except that I'm trapped down there with bubbles of gas-like explosions of smells. A woman on the elevator was eating garlic the night before and I nearly faint with cold sweats before I escape her.

In the lobby, I smell again that awful, sticky, hot scent I can't place, and I say to my mother, "What is that smell?"

She gives me a quizzical look and says, "I just smell chiles and onions." Her eyes narrow. "You look a little green this morning, child. Are you okay?"

I shake my head. Without thinking, I touch the top of my stomach, that bruised place, and yank my hand away instantly. "Just a little tired, I think. Maybe a touch of food poisoning."

"Might be. Might just be that all this rich road food is disagreeing with you." She hands me a piece of Juicy Fruit, which I unwrap with gratitude.

I'm all right in the car. I get us out of Santa Fe and on the road to Gallup without incident. The sky is dark and cold this morning, threatening more snow. "I forgot to look at the weather forecast. Did you hear it?"

Eldora shakes her head. "Doesn't look good, though, does it? The weather hasn't been great for us. You'd think April would be better."

"Mother, you've lived in this part of the country for forty years. It always snows in April."

She lifts a shoulder. "Never seems like it should, though."

There's a hot smell coming off the engine this morning, like oil burning too fast or something. It's bothering me a little, but I can drive anyway. My mother is quiet, and doesn't nag me to get out for a cigarette. She's somewhat hungover, I suspect, going by the tender way she holds her head, the lack of chatter spilling out of her. I consider asking her if she's ever going to give it up, and think better of it.

Traffic is light, the clouds low and dark over the mountains. I'd forgotten the reservations along the road to Gallup. The pueblos start north of Santa Fe, with the most famous and one of the most photographed places on the planet, surely, Taos Pueblo. From Taos, they lie in a waterfall across the desert, most with the names of Spanish saints: Santa Clara, Santo Domingo, San Felipe. I remember it seemed there was nothing to see when I was a child. I'd been so excited to see the pueblos, and we never even glimpsed one.

Now there are big, prosperous-looking casinos perched along the highway. Every pueblo seems to have its own, and every parking lot has plenty of cars. To my mother I say "You could do some gambling through here. They must be raking in a fortune."

"Pretty smart," Eldora says with a nod. "Turns the tables on white greed, doesn't it?"

So to speak, I think, but don't say. In truth, I tend to discount the depth and experience of my mother's intelligence, and this statement has taken me by surprise. I know better. She reads all the time. "Did you grow up in Indian country?"

"Yeah." She takes a breath. "Reservations were sorry places in those days, I'll tell you."

"It was the dark ages of Indian affairs."

"Like there's been a bright age?"

I smile softly. "Touché." I pass the giant, shiny new casino with its packed parking lot. "Did you want to stop at one of them, check it out?"

"No, I'm ready to get to Las Vegas."

"The real thing?"

She lifts a slim shoulder. "I guess. I'm not really going there to gamble." She lowers her sunglasses. "Are you worried that I have a gambling problem, India?"

"No, not at all. I worry about your drinking and your smoking, but not your gambling."

"Well, good. I've never been crazy with it. I like playing the slots for fun, but I stay within my limits. I stick with my drinking limits, too, sugar. You might not think so, but I pay attention. I know it's not good for me."

I can't think of anything to say and simply nod.

"It's flirtin' with disaster, I get that." She clears her throat. "The smoking, too. Believe me, I think about it a lot. It's just so hard to imagine giving up something you've been doing practically your whole life."

"I know."

"I'm glad you never took up smoking."

"Gypsy smokes enough for both of us." I grin at her a little. "Whatever will the tobacco industry do if they cure schizophrenia?"

She's silent for a minute. "Wouldn't that be something? If they figured out how to cure it?"

"I can't even imagine."

"That's what I thought was beautiful about your daddy's fight. He really did believe that if enough people made enough noise for long enough, maybe someday they could come up with a cure. Or at least better drugs." She abruptly clears her throat and looks out the window. "He had more faith . . ." Ducking down, she picks up her purse, starts digging through it. When she speaks again, her voice is wavery: "Than anybody I ever met."

"I miss him a lot, too, Mom." I turn the radio down a little so she can talk about him if she wants. "I made some chocolate-covered cherries for Jack, just so I could think about Daddy."

"That's beautiful, India."

"I should go through his paperwork and see where he was involved, see if I can take up some of the work he was doing, anyway."

"We all give in our own way, honey. You don't have to do exactly what he did. Just find your own way."

The oil smell is working on my stomach a little. "Can I have some more gum?" As she's pulling it out, I add, "What do you miss, Mom?"

"His laugh," she says without hesitation. "His silly jokes. The way he'd whistle when he took out the trash. He was a very happy man, you know?" Unwrapping some Juicy Fruit for me, she says, "But if you really want to know, what I miss most of all is the feeling of his arms around me at night. It's hard to go on without that, night after night after night."

"Maybe you should date a little."

She doesn't say anything for a long while. Finally she says simply, "It wouldn't be the same."

I feel ashamed of myself. After a few miles, I say, "Mom, how did you end up in Las Vegas finally? You haven't finished your story."

"You don't have to humor me, India."

I laugh. "It's hardly that. C'mon. Tell me a story to keep me awake on this drive."

"Maybe later, sweetheart, all right? Just this minute, I'm tired."

In alarm, I glance at her. "Do you want to get out, have a smoke or something?"

"No." She closes her eyes and leans her head back. "I'll be all right in a little while."

PART FIVE

Home of the Movie Stars

Formally opened December 17, 1937, the El Rancho Hotel was built by the brother of the movie magnet, D. W. Griffith. Drawn by the many films made in the area, Ronald Reagan, Spencer Tracy, Katharine Hepburn, and Kirk Douglas were among the stars listed in the guest register. Autographed photos of the stars, Navajo rugs, and mounted trophy animal heads adorn the magnificent two-story open lobby with its circular staircase.

CHAPTER
TWENTY-SEVEN

India

It's only a three-hour drive to Gallup. An odd, thick sense of dread is building in me as we approach the town, and I'm thinking maybe we should just go on to Las Vegas today. It's another six hours, but we can do it. As we enter the town proper, looking for the address I found for the homeless shelter, I feel almost strangled with . . . what? Dread, sorrow, something.

"This is where Gypsy ran away the first time," my mother says. "Do you remember?"

"Yes." We couldn't find her for more than six hours, and when we did, she had a bruise on her cheek. She never did tell us how she got it. "I don't want to talk about that right now, though. We just need to find this shelter."

"I'd really like a break before we do that. A cup of coffee? There's a diner right there."

I drive by without stopping. "I want to check the shelter first."

"For once, India, I'm gonna say no. Let's stop, get out, stretch our legs. The shelter isn't going anywhere." She points with one long-nailed index finger at a big neon sign on the main drag. "There. Stop."

She is my mother. I was an obedient child. Some habits you just can't break. We get out of the car, and I find myself scanning the sky. A cold wind has the bite of winter in it, and the clouds are heavy and ominous. Damn.

We walk into the diner and that awful smell hits me again, that sweaty something that makes me tell my mother, "I'll be right back."

At a near run, I make it to the ladies' room, which is bright and cheerful with Navajo diamond patterns on the wall in border paper. In the toilet, I throw up impressively and wonder how much a person can throw up every day before it ruins her throat. Like bulimia. The thought makes me smile as I flush the toilet, wipe my eyes, rinse my mouth. I expect to look as wan and clammy as a person who has been throwing up all day should, but my face in the mirror is surprisingly robust. Roses in my cheeks, the whites of my eyes as pristine as freshly bleached sheets, a dewiness to my sallow skin.

From the cosmetics section of my purse, I take out a lipstick, comb my hair, eat a mint. Put everything back exactly where it was.

Raising a brow, I step back to take a longer look at myself. It's not an illusion. I look hot, as in sexy, as in younger than I've looked in ages. "Wow," I say, touching my still unrevealed belly, my lusher breasts. "Not bad, kiddo." Until I say it aloud, I don't realize I'm talking to the kid.

Damn. I want this baby. I want to see what she'll look like. I want to hold her and touch her and smell her. I want to see Jack's eyes or hair or fingernails mixed up with my nose and neck and toes. How selfish is that?

It brings tears to my eyes. "Oh, stop it!" I've been as weepy as a willow and I'm tired of it. I can just see me going through a whole pregnancy with tears streaming down my face.

I suddenly, painfully, want pie. Cherry pie.

My mother has settled in a booth by the window. All around her, men send covert glances in her direction. God, it used to drive me crazy! No matter where we went, the male of the species admired my mother, even when she was forty and I was in my teens and you'd think I might get a few appreciative glances of my own.

There is an especially handsome Indian man sitting two tables away who makes no secret of his frank measuring. I know he's Navajo rather than some other nation because of the way he's wearing his hair, in a traditional bun. The hair is salt and pepper, thick and shiny, and I suspect it would be spectacular if he freed it. In his late fifties or early sixties, cheekbones like mesas, full lips and broad shoulders. He looks . . . substantial. There are turquoise and silver cuffs on his sturdy wrists. His hands look as if they could manage everything from horses to dishes to women. He's wearing no ring.

As I cut through the restaurant, trying to breathe through my mouth so I don't have to inhale that sweaty scent of meat cooking, I notice my mother noticing the man. She touches her hair, looks his way as if by accident. He nods with respect and a very, very small quirk of his lips. She smiles.

I like him even more when he doesn't fall to his knees and worship her. His acknowledgment is not dazzled, but a very slight smile of his own, a knowing sort of expression. He's been worshiped now and again himself.

Sliding into the booth, I blink coquettishly at Eldora. "Oooh," I say, with a wicked grin. "Not bad."

She straightens, demurely looks down, touches her face. "Don't be silly."

The waitress has a dark round face and hair to her hips. I ask for cherry pie.

"Before you eat?" my mother asks.

"Lunch is lunch."

"It smells wonderful in here," Eldora says to the waitress. "Is that chile?"

"Fresh this morning," the waitress says.

Chile, I think. Great. It's the combination of chiles, onions, and meat that are making me so sick. I'll be very glad to get out of New Mexico.

"Do you mind if I have some, India?"

I look at her. "Why would I care?"

"The smell seems not to be agreeing with you."

Startled, I meet her eyes, see her knowledge. New raindrop tears show up in my eyes. "No, it's fine. Go ahead." But having thrown up, I'm very hungry again. "Maybe I want something, too."

"We have a Navajo taco with beans," the girl says, pointing the eraser of her pencil at the menu. "Beans are good if you're having a baby. Lots of iron."

Do I have a sign on my face that says I'm pregnant? I'm disconcerted and don't know what to do with my eyes or my hands. Or how to answer. "All right" is what I finally come up with.

"The chile for me," my mother says. "Coffee, and then some cherry pie after."

The waitress grins. "You got it."

When she leaves, I can't look at my mother for a moment, and busy myself by checking out the customers and the setting. It's no longer Spanish New Mexico, which is how both Tucumcari and Santa Fe feel. Gallup bills itself as the heart of Indian country, and it's true. Around us in the booths are Indian faces, young and old, fat and thin. The soft murmur of Indian accents, which are not the same as Spanish, fills the air. I close my eyes and listen to it, thrilling to the up-and-down cadence. I should have told those Irish girls to come to Gallup. I should bring Jack here. He would love it. This is the Indian west, which for him holds an almost mystical significance.

"When we came here when Gypsy and I were little," I say, "she decided this was the center of the communications from the stars."

"What do you mean?"

I'm relieved that she's not going to push me about the other subject. "You get the delusions, right? Or hallucinations or whatever. Gypsy's world?"

"Not really. I mean, I know she thinks she's Indian or Spanish. I know she has that weird thing about never cutting her hair and she has your language. Is there some key to it all?"

I blink. "You really don't know?"

"How would I know? She doesn't talk to me when she's delusional."

"Well, it's quite cohesive and complete. Like a whole world with unbreakable rules. There's like a confederation of people in the galaxy who use Earth as a sort of airport and message center. There are a lot of people who live here among us, and they use crosses to communicate." It's hard to say this with a straight face, and my nostrils quiver as my mother starts to blink. "Don't make me laugh. I know it sounds ridiculous, but to her, it's totally real."

She lifts a hand, palm out, shakes her head. "I'm not laughing."

"The extraterrestrials take Indian form, and that's why she likes coming to this part of the country."

"And the round food?"

I raise my eyebrows. "Earth food. Round planet, round food. It's not good for her."

My mother starts to chuckle. "So, there are some square planets somewhere or what?" She covers her mouth. "Rectangles?"

A giggle rises in my throat. "I know. Pyramids?"

She does laugh at that, but not in a mean way. "You're right. It all makes sense. Except—" her smile fades. "She used to be so afraid of me when she was delusional." She taps her unlit cigarette on the ashtray with some irritation. "It doesn't make sense."

"You're wrong. The first time she was delusional, you betrayed her. Twice."

"I was the only one who knew she was delusional!" Eldora protests. "I spent weeks trying to get your father to let me take her to the doctor."

"Not when she was seventeen, Mom. Her first psychotic break was when we made that trip when we were eleven."

She's no dummy, my mother. I watch clarity blossom in her eyes. She sinks back against the booth, looks toward the open restaurant, blows out a drag. "Of course," she says quietly.

"I wish," I say slowly, "that she could just have the good parts of the delusions. It wouldn't hurt anything if she could just believe in this harmless little fantasy, that she was part of an alien race that was superior and smart and so clever they had the whole world fooled."

"I know."

The truth is, though, she doesn't stay there. She enjoys it for a little while, and I sometimes think it's the longing for her friendly world that makes her go off the meds. It's just that it ends up getting darker and darker, with assassins coming after her, and evil beasts from other worlds coming through graveyards to suck out her blood. She is still a queenlike figure, but she's wanted by some evil empire. The tortures of the damned await her if they get her.

It's been nearly a month this time. Long enough for the bad guys to be after her. I rub my forehead. "I wish we could find her."

The waitress brings our coffee. My mother puts her cigarette down and stirs in some Sweet 'N Low. "Do my cigarettes make you sick?"

"Actually, no. It's only that . . . chile and meat smell. It's awful."

"For me, it was perfume. I could not stand the smell of perfume." She's waving her unlit cigarette around to illustrate her words. "And you know me. I love the stuff."

"Do you want a light, Mom?"

"Oh, I'll get one in a minute. My lighter died."

I stir my coffee around and around. "How did you know that I was pregnant?"

She chuckles. "Good God, India, you've been barfing at everything since we left." Her face goes tender. "And it's not like I don't know you, sweetheart. I could tell something was bothering you for a while."

I take a breath. "I don't know what to do."

"What does Jack think?"

"I don't know."

"You haven't told him?"

"Well, just barely. Just before we left."

"And he hasn't said anything?"

I duck my head. "I kinda didn't let him. And as I said, we never had any kind of agreement about any of this."

"I see."

The handsome Navajo appears at the side of our table and holds out a silver lighter. "Allow me," he says in a lilting, beautiful voice.

Eldora laughs slightly, a breathless, lovely sound, and lets him light her cigarette. "Thank you." She transfers her cigarette to her left hand and holds her right out to him. "I'm Eldora."

"Joseph," he says. "I won't keep you, but here is my card. Stop on your way out if you like."

"Thank you."

He goes back to his place, and it's suddenly clear by the detritus on the table around him that he must own or at least manage the place. As he sits back down, my mother gives me the tiniest smile and just barely winks with the eye away from his side of the table. She passes the card silently across the Formica.

Joseph Tsosie, it says in Art Deco script. Photographer.

Only my mother. But for once it doesn't irk me. "Good for you." Feeling generous and not a little curious, I say, "Now will you tell me your Las Vegas tale?"

"Not here, sweetie." She cuts her eyes toward Joseph.

"Ah, okay. At dinner, then?"

She bows her head for a minute, taps her thumbnails together. "Sure."

~

My good mood dissipates as we pull up in front of the homeless shelter. Gallup has come a long way in the last few years, trying to improve its image, but the truth is, there are still a lot of alcoholics lying around the hidden places of the town, and on the roads spidering out to the outlying Indian lands.

The casinos along the road here are sort of shiny and positive and forward-thinking. In Gallup, where white and Indian dreams clash, you feel the losses. The Navajo were brilliant with peach orchards, but the Spanish burned them, and God knows you can't grow a peach tree on the high desert. These are lands nobody wanted, so they gave them to the Indians.

Somehow I can feel that bloody past here.

Under the lowering sky, the homeless shelter looks squat and depressed. A wind has whipped up, too, pushing discarded cans and scraps of paper across the pavement. A man as skinny as a straw, in a greasy corduroy coat, bends his shoulders against the gusts, his long gray-and-blond hair blowing in his face as he tries to smoke. I worry about the hair catching fire.

Eldora gets some extra packs of cigarettes out of the trunk and gives one to the man at the door. There is such a vacancy in his eyes that she doesn't even ask about Gypsy, just gives out the cigarettes and keeps walking. I think with surprise that she would be good at working the shelters. There's no judgment in her.

Inside, it's the same story as all the others. A layer of grime that comes from too many unwashed and uncared-for people coming through the doors day after day after day, sour smells of things rotting, not enough volunteers to cover everything no matter how many appear. The person we talk to is a young woman, earnest and not yet lost to despair. She hasn't been at the shelter long, so she has not met Gypsy in the past.

She does know Loon, however. A shadow crosses her face before she can hide it. "Loon. A Sioux, right?"

"Yeah."

She exchanges a look with a girl working on a clipboard of forms. "He's been here quite a bit. We have trouble with him, frankly. He has flashbacks and they make him dangerous."

I blanch. My mother takes my arm. "Never mind, honey. You can't change it. You'll let us know if Gypsy shows up?"

The woman nods. "Sorry," she says to me.

There's no way to take away the fear her comments have stirred. And as we step out into the day, it's also plain that we're not going any farther tonight. Thick snow is swirling out of the sky, a second front in as many days. In April! Much as I'd love to just get to freaking Las Vegas and have this road trip done, the miles across Arizona are desolate and underpopulated and I'm not about to get stranded in a blizzard out there.

"Damn this snow!" I say.

"There's no help for it. Let's just get a room."

~

We get rooms at the El Rancho. It's a quaint little hotel in the middle of the desert, famous for once being home to movie stars on location. There are antelope and deer heads on the walls, along with wagon wheel accents and the ubiquitous Indian print fabrics, but I have to admit I rather like it. My mother and I both head for naps. I unpack, sorting dirty clothes from clean, lying the dwindling underwear in neat piles in the top drawer. In the bathroom, I close the door and brush my teeth and leave the toothbrush out on the sink to air-dry. More hygienic.

I fire up my computer in the quiet of my room and check email. It's an agonizingly slow connection, and I only look over the list for an email from jshea@sheaenterprises.com. There's nothing. I post a quick paragraph on my blog about our trip and turn off the computer.

Next, I call my answering machine at home and I'm electrified when the voice mail robot says, "You have two new messages. Press one to hear your messages now."

"India!" says my sister's voice, breathless and manic. It sounds like she says, *"Garble barbell garble gobble bobble barbell."* She starts to cry, but keeps talking, still in the mysterious language. At the end, she says in English, "Call me."

"How?" I ask the recorded message. "How can I call you, Gyps?" I save the message and listen to the next one. It's from the man at the Espanola homeless shelter. "This is Ramón Medina. Your sister showed up again tonight. I tried to get her to stay so we could call you, but she grew agitated and delusional and we had to let her go. I did tell her that you and her mom were looking for her, but she wouldn't stay. Sorry."

Damn.

I hit the code to play the saved messages on my voice mail. Both of the messages Gypsy left for me in the twin language are there. The happy one I received before Eldora and I left Colorado Springs, and the one from today or last night or whenever she left it.

Pressing the button to replay them, I close my eyes and listen very carefully. Maybe there is some clue I've missed, some secret I can unravel, that one single bit of code that will make it all miraculously clear.

I do it over and over, not trying to grab anything, just letting the syllables play over my mind. And suddenly, there are wisps of things. A jolt of almost and then another.

Maybe it's being on the road like this, remembering when we watched all those television shows. A blip of a television commercial runs through my memory, "I'm a pepper, you're a pepper, he's a pepper," and it runs into a rhythm that almost takes me down a lane I know. I reach for it, feel the red gravel beneath my feet, smell rain coming from the west: We are walking near the Garden of the Gods, long before there were sidewalks built there.

I'm a pepper you're a pepper he's a pepper . . .

Holding the phone close to my ear, I stand up and pace as far as the phone cord will allow me to go, humming under my breath, pressing the code to hear Gypsy's message again. It does sound like Spanish in a way, a softness to the syllables, but as I listen, I realize it's just the lilt, the up and downness, an imitation Spanish accent, like the tune of a song with words that you don't know.

Peter Piper picked a peck of pickled peppers . . .

I can see us walking, kicking gravel. The mountains, burly on the horizon, the sky lowering with a coming thunderstorm, the smell of damp sandstone.

Red rocks, red road, red room, red shoes.

For a minute, again, it nearly comes through. I almost have the code.

Then it's gone, as abruptly as if my brain has slammed a drawer shut. I'm left listening to the sound of my sister weeping in fear and loneliness, speaking a language I have betrayed her by forgetting.

The last thing I have to do is call Jack at his office, but his secretary says he's already gone home. When I try his house, he isn't there, and listening to the phone ring at the other end, seeing that phone sitting on the counter of his apartment kitchen, makes me feel even more lost and hollow. New York seems a million miles away. I touch my belly with the flat of my palm and remember lying on the floor at the foot of my sister's bed in a hotel room in Santa Fe thirty years ago, and I just want to cry and cry and cry.

Trouble is, crying doesn't help anything. As I lie on the bed, staring at the ceiling, I wonder where in the world I can find someone to help me decipher my sister's language. Somewhere, someone can help, I just know it.

CHAPTER
TWENTY-EIGHT

Eldora, 1959

There is still so much I have to tell India, and I'm not sure how to do it. What I want to keep to myself, what I have to face on my own without including her, what I need to tell her so she'll understand the whole business.

We're both sick to death of hamburgers and such things so we go to the supermarket and pick up some fruit, cheese, and bread and bring them back to the hotel. There's a nice little sitting area by a fire and we spread out there. We pretty much have the place to ourselves anyway. There's snow. It's the middle of the week. Not yet tourist season.

"I kinda like this spot, really," I tell India, looking around.

"It's famous enough."

"You should write a web page about Route Sixty-Six," I say, wrapping a piece of turkey around an olive. "Talk about all the good places to stay."

She lifts a shoulder and the opposite eyebrow, the quintessential India gesture. "I've been describing our trip on a blog I keep."

"What is that?"

"A sort of public diary. I don't write anything personal, just my travels and experiences as a web designer." She gives me that wry smile. "It's *très* hip, you know."

"You'll have to let me read it."

"Doubtful." It's not mean, just straightforward. I can appreciate that.

If I haven't said so, I would just like to say I purely love this woman's face. The dark eyes, the arched flying eyebrows, the strong, generous mouth. She's vividly, vibrantly beautiful, and the pregnancy has given her a zesty look. "Are you feeling a little better this evening?"

"Some." She dips cauliflower in ranch dressing. "Tell me about going to Las Vegas now."

A rumble of choices goes through my stomach. Maybe this was all a stupid idea. Maybe she doesn't really need to know it all, just the parts about—

No. Without all of it, she'll never understand the pieces I've got to tell her, now that she's pregnant.

"All right." I tuck my feet up under me and begin.

~

The first time I went to Las Vegas, I was home. It was like somebody made up a city just for me. I went with a couple of girlfriends, secretaries who flew in on weekends to hang around the casinos, and we arrived on the Strip just after dark. You've seen a thousand pictures. You know all about it.

But I didn't.

It was noisy and hot, and there were crushes of people, all dressed up and a little too bright, as if they were trying to match the blaze of neon. I'd grown used to fancy cars and glamorous-looking people in Hollywood, but Las Vegas was like a musical where at any minute the people would burst into song and dance. I stood there in a borrowed cocktail dress, wishing for a pair of ruby slippers to dance me over the stage sets.

Instead, I sashayed through the open doors at the Sands. It was the moment my real life began. I had that feeling in my chest. This was why I'd left Elk City.

For rich carpet stretching through a glittering room full of people and light and cocktail waitresses in tiny uniforms that showed lots of skin and leg. For the noise of slot machines clanging, and the sound of money falling, and gamblers shouting curses or cheers. For the smell of dreams and sweat and bourbon, for perfume coming off the gleaming hair of the most beautiful women I'd ever seen. For feathers and furs and diamonds, for the ruby velvet on the walls and the ruby shine of rings and the ruby-rich voice of cocktail singers. For cards shuffled and dreams drawn and broken in a second.

I wandered around with a cocktail in my hand—I was only seventeen, but I knew how to look a lot older—and soaked it all up. It had been eight months since I'd left Elk City, and I was ready for a change.

Cliff wasn't cruel or stupid or mean, which a lot of men are. He set me up in Hollywood, just as he promised, and I only saw him about once every couple of months when he'd drive in and act out his fantasies, which made him feel so bad, and usually consisted of something mild, like having me wear an old blouse he could rip open to show my breasts. Or having me wander around the apartment fixing us a meal wearing ordinary clothes but no underwear. He was absolutely miserable doing it, all of it, but he couldn't stop. Sometimes he'd cry about his wife and all the wrong he was doing her, then he'd have me again. I just put up with it. He'd held up his part of the bargain. I upheld mine. I never complained. I petted his head when he was weepy and did what he asked.

In the meantime, I made friends here and there, and did what I could to see about getting into the movies, though I have to tell you that what was absolutely gorgeous in Elk City wasn't much better than ordinary in Hollywood, California.

I never went back to LA. That night, I wandered over to a craps table, just to watch the action, and there were men gathered around it who had the same look in their eyes as the men who used to stop in Dina's café, but I was older now. I knew a little bit more about what made folks tick. I'd learned that look in their eye was, plain and simple, figuring out that they'd die without doing half of what they wanted or thought. They'd figured out they weren't as mighty as they'd believed they would be.

There was a lot of excitement coming from some little round tables in a strip down the middle of the casino and I stopped there to see what was going on. There were six men gathered around the table, along with a dealer passing out cards. The men had a cleanliness to them that I associated with a lot of money—nails neat and filed, jaws shaven painfully close, the collars of their shirts starched and standing up.

One wore a cowboy hat and a string tie, which I hadn't seen for a while, and it made me smile. I knew he was a Texan before he ever opened his mouth. A big man, beefy but not yet fat, with a diamond the size of my shoe on his right hand. He was winning, by the look of the chips in front of him, and having a grand old time. He caught my eye and said, "Come on over here, sister, let me show you how it's done."

So I did. I stood there beside him and listened when he told me what he was doing. The money those men threw away made my head spin—thousands and thousands of dollars on the draw of a card. Insane.

But it was exciting. The Texan kept up his winning streak until way past midnight. By then, he'd been drinking a bit and made a few bad calls. When his pile of chips was about half what it had been, he took his hat off, wiped his brow, and said, "Well, I reckon I'm all done in for this evening." He winked at me. "Didya learn anything, darlin'?"

I blinked. "I'll let you know."

He chuckled, putting chips in his hat. "How old are you?"

"Twenty-one."

"And I'm sixteen," he said with a tilt of his mouth. He picked up some of the chips and pressed them into my hand. "That's for keeping an old man company. Don't get yourself in trouble around here, sugar, you hear?"

I curled my hand toward my chest with a little smile. "No, I won't," I said, and met his eyes. "I'm smarter than I look."

"I reckon you are," he said, and lifted his hand. "You be good then, honey. Buy yourself something pretty."

When I took the chips to cash them in, it turned out they were $100 markers, and he'd tossed six of them at me like they were nothing. I blinked at the cashier and then I laughed and tucked the bills into my bra.

When I walked away from the cage, another man approached me, a casino employee in his mid-thirties with a crew cut and hard eyes. "Hi, there," he said, holding out his hand. "I'm Rick."

I took his hand, warily. Had I done something wrong? I decided to play it cool. "Eldora."

"I'm the pit boss around here. Can I buy you a cup of coffee, maybe some breakfast? I have a little proposition for you."

I was starving. "I'd love some food."

His smile made his hard face look a little less intimidating. "All right. Let me tell my boys what's going on, and we'll go get some steak and eggs, how 'bout that?"

Over plates of eggs and thick steaks and hash browns at an all-night diner, Rick laid out his proposition. "I was watching you tonight."

"Yeah?" I still wasn't sure I wasn't about to get in trouble.

"What you did tonight, standing there by that old rancher, cheering him on as he played big money, that's worth something to the casino. You're not only gorgeous, but you're a natural."

I inclined my head, stayed quiet.

Rick took a bite of his bacon. You could see he was somebody who hadn't had much as a young man, but was learning. He forgot to put his napkin in his lap, then did it. He held his fork like a shovel, then remembered to do it the right way. I liked him for that. His voice carried an accent I didn't know, but found out later that he was from New Jersey.

"All I'd want is for you to show up at the casino a few nights a week and let me point out the high rollers. I'll see to it that you get some compensation—food, drink, a room in the hotel if you like."

"And all I have to do is stand there by the high-roller guy and cheer him on?"

"Yep."

"What if he wants more than that?"

He lifted an eyebrow and smiled very slowly. "You're not as naive as you look, are you?"

I let that go. Waited for his reply.

"There's prostitutes by the dozens around the casinos, sweetheart. You're way above that." He grinned. "What'd Tex throw at you tonight?"

"That's my business," I said, but I couldn't help the smile that curled up my mouth.

He chuckled. "Good for you." Buttering his toast, he said, "So what do you think?"

"I think I need a place to stay while I see what this town's all about, and I wouldn't mind trying your offer for a little while."

"Good. I'll get you a room when we get back." He measured me. "And a fake ID."

"That would be nice," I agreed.

~

And that's how Rick Marconi and I become friends. Within a few months, I had more money than I'd ever dreamed I'd see in one place. Enough to get myself a nice apartment, which gave me some freedom, too. I didn't have to stick to the Sands, though I always showed up there once a week out of loyalty to Rick.

I learned to play poker and craps, roulette and even baccarat, which was where the truly enormous amounts of money were spent. I watched and learned—watched the men to see how they played their games and what they most wanted while they were playing. I also watched their wives and girlfriends, particularly those who sat, bored and smoking, discreetly sipping far too many martinis, while their husbands and lovers played the big games. The women played slot machines, mostly, their coiffed hair and sleek legs going unappreciated by the men burning with another sort of lust around the tables.

I copied them, those women. Learned how to dress elegantly and with a sense of style, learned how to walk and talk and do my hair. I'm sure I didn't fool any of the women, but the veneer was enough to please the men.

In time, I had created a niche for myself in Las Vegas. There is no proper word for it in the world today, although if you read historical novels as much as I do, you'll know there've always been women who were mistresses to men of power. I learned how they did it, and I saw how much higher a position I occupied in the world by refusing to be a wife. I had my freedom, money, all I could desire.

Since there was no one to teach me the rules, I made up my own. I settled on a patron, one at a time, and he would pay my bills. He would not be a local, and he would be married, and my only promise to him was that I would be available for him when he came to Las Vegas, or if he wished to vacation without his wife somewhere else.

On my own time, I was free, though I never came right out and said it. In actual experience, I did not often have more than one man in my life at a time, and I never was one to sleep casually with men passing through. It always seemed to take too much of a piece of me to have one-night stands, casual encounters. If I was going to make love to a man, I wanted to know him a little.

One of the other rules was that I stayed away from men I found too compelling. No one too young, too handsome, too alluring to me for whatever reason. If I felt that zing, I left him alone. I preferred older men, usually at least forty, most in their fifties or thereabouts. I'm not sure what it is about that age for men, but they get scared and lonely and need sometimes to have a young woman's legs around them.

There was one exception, and I only let him through because he was an honest-to-God prince, a young Arabian with eyes like Omar Sharif who loved my red hair and long legs. I loved his low laugh and his clever wordplay and his virility. He bought me rubies of all sorts, saying they suited me. We traveled to lovely places, once all the way to Hawaii. He loved champagne and loathed bacon and I was lucky to find him. He was my lover, off and on, for most of the time I was in Las Vegas.

Until I met the man I fell in love with. The man who would be my downfall.

I didn't tell India that part. Not then.

CHAPTER
TWENTY-NINE

India

It takes my mother some time to tell her story and I can see it's made her depressed. Something has, anyway. There's that vulnerability around her eyes, a little shake to her fingers as she lights her cigarette. Trying to cheer her up, I say "So that's where all those dresses came from."

"Yeah." She smokes thoughtfully. "I bought them all myself, you understand—most of them, anyway—but I had to have pretty things, you know?"

"Of course." I think about the Thunderbird, about how exciting it must have been in those days in Las Vegas. "A prince, huh?" I smile at her.

Dark and snow have settled around the hotel, along with a blustery wind that piles the fat flakes into miniature mountain ranges across the sidewalk. The yellow glow of a lamp touches the sheen of my mother's hair, and gives her blue eyes the lure of topazes as she looks at me. "It was all pretty empty in the long run." She gives a little shift of her shoulders. "All those men running from their lives. Their wives."

"Were they all married?"

"A man who isn't married doesn't need a mistress." She inhales from her Salem, wiggles her nose. "In those days, India, everybody was married. It was just what people did."

"Including you, eventually."

She doesn't meet my eyes. "Eventually."

"How old were you when you first got to Vegas?"

"Seventeen."

"And when you met my dad?"

There's the slightest hesitation as she plucks an imaginary hair off her skirt. "Twenty-three when I got married." She grins. "I thought I was so old, too. My mama was fifteen when she married."

And here I am forty and pregnant for the first time, never married at all. "Times do change."

"You're not bothered by all of this?"

Because she's asked so directly, I take some time to consider. I probe around in my belly and chest for resentments or little bits of betrayal over the lies she made up about her past. "No," I say after a minute. "Things never quite made sense."

"I swear I wasn't a prostitute." She holds up three fingers. "Scout's honor."

"I believe you. But—" I take a breath. "It frankly doesn't look that different to me."

"It is, though," she says, strongly. "A mistress makes her own rules. A prostitute is at the mercy of men."

"And you weren't?"

"No. I won't argue that I had to use them—there wasn't much else available to a woman of my background and education, you know? At the time, it was just about the only way for a woman like me to turn the tables."

"Like the Indians and their casinos?" I smile.

"Exactly."

Silence flutters down like the snowfall. In the fireplace, a log snaps and sends a spray of orange sparks into the air. The smell reminds me of summer camp and bunk beds and s'mores. "Fires make me think of Gypsy telling ghost stories," I say.

"She was always so good at it."

I fold my hands between my legs, stare out at the snow. "God, please let her be okay."

"Amen."

~

Back in my room, I try Jack at home again and reach his answering machine. There is no email from him, but I'd told him that my access was quite patchy on this trip. Rare for him to be so completely out of touch, but then maybe he's feeling as conflicted as I am.

I had really been looking forward to talking to him, however, and after the disappointments and struggles of the day, it's enough to make me feel genuinely weepy. I call his cell phone, which ordinarily I would not do, and leave a short message. "Hi, Jack. It's me, India. I'm in Gallup tonight, at the El Rancho Hotel. It's been a long day of driving and disappointments with my sister." I hesitate. "I would purely love to hear your voice tonight, so if you're not too late, give me a call."

There's nothing to do but turn on the television. I flip through the desultory offerings, bored with all of it, wishing for my own house, my big computer, a deep hot bath, maybe a nice DVD from Blockbuster. It's funny to me that I imagine the apartment in Colorado Springs, not the one in Capitol Hill. I'm not going to stay in an apartment if I stay in the Springs, but somehow I've lost my longing to live in the high-intensity, high-traffic, high-stress world of Denver.

The recognition arrives with a solid certainty. I'm not going back to the big city and my fast-paced life and my artsy friends. Something in me, in my life or heart or soul, has shifted. I imagine a house on the west side of Colorado Springs, maybe Manitou or Old Colorado City, an agreeable Victorian or Craftsman-style house. Maybe a big Victorian with room for me and my mother, Gypsy, and a baby. We could all take care of each other. Gypsy would never miss her meds. My mother wouldn't drink herself under the table at night. My baby would have love and kisses from morning till night.

It doesn't seem so bad.

"God, India, you are losing it," I say aloud, and flip the channel button. Finally, here is the weather channel, showing the small scattering of pink storm over the northern and western sections of New Mexico. It seems to have moved beyond Gallup, and in surprise, I get up to peek outside my windows. The snow has stopped entirely, leaving feathers of powdery snow scattered over the grassy areas. The sidewalks and streets are clean.

Close to the glass, however, I can feel the cold, and I think of Gypsy. Tomorrow, I'll ask my mother to brainstorm with me on our language. Maybe she has a clue.

A knock on the door jolts me, and I glance at my watch. It's nearly ten-thirty. "Who is it?"

"Just me."

I open the door to find my mother looking the slightest bit disheveled, a water glass of bourbon and Coke in her hand. "Is everything all right?"

"Feeling a little lonely is all. Can I come in for a few minutes?"

"Yeah, sure. What's wrong, Mom?"

She sighs, settles on the chair. "It's just harder some days than others, that's all. Do you remember what happened to your daddy's ex-wife? Bea?"

"She died when we were kids."

"Yeah. While we were gone. Ripped your dad's heart out. He felt so guilty about her."

I nod, unsure how far I want to go with her down memory lane once she's started drinking.

She rubs her forehead, hard, the ice in her glass clinking. "I've been thinking a lot about how awful I was on that trip, India. I don't know what came over me, honestly. I'd been fine, and all at once, it just

Barbara O'Neal

seemed like everything was a trap, and I didn't know what to do." She sips her drink, a very, very tiny sip indeed. "Sometimes I wonder if you'd have been better off if I'd just left you two with your daddy."

Her smile is so sad I can't stand it. "Oh, Mom, don't say that."

"No," she says with a sigh. "I'm not gonna get all maudlin on you, honey, I swear. I'm just feeling them all tonight, all the choices. All the turns I took."

"I can understand that."

"It's just . . . what does it all add up to, in the end?"

What can I possibly offer her? "Mom, those are pretty big questions for anyone, any time. They're probably too big for a night when it's snowy and cold and you're depressed and so am I. Let's see how things look in the morning, huh?"

She wrinkles her nose, stands up. "You're awfully good to me, India. Thank you." She kisses my head and makes her way to the door.

"Mom, I love you, you know."

"I know," she says quietly. "Love you, too."

As the door snicks closed behind her, my phone rings and I feel a surge of purest hope, a white shaft through the gray layer of depression. "Hello?"

"Hello, India," says Jack, and the sound of his green voice on this wintery night is one of the finest things I've ever heard.

Maybe I'll have to give him up. Maybe it won't work out in the long run. Maybe my heart will be broken in the end, but tonight, this minute, he is on the other end of the phone.

"I am so happy to hear your voice, Jack Shea."

"I miss you."

"Me, too."

I hear the squish of a can opening and the sound is as comforting as a lullaby. "Tell me about your day," he says. "Where are you?"

I settle on the bed, tucking my feet beneath me, and close my eyes. "Gallup," I begin.

CHAPTER THIRTY

Eldora, 1973

When I'm alone in my room, I have to ask myself some hard questions. I had not really intended to tell India everything, only the parts that concerned her.

Now she's pregnant, and I guess I'm going to have to let it all come out. It hurts my heart, and it will hurt hers. More than I could wish.

The weather outside is bitter and punishing—snow, wind, all the sharpness of winter. My thoughts are with Gypsy, now and back then, and with my own regrets, which are long enough to keep a priest going for quite some time. I've made peace with a lot of my choices, being as I didn't have so many as you might think.

But there are others that still taste like bitter apples in my throat, some that rise like the furies to torment me late at night. Gallup, New Mexico, houses one of the most bitter of them all.

Don't ask me what happened in my head back in Santa Fe. I had fully intended to go home to Don from there after saying goodbye to Glenn.

I didn't. Not even when I got back to the room and found India asleep at the foot of her bed and Gypsy sound asleep in the bathtub.

Not even then. When it was plain my daughters had been frightened and lonely without me. When I knew they were missing their daddy and their home and their things. When—

God.

There are things you look back on and you just don't know why. I don't know, that's the truth. I regret it. I regret everything that happened through that stretch of days. I don't know what was wrong with me to make me go so crazy. A friend of mine, who has heard the story says I ought to go get some counseling, let it all out, and forgive myself. But I'm not about to forgive myself for such bad behavior. I don't go around slicing little marks in my skin from morning till night, either, but there are some things you're just required to carry. I'm ashamed of myself and I have reason to be.

I'd planned to be in Las Vegas with Glenn by nightfall—a hard day's drive but doable. The girls would have their own rooms in his Las Vegas house, and maybe they'd be excited by his swimming pool and everything would be on the way to normal. That's how I was thinking, that running off in the middle of their lives, dragging them out to the desert without even their things, was perfectly normal, that a swimming pool would make up for losing their daddy.

But India could be intractable and Gallup was on her list of towns we had to see in her Route 66 tour. She showed it to me on the map, circled in a red heart because it was the Heart of Indian Country. Gypsy, too, was excited.

They wanted to stop at the lava beds at El Malpais, so we took the detour and drove down to the badlands. A desolate place, but India sure liked it. She was funny, pacing around with her little toy six-shooters and her neckerchief tied just so and her hair in pigtails. She and Gypsy did each other's hair every morning.

After that, we stopped at the Continental Divide, too, which wasn't nearly as impressive as a person might think. I guess I was feeling guilty, because I pulled over at every two-bit tourist stand the whole way to Gallup. And if you've never been that way, there are a lot. I was disappointed this morning to see it was mainly casinos nowadays. The old places were tacky as stick-on fingernails, but they had some heart to them.

After we stopped at the Continental Divide, the car started acting up a little bit. Spluttering and bucking, and finally overheating so much that steam was pouring out from underneath the hood. I was lucky it happened when it did, not more than a couple of miles outside town— if it had happened an hour before or an hour beyond Gallup we would have been stuck in the desert, three females without any help. And remember, there weren't any cell phones in those days.

I flagged down a trucker who drove us the rest of the way into the little town, which was really depressing, I can tell you. It's better now than it was. In those days it was a grimy reservation town with a lot of drunks all over the place and the smell of despair like soot in the air. I hated it on sight, but the girls were enchanted by the real Indian shops. Probably by a sense of something real, honestly. They have good bullshit detectors, those girls. They liked Gallup because it was the real thing, grimy and hard as it was.

The car had a broken radiator and the service station man said they'd fix it but it'd take overnight. There was no way of reaching Glenn, who'd driven his own car ahead of us and wouldn't be in Las Vegas till later that evening. We were stuck in Gallup, and we just messed around all day. India was in a pissy mood, which I can certainly understand now, but at the time she seemed to be doing it deliberately, misbehaving just to get a rise out of me.

It was India who insisted we had to call her daddy. I'd already gotten us all some supper at a tacky little Route 66 restaurant that reminded me entirely too much of Dina's in Elk City, right down to the chicken-fried steaks and the decor on the walls, all cowboys and lassos and neon. Terrible. It made me purely claustrophobic.

The girls had milkshakes. They were both sunburned from being out in the sun all day. They begged me to let them go swimming after supper in the motel pool. I let them, too tense to put on my own suit and go with them. I was nibbling my bitten nails and smoking cigarettes one after the other, thinking about getting something to drink so I could sleep. I didn't, but I had a strong longing that night, I can tell you.

Finally, we went back to the room, watched *Love, American Style* and *Room 222* on television, and then India started agitating to call her daddy. I ignored her at first, pretending like I was reading. I used to do that a lot in those days, when I was tired and the children were wearing me out; I'd disconnect with a book in my lap. It wasn't like I didn't really hear them—I heard their voices and the tone, so if anybody was in big trouble, I'd know—but I could put them on the other side of a wall for a little while and let them sort things out on their own.

But that night, India came over and put her hand over the pages of my paperback and said, "Mom. We haven't talked to Daddy since we left."

So what could I do? I had to call him. Well, I might have been able to get out of it. I don't know that I wanted to talk, exactly, but it did seem like a kindness to at least let him know what was going on. How I'd do that with the girls in the room was a little tougher to imagine, but he'd get it.

We had to call collect, and he answered on the second ring, sounding so ragged a fingernail screeched down the middle of my chest. The operator asked if he'd accept the charges and for a long second, he didn't reply.

"Sir," said the operator again, "there is a collect call from Eldora Redding. Will you accept the charges?"

Finally he said, "Yes."

"Hi," I said with false joviality. "There are two girls here who are dying to talk to their daddy." And before he could say a word, I handed the phone to Gypsy. In her throaty little voice, she said, "Hi, Daddy. We saw a red-tailed hawk today! It was so pretty."

Next to her, India was dancing from foot to foot, her socks falling down her skinny calves as always. She hissed, "Let me tell him about the silversmith!" Gypsy scowled and waved her hand away, but I knew she wouldn't give away her sister's secret. In her dignified way, she told him about some postcards she bought in a little store and about her apple pancakes at breakfast. They were wearing little T-shirts and I could see the first swollen buds of their nipples beneath their shirts. They'd be twelve in a couple of months. It was probably time to have the talk about periods.

And for the first time it hit me that I was this old when I lost my mama for good. She'd been sick off and on for years, of course, but she was always there until then. I could go lie down next to her in bed if she was poorly, and when she was well, I helped her with the laundry and my brothers, feeding the next-to-the-littlest ones while she nursed the youngest.

I felt so big then, I thought, looking at my little daughters. I remember coming in to find them on the floor and in the bathtub last night. What kind of mother had I become? I wanted to cry about it, but instead I got up and brushed my hair, lit a cigarette, turned the channel on the television to see what else was on. Only one of them came in clearly. The other one was snowy.

India got on the phone next and excitedly told her daddy about the silversmith we saw in Albuquerque, and about the woman who showed her beading in the plaza yesterday and about the Magic Fingers. Then she wanted to know how his days were going and what he'd been doing, and she listened.

In the end, she said, "Okay, Daddy, good night. I love you lots and lots!" Then she held out the heavy receiver to me. "He wants to talk to you, and he said me and Gypsy should have some candy so you should give us quarters to go to the machine."

"All right." I dug out the quarters. "Stay away from the pool, you hear me?"

"We're not babies," Gypsy said with disgust, and nudged her sister with a roll of her eyes. "We'll sit in the lobby in those big chairs."

I nodded and put the receiver to my lips. "Hi. They're gone."

"Eldora, I have some bad news."

His tone was so terrible that my heart caught hard. "Who died?"

He cleared his throat. "Bea."

His ex-wife. "What?" It didn't make any sense to me. "How? What happened?"

"She came by here yesterday all dressed up. Had on her lipstick, a pretty dress, and I could tell she was happy, you know?" He paused, and with a sharp, painful sense of clarity, I could see his face as plain as day, the way he'd be pinching the bridge of his nose, the way his blue eyes would have bewilderment in them. "I asked her where she was going all dressed up so pretty. And she said . . . she said . . ."

Oh God. "Take your time."

He was weeping silently. I knew it by the utter depth of quiet on the other end of the line. Finally he went on. "She said she'd come by because she knew you'd left me. She wanted to go out to dinner."

Oh God oh God oh God.

"I asked her to come in and have some tea. I swear that's all it was gonna be, Eldora. But she started kissing me and I was so sad about everything and I let her. I let her. I let her touch me and I let her take me to bed and then I felt so bad and told her it just couldn't ever be again, that I loved you, even if you didn't love me. And she went home and put her head in the oven and turned it on. She killed herself, Eldora."

"Oh, Don," I said in a whisper.

"It's my fault."

I felt the thick tears in my throat, but I had no right to weep over her. "No, it wasn't." And I wasn't even going to say whose fault it was, because it was too much attention on me and my stupid self. But I thought of her standing there in my backyard.

I thought of her. "She loved you so much, Don. I never saw anyone who loved—"

He was weeping again.

"I was coming home, Don. Really. My car broke down," I said. "The radiator broke. I tried calling you this morning but I couldn't get through."

"Eldora—"

"I'm trying to tell you that we'll be heading back tomorrow morning. They got me a new radiator and the car is fine. You hold on, honey, okay? I love you. You can count on me."

"Eldora, I thought you were gone for good."

"Oh, honey," I breathed, "how could I ever leave you?"

PART SIX

THE FLAMINGO HOTEL

Bugsy Siegel's desert dream, the Flamingo, has anchored the Las Vegas Strip since they started rolling dice in 1946. This self-contained casino and resort offers everything an adventurous vacationer could want—including a Wildlife Habitat and a 15-acre Caribbean-style water playground. 3,530 rooms.

CHAPTER
THIRTY-ONE

India

The morning is classically Southwestern spring weather: brilliantly blue skies stretched like rubber over the bowl of the horizon, the snow melted or melting in a cheery drip-drip-drip from the roofs to the ground. I run by the homeless shelter on the way out of town, but we don't even eat in Gallup. Both of us are anxious to get to Las Vegas.

"What's your general plan when we get there, Mom? Are there special places you want to see? I booked rooms at the Flamingo, I thought you'd enjoy that, but we can stay somewhere else if you'd rather. What was there when you were there?"

"Oh, there was lots there. I just don't know which ones are which these days. They're always having an implosion and building a new casino. Who can keep up?"

"That's true," I say to be agreeable, but what I know of Las Vegas can be summed up in a few words: neon, Elvis, wedding chapels, and the mob.

"F'instance," she says, "the Bellagio went up over the place where the Dunes was. And I know they imploded the old Aladdin and built a new one, but it wasn't there when I was."

"What were your favorites, back then?"

"Hmmm. The Sands, of course. The Sahara was very big and important. Sometimes it was fun to go up to the Tropicana, but I didn't, much. Each of the casinos had their flavor, you know? I never much cared for the Trop."

"So, do you want to visit those places, or just look around, go shopping, gamble? I don't know what we'll be doing when we get there."

"You don't have to tag along, India. You can look at whatever interests you. I'd like to take you into the Sands if it's still there. It's kinda special. Have you ever played slot machines?"

"Nope, can't say that I have."

"You might enjoy it. And I expect you'd probably enjoy the big, fancy resorts they've been building. The New York, New York, and the Luxor and the Paris and . . . what's the other one?"

I'm chuckling at the names, which I must have heard but have not filed. "I have no idea, Mom."

She snaps her fingers, frowning. "You know. It has canals and a palace."

"Venice?"

"Yes! That's it. The Venetian."

"Venice in Las Vegas?"

"Is that any weirder than New York in Las Vegas?"

"Guess not." I shift the heater vent to blow on my cold hands.

We're quiet for a while. "You think Gypsy's okay?" she asks me suddenly.

The word is out before I know it will be: "No."

"Me neither. I had bad dreams all night."

"So did I." Howling winds. Coyotes and graveyards. One woke me up, a blood-soaked wash of color, noise, fear; a jumble of images I couldn't sort out. I sigh. "God, I wish we could find her!"

"I know, but other than what we're doing, I'm not sure what else we can possibly do, baby."

"What about our language? Mine and Gypsy's. She left me another message in it. I keep thinking if I could just figure it out, maybe I could piece it together."

"I'm sorry, honey. I never did understand it. You two made it up and that's the way it stayed."

"You don't remember anything about it? A certain kind of sound or a rhythm or something?"

"Yeah, there was a rhythm, a rolling kind of sound. Or no, not rolling. Lilting. LalaLAla LalalaLA."

Letting the sound percolate, imitating it under my breath, I shift to go around a U-Haul chugging down the highway. A weary-looking dad in a fishing hat is leaning over the wheel. Poor guy. Chewing on my inner cheek, I shake my head. "That didn't shake anything loose, either." I take in a breath. "I'm so worried about her this morning!"

"Don't think about it, sweetheart. Maybe she'll call or show up at one of the shelters, but if she doesn't there isn't anything we can do but pray for her." Her hand on my wrist is comforting.

"Tell me some more about Las Vegas, then, Mom. Who gave you the Thunderbird?"

"How do you know I didn't buy it myself?"

I give her a look.

She grins, and it's a half smile, dashing and pretty, making her eyes look mischievous. "Well, you're right. It was a present."

"From?"

For a long moment she's quiet, looking out the window, and I can feel her wish for a cigarette to punctuate her tale. After a time she opens her purse and takes a photograph out of her wallet. "Him," she says, holding it up so I can glance at it in long bits.

He's dark and beautiful, with thick black hair sweeping away from a high forehead and an elegant, bold Roman nose. His dark eyes are knowing and somehow familiar. He's wearing a white dinner jacket. "Wow," I say. "He's gorgeous."

"His name," she says with a hint of sadness, "was Alex Morelli. He was my downfall, and I was his."

CHAPTER
THIRTY-TWO

Eldora, 1960

In Las Vegas, this was my life:

Late in the afternoon I'd lay out my clothes for the evening—dress, shoes, bag, accessories. I especially liked the intimates: champagne silk and black lace bra and panties. I kept the advice of Mrs. Pachek from the department store in Elk City and bought good foundation garments, but I found them in elegant fabrics and colors. It's a decision I've never had reason to regret.

Once I knew what I'd be wearing, I ate a cold supper of some sort, shrimp or tuna mostly, often cold cuts. In those days, I never had to watch a single thing I ate, but I discovered I felt better longer if I kept my portions small in the heat of the day. I'd have my main meal late, usually at one or two in the morning.

After the quick supper, I'd shower and smooth my skin, my hair, put on my face, and then get dressed. By eight, I'd be in the casinos.

My world. The richness of carpets stretching through the labyrinth of tables and machines and people, the cocktail girls in their tight uniforms and short skirts; the players with worry or hope or weariness around their eyes. The slightly sour smells of sweat and spilled alcohol, the spice of colognes and exotic perfumes, the bite of cigarette smoke. One of the reasons I love going to Cripple Creek so much is that smell, and the sound. The sound of slots and cards and voices, excitement and music. These days there's an electronic angle to it; in those days it was more clattery. But it's still the sound of money falling home.

Nothing like it.

The night I met Alex I was sitting in the Riviera in a cloud of blue cigarette smoke. There was a singer, someone I didn't know, and the sound of the barman clanking bottles.

He approached me in the blue-dark room, and offered a flame to the end of my cigarette. "Alex Morelli," he said, and I knew immediately who he was. A casino boss, a made guy as they said then. Connected, wealthy, ruthless. I'd heard of him, had heard that he was charming. But no one had ever said how beautiful he was.

I nodded, as if I didn't know the name, blew smoke into the darkness, pretended he did not move me. He sat down on the barstool next to mine. "You won't tell me your name?"

"I think you know it already," I said, and took a tiny drag on my cigarette. "Just like I know who you are."

When he smiled, he had a dimple, deep in his dark, smooth cheek. "You're right. Your name is Eldora, and that makes me think of Eldorado, and gold. You've been in town three years and are sometimes seen in the company of a certain Arabian prince."

I raised an eyebrow and shifted, knowing his eyes would fall on my neck and shoulders, and lower, to the swell of my breasts. "And you are a well-connected man with an interest in many casinos, but particularly the Sands and the Sahara. And you have a very beautiful wife, a Sicilian with a temper."

He nodded. "Will you come to my suite for a steak?"

"No."

"That's probably wise," he said, and put the lighter in my palm. "But I hope you will change your mind."

Even then, I knew that I would. There was chemistry arcing between us like the Fourth of July. I could almost taste him as he looked at me, and I know it was the same for him. Who knows why that happens, why anyone falls in love with anyone else?

That night I resisted him. And for ten more attempts afterward. You must remember my situation. I was quite comfortable in my world, sitting close to the knee of an aging rancher who was playing big or the elbow of a businessman who'd just rolled the dice for the big time. The pit bosses were my friends, and I was loyal, and they knew it. I'd only happened into my liaison with the prince, but it was a perfect arrangement. I liked him, I did not find his touch repugnant, and there was genuine pleasure in our laughing together, but there was no spark from my side. I was in no danger of losing my heart to Rajid. He also only came to town once every few months, so my time was my own for the most part. He paid for an elegant set of rooms in the Dunes, where he sometimes required me to host elegant little suppers for associates. It wasn't a hardship. I discovered those years in the diner had taught me a lot about things, and the years in between, watching the wealthy wives of high rollers, I'd learned a great deal more. I had a talent for making people comfortable.

And I did not lack for girlfriends. There was a showgirl named Jackie, a beauty from the South who'd left a baby and an abusive husband behind in Biloxi; Kitten, the hairdresser who'd come to Las Vegas from Bakersfield and loved the glamour of being backstage with the breathlessly beautiful women who shone on the stages. Kitten showed me how to apply makeup as if it were done by an expert. She adored my rooms and my prince. She was not a particularly pretty woman, but we were of a size, and she loved getting some of my clothes when I tired of them.

Anna was my best friend. We met one night at the slot machines at the Sands, both of us wearing identical creamy white cocktail dresses that suited our redheadedness. She was peeved at first, but I made her laugh, and we had martinis, thanks to a handsome bartender named Bill who was known to look out for the locals.

Anna was the second wife of a casino executive, a former showgirl who knew the ins and outs of the city. She was the one most horrified when I confessed that Alex had been pursuing me.

"Have you heard all the stories about his wife?" Anna asked me.

"A few. She's jealous and temperamental."

"And beautiful and possessive and crazy. Most of these wives are good girls from New Jersey. They look the other way when their husbands have affairs. Not her. She's spoiled and haughty and her father is a big-time mob boss, so she gets away with murder. That's also how Alex got connected."

I lit a cigarette. "I get it, Anna. I get it."

So I stayed away from Alex Morelli. Ten times I ran into him and ten times I eluded him.

The eleventh was a night in full summer, nearly midnight after a show at the Sahara. I was by myself, outside on a little patio where the air was coming cool from the desert at last. I stood against a balustrade, taking tiny, tiny sips of a martini so it wouldn't give me a headache the next day, and listening to the music coming through the open doors.

"It seems," he said from behind me, "that we are fated to meet."

His hair was loosening from the way he combed it back from his face, and a lock fell on his cheekbone. Every molecule in me shivered and he saw it. "You are so beautiful," he said quietly. "Will you just dance with me one time?"

I looked around the open area and there was no one watching. "Once," I said, and shivered as I stepped forward, as I felt his hands light on my own. I looked up to him and my breath caught. He put my glass down on a nearby table and we stepped close to each other. I felt the front of his thighs along the front of mine, and the brush of his chest in the air just beyond my breasts.

We danced in a slow, easy way, our eyes locked as we moved. At the end of the song, he stopped and I saw him swallow. When I would have stepped away, he said, "No," and kissed me.

And that, as they say, was that. It was magical, that kiss. Everything in me came alive, as if I had swallowed iridescent paint and it glowed along my ribs and my belly and hips, and came out of my mouth in powdery puffs of barely visible glitter. His tongue touched mine and all the desire I'd never felt for others coalesced in a burning need for this man.

"I haven't slept in six months for thinking of you," he said, and his hands were big around my face. He smelled of Canoe, a scent I still associate with a shiver down my spine. "I don't know why. It's crazy. But I have to know you."

He took me to a hotel toward the north end of the Strip, not as often frequented by his crowd, the Thunderbird. There, we made love for the first time, and long into the night, we drank champagne and talked. We talked about everything, about big dreams, his and mine, about the hard-luck tales that brought us here—his not so different from mine, nor his way of managing it. He was from a bad world in Newark, New Jersey, and left school at fifteen to make his way up the ranks of numbers runners. He seduced his boss, emotionally, and then his boss's daughter, physically. He used his wits and his good looks, just as I had.

He was straight with me. He told me he could never leave his wife, that not only would his career be over, but probably his life. He said it with a smile, but it put a knife through my heart.

"I'm not as worried about your father-in-law as I am about your wife."

Alex, lying with the sheet tangled around his waist, nodded. "That's why we have to be careful. She's crazy, and I don't mean like the kind of crazy that makes you have a fit or throw things. She's the only person who really matters to herself, you know what I mean?"

I nodded. "We'll see how it goes, then, huh, lover?"

He swallowed, his nostrils flaring. "No. This is for us."

And I knew it, too. I tasted my soulmate on his lips. It made me weep, and when he made love to me and kissed the tears on my face, licking them away, one by one, I knew I had lost myself to him.

CHAPTER
THIRTY-THREE

India

And suddenly, here we are: Las Vegas.

I've seen it a thousand times in pictures and on television and in movies. The desert sun has sunk low in the wide sky by the time we get there, and the lights are just beginning to stand out against the dusk. It looks both exactly the same and not at all what I'd been expecting— both more overwhelming and less tacky than I'd imagined. The sheer scale of the hotels is overwhelming—they ramble for the length of city blocks, one after the other rising into the violet-stained sky, thousands and thousands and thousands of hotel rooms. We pass the New York, New York and I think of the first time I flew to the city to see Jack, and how entranced I'd been. The casino makes me laugh at the delight and absurdity of it. It's a marvel of design.

When we first spied the Strip, miles and miles away—a sudden sprouting of buildings visible from a very long way away—my mother said, "Everything is so tall!" Since then, she's been absolutely silent.

It's easy to find the Flamingo and find a place to park. We enter from the eastern side, and my mother has on her cat-eye sunglasses. She takes them off as we approach the doors. "Now, there," she says, gesturing with an earpiece toward a three-story wing of rooms with a George Jetson Design Approval rating of 8.5, "that's what the old Las Vegas looked like." Her eyes follow the rise of the towers all around us with awe. "Gawd. Imagine how much money is pouring into this town."

"Can't go wrong capitalizing on vice."

There is such a huge amount of money and the hotels are so gigantic that I am expecting the usual Hiltonesque spirit inside. That hush of soft good breeding, invisible service, sleek operations. And the tone of the doorman is the same, but inside, everything is different.

It's a slam of noise and light. We have to walk quite a distance to the check-in desk, following a path woven into the carpet. It loops through acres and acres of slot machines, all binging and clanging and ringing. There's a funny electronic undernote I hadn't expected, a happy sort of sound that makes me want to walk a little more jauntily, and I wonder with narrowed eyes if someone has done research into the sounds humans find appealing.

Of course they have.

As we pass a deck of machines, an alarm goes off and a light on top of a slot machine starts flashing red and white. An Asian woman with heavily lined lids and expensive shoes turns without much excitement to look for an attendant.

"She just won big," Eldora said. "The light goes off when the payoff is too big to pay with quarters."

It's dizzying and disorienting, and even as I think it, I know it's supposed to be, that the sounds and the lights and the artificial darkness of no windows combine to keep people dropping money into those little slots. The machines stretch in beeping silver splendor as far as I can see in any direction. Zillions of them, and in every casino, there are zillions and zillions more. Slot machines into infinity, and people feeding pennies, nickels, quarters, dollars into them. It's more than my mind can take in.

Next to me, Eldora has slowed, her eyes narrowed as she looks at one machine, then another, and another. "Here's my favorite," she says, and stops in front of one with Mylar-looking diamonds on it. "Hold on for just a minute, will you? I'll just play a couple of dollars."

I'm curious anyway, and it's not like we have anything to do but this. "Sure." I settle on the stool next to her.

She feeds the machine a five-dollar bill and punches the button. The reels spin around and around, making that happy, anticipatory electronic music. Nothing lines up. Eldora punches the button again, and gets three bars, which feeds her fifteen coins.

"Nice," she says.

Hits it again. Nothing. Again, which gives her a cherry and six coins. She's up to forty-three coins from twenty-five. This has my attention.

But then it's nothing, nothing, nothing, nothing, nothing. She gets another cherry along about eighteen coins, and plays a little while, but before long, she's lost the five dollars and we're walking away.

"I couldn't stand to just feed my money to those monsters," I say.

"There are some tricks to it. You want to find a machine that's paying pretty regular. Eventually, you'll nearly always lose whatever you've brought in with you, except maybe on video poker, but the trick is to find a machine that'll let you play for a long time on your five dollars or whatever. That one was a little bit cold, but it paid out right away, so it had me going for a minute."

"The secrets of slots," I say.

She smiles. "Laugh if you will, but it's been working for me for more than forty years."

Check-in is fast and easy, and on the elevators to our rooms, my mother says, "I'd like to just wander around a little on my own, if you wouldn't mind. We can meet for supper later on, maybe eight or so?"

"That sounds good. I'm tired." I'd also been hoping for a message from Jack when we checked in, and I'm fighting disappointment that there's nothing there.

I leave my mother on her floor and go up to my own, and on the way, get lost in the labyrinthine circles of rooms. I have to backtrack twice and finally I'm in near tears when I stop a maid, who gets me pointed in the right direction.

Headed firmly toward my room at last, I wonder how many maids it takes to clean this hotel every day. How many maids in each hotel? How many waitresses to bring cocktails and Cokes to the gamblers, how many more to staff the buffets and restaurants? How many cooks, security guards, cabdrivers? It's astonishing to think about.

With a swipe of the electronic key card, my door blips a green light to let me open it, and I think: *What if there was an electrical outage along the Strip, as there was in New York recently. What would happen? How could the people in the casinos find their way out? How could the guests get out of here?*

It's making me feel panicky and with a jerk, I open the curtains to give me a sense of space. I'm overlooking another casino, and the street, and in the distance the mountains, limned along the jagged top edge with the last dying rays of the sun.

Breathe.

After washing my face and settling my things, I pick up the phone and dial my voice mail. Nothing from Gypsy. One message from Jack. "Call me on my cell as soon as you get to Las Vegas," he says.

Which I am more than happy to do. I'm feeling overwhelmed and emotional and even very close to weepy. Is this what pregnancy will do to me? Am I going to be a fainting-violet person for the next six or seven months?

No. Because I can't do this, have this baby. As Jack's cell phone rings in my ear, I'm so worn out that I can't even think of the reasons why I thought I could or couldn't. None of it makes any sense.

"Hello, this is Jack. Leave a message."

My heart plummets. I'd been so wanting to hear his actual voice. "Hi, Jack, it's me. We're in the Flamingo, give me a call. Room 1462. I'll be around for a couple of hours, then we're going out."

I hang up and stretch out on the bed, which is big and firm and rather deliciously comfortable. As if the cells in my body have each been holding on to their own tight coil of tension, I feel a sudden wave of release. If it were water, the bed would be soaked.

It seems impossible that it has only been four days since we left Colorado Springs. I feel as if I've been with Lewis and Clark, as if I've seen the entire history of the twentieth century. My hands rest on my belly and I absently rub my thumbs together, thinking of my mother as a young woman sashaying through a casino with her hair in a bouffant style, one of those glorious dresses on her curvy bod. It makes me smile softly.

Amazing.

A knock jerks me out of a doze. "Hang on," I say, and take in a deep breath, blink hard as I roll off the bed heavily and pad to the door. It's likely my mother, but I really did get the impression she wanted to get out by herself. I peer through the peephole.

And yank open the door to Jack, standing there in his black leather coat, his hair falling in that rakish way across his forehead. Just the sight of him makes me very nearly swoon. I put a hand to my head, and then he's there, with one arm around my shoulders, and his nose next to my cheek. "God, I've been worried to death."

The smell of leather from his jacket, the perfume of his skin, the exquisitely pleasing sound of his cello voice in my ear slam my senses, and I turn to him, throw my arms around his shoulders. "Oh, Jack, I miss you so much when I don't see you!"

He's kissing me then, his hands on my face, my arms around his neck. It's moments before we are lying on the bed together, moments more before we are naked, kissing, burrowing into each other, closer and closer. It makes me want to cry.

Afterward we lie together in a tangle of limbs, my head on his chest. "When did you get here?" I ask.

"Last night. I was expecting to surprise you then."

I groan. "Instead I spent the night in grim Gallup, with a snowstorm."

"I made do by taking a survey of the costumes of various casino cocktail waitresses."

Chuckling, I raise my head to look at him. "And what did you discover?"

"I quite like the Paris ones, but the Venetian wins."

"Mmm." His hand smoothes over my upper back. His lashes are black on his cheeks. I touch his mouth, seeing my girl with black curls tumbling down her back, her little red lips. How did I allow myself to fall so in love?

But I have. It fills me like the water of a stream, rushing clear and honest and true through the heart of me. Resettling my head on his chest, I say, "How do you like it? I know you've always wanted to visit."

"Dazzling. Everything is so big, so bright."

"Supersized."

A small laugh. "Yes, like America." He slides down, faces me, tugs the cover over our heads so that we're lying face-to-face in a cocoon. "How are you?" he asks quietly.

"Better, now that I'm looking at you."

"I went mad, worrying."

"Me, too."

"What do you want to do, India?"

"Let's not talk about it right now, okay?" I put my hand on his lean, handsome cheek. "Let me just enjoy the moment."

He kisses my brow. "All right, then." He pulls the covers from our heads, but we don't get up. "What's the plan for this evening?"

"My mother wants to see some of the places she used to frequent."

"I'll look forward to that. She can give us the historic tour."

I laugh. "Something like that." I pause, thinking about all she's told me. "What an amazement she's turning out to be. Do you know she had an Arabian prince as a lover for a time? And another great love, a mobster."

"How exciting." He tucks a lock of my hair around my left ear, his fingers trailing along the edge. I see the weariness around his eyes, see the fact that he is not young, not by a long shot. "Did you bring along one of those dresses?"

"No, but you will love them, I promise. Next time I come to New York, I'll bring one."

He nods. "You look tired."

"I am."

"Perhaps you should nap a little."

"I don't want you to go anywhere."

"No," he says. "I'll stay right here."

CHAPTER THIRTY-FOUR

India

My mother is waiting for me by the front desk. She's dressed in one of the cocktail dresses, a blue silk number with a neckline she's draped expertly with a gossamer scarf. Her figure is excellent, full of breast and narrow of waist, those long, long legs ending in naked high-heel sandals. She's smoking a cigarette, perfectly at ease as she watches the people stream by. She looks like a movie star, aging but still gorgeous. People peer at her, trying to figure out if she's someone famous.

She catches sight of me, then Jack, and a smile spreads over her mouth. "Jack!" she cries, and kisses his cheeks as if she's known him forever. "I'm so glad to see you again! What do you think of our Las Vegas?"

"Astonishing."

"Do you play the games?"

"A little roulette." He inclines his head, giving her the half smile that slays me every time. "Mainly I save my gambling for the business world."

"And love?" she inquires, arching a brow.

He winks at me. "That, too."

We head out into the evening, plunging into a Saturday night crowd that has the same background feeling as New Orleans. I think of the ad for Las Vegas that ran a couple of years ago: "What you do here, stays here."

Sin City.

Jack offers an arm to each of us, and I admit the evening is pleasant. We take the car farther down the Strip, and get out by the Sahara, where Jack can slink through, looking for the movie scenes of his youth. We eat fresh fruits and sandwiches at an excellent buffet, and while Jack plays roulette for a little while, my mother shows me her methodology for finding a "hot" slot machine.

"Everybody gets their special favorites," she says, gesturing like Vanna White toward the machines. "Your daddy liked the ones with the sevens that line up—sevens felt lucky to him. I tend to like the ones with the doubling points—the double diamonds and ten times wins, that kind of thing. They're not so boring, you know?"

I nod. There is a dizzying variety. "Try a double diamond then."

"All right, so then we wander and kind of let one call us."

"Call us," I repeat with skepticism.

"Yep." She sashays down the rows, her red-tinted hair gleaming against her white neck, looking at the machines, focused in a way I haven't seen in her except when she's picking fabric samples or paint chips.

Men admire her, taking a second between spins on the machines to get a full look. She sometimes winks at this one, or smiles at that one. She could have a roomful of retirees at her beck and call if she so desired.

For one second, I can see her at twenty, nubile and breathtakingly beautiful, commanding the attention of the men around poker or baccarat tables, capturing the attention of a prince.

But that girl could have nothing on this seasoned beauty. No way she knew anything close to what this one knows. It makes me look forward to my own maturity.

"Here's one," she says, stopping abruptly. "This one is a double diamond and a ten-time pay."

"Ah! But why this one?"

She lifts a graceful shoulder and feeds in a ten-dollar bill. "Just feels right, that's all."

But for the first few spins, it doesn't seem as if it will be any good. She wins nothing in the first five spins, and shakes her head. "And sometimes you're wrong."

I grin.

"Really. One of the other things you've got to know is when to say when. You get caught up in your ego and hunches and you're doomed. There's nothing wrong with intuition, but you've got to use common sense, too." She punches the button. "I'll play until I'm down five dollars, then quit."

The rollers swing into place: a cherry, a cherry, and then a diamond. The little counting noise spins into action, and when it's finished, she has 624 coins—the six dollars she had left, plus the payoff for this round.

Next to her, a man says, "Nice."

"Thanks." My mother stands up and gestures for me to sit on the stool. "Now you play. We're not going to blow it all, but you may as well get some of the rush out of it. I have a feeling this is a real nice machine."

So I settle in and play her slot machines. It's surprisingly relaxing and enjoyable—who knew? I win and lose, and when we're down to 575 coins, my mother calls it quits. "Let's cash this in and go for a little walk, huh? All this smoke can't be making you feel good."

"Okay. I'll find Jack and let him know."

"I'll be right here by the money cage."

Jack is hotly engaged, not in roulette, but in poker. The lock of hair on his forehead is loose and rakish and he should be smoking a cigar. "Is this a good time to tell you something?" I ask.

"Of course!" He takes my hand.

"Are you enjoying yourself?" I ask.

"More than I would have expected," he says.

"My mother wants to go for a walk. Do you want us to wait, or what?"

He's watching the game from the corner of his eye. "I'm winning just now. Would you mind if I met you back at the hotel?"

"Not at all."

"All right then, I'll see you there." He squeezes my hand. Not even in Vegas would he find kissing in public acceptable.

My mother and I head into the night. "I was going to go down and look at the Thunderbird, but the woman in there just told me it's gone."

"Why did you want to go there?"

She sighs, tugs on the end of her scarf. "For that, sweetheart, I need a drink."

I point to the cocktail lounge. "There?"

"No, let's get out of here. I think there might be something a little farther on." She's agitated as we walk, lights a cigarette, fiddles with the ends of her scarf. There's a sidewalk vendor selling soft drinks and hot dogs. Several park benches are arranged around it. "Let's just get a Coke, shall we?"

Her nervousness is making me nervous. "You don't have to tell me if you don't want to, Mom."

"No, I need to." We settle on the benches. "The Thunderbird wasn't far from here," she says, pointing. "I really did want to see it again."

CHAPTER
THIRTY-FIVE

Eldora, 1962

I had never been in love, but I fell head over heels for Alex Morelli. I loved everything about him—the deep timbre of his laughter, the way he sang bawdy little songs in the shower, the sight of his long back when he was asleep.

It went on for three years. And I will say they were a good three years. Our symbol was the Thunderbird, which is a Navajo symbol for "happiness unlimited." We met at the Thunderbird hotel, and he bought me my Thunderbird car, and we even had some special stationery printed with Thunderbirds on it. I kept my rooms at the Dunes, which Alex discreetly paid for through a special account. I still went out with my girlfriends and sat with a high roller once in a while, but mainly I lived for Alex, and he lived for me.

Happiness unlimited.

We had a lot in common. Movies had given us a vision of a world beyond where we'd been born. His mother was a drunk, and his father had left them when he was young. We liked cards and cigarettes and martinis served icy cold. We traveled some and I loved that most of all—we went to Palm Springs a few times, and to New York City a couple of times, and once all the way to Vancouver for a secret, week-long tryst. We said it was our honeymoon. It felt like it.

But Las Vegas is a small town. The secret was bound to come out. Perhaps one or the other of us helped it along once in a while, even, hoping to bring things into the open. A quick divorce, a resolution, a fresh start somewhere else—we dreamed of disappearing in Europe, to Monaco, or one of the other gambling meccas we'd heard tales of. With his knowledge of casinos, surely there was somewhere we could be happy and productive.

I'm sure we both knew it was a pipe dream, that our time together, one way or another, would be brief. It lent the days a certain sweetness.

It ended where it began, at the Thunderbird hotel on a February night. Alex was making love to me. We were laughing, though I have often tried to remember why and can't seem to pull the details into my living memory.

His wife, Sofia, burst into the room. Alex jumped up and tried to hide me from her, but she shot him before he could get very far. I squeezed my eyes tight and waited, but she didn't shoot me.

She lowered the gun. A beautiful woman, with lush red lips and eyes like a Moroccan harem girl. I was starting to shiver with reaction, and there was hot fluid pooling at my midsection, and Alex's head was on my knee. His eyes were open, and my hands trembled as I touched his brow. And still, she just stood there, looking at me, the gun dangling in her hand.

There was a strange, whining sound in the room, and I figured out it was me, whimpering, oh God oh God oh God oh God.

I loved him so much, but it was too deep, too wild, too unbeliev-able for tears. I raised my head and looked at Sofia, who was beautiful and pouty.

"Get it over with," I said.

Sofia shook her head. "No. I want you to live with this for the rest of your life. I want you to wake up screaming when you're sixty-five." She smiled and dropped the gun on the floor.

It seemed that it took hours for the police to come. Hours I sat with my lover's blood pooling in my lap, hours I stroked his face and breathed in the smell of his hair and said my goodbyes. The blood was hot, but it cooled quickly. I was a mess by the time the cops came. I don't remember much about the rest of the night, just waking up in my friend Kitten's apartment the next day and realizing I was in big, big trouble.

CHAPTER
THIRTY-SIX

India

"Jesus, Mom. How did you stand it?"

She lifts her shoulder, wipes a tear from the corner of her eye. "What could I do, really? Live with it or not live with it." Wind rattles the palm fronds overhead. "And there were some more pressing problems." She looks at me. "This is the last part of the story, India."

I'm afraid when she says that. But she is my mother, and there has been murder and mayhem in her life, and I always thought she was just irritating and cloying. For the last time on this trip, I say, "Tell me."

CHAPTER THIRTY-SEVEN

Eldora, 1962

The murder made the papers, and by morning, my name was mud. One thing a mistress must be is discreet. Having my name splashed across the headlines in connection to such a lurid story pretty much assured I'd never have another patron in Las Vegas again. Sofia was arrested and she'd eventually do some time, but in the meantime, her papa was pretty pissed off. And he was connected enough that he got whatever he wanted. I lost my suite at the Dunes, though the manager was nice enough to give me a few days to pack things up.

Kitten let me stay with her for a week or two, until I could figure out what my next move should be. Not that there were a lot of choices. I did have a small amount of money tucked away, along with the jewels I'd been given and bought for myself over the years.

If not for a certain other problem, I might have just gone back to LA until it all died down, or found myself a partner and opened a restaurant or something. Unfortunately, there was a rather huge pressing problem: I was pregnant.

The world is not the same place it is now. Abortions were illegal and dangerous, though I could have found a doctor to do it if I'd chosen to look. The truth is, though, I wanted my baby. I was utterly destroyed by Alex's death, and the only silver lining was the truth of his seed in my womb. I couldn't realistically do it on my own. That left one option: I'd have to find a man to marry me. Quick.

That weekend there was a convention of engineers in town, and I dressed up in my finest dress, perfumed my hair, and walked straight and saucy into the casinos, looking for the right man. I steered clear of the places where I'd be immediately recognized, the places where my pit-boss friends would hustle me out in three minutes—the Sands, the Dunes, the Flamingo, the Thunderbird. Instead, I cruised the Riviera and the Tropicana, which I'd never much liked. I knew exactly what I was looking for.

The man would be middle-aged, probably from the Midwest somewhere. A good man, one who mowed his lawn and had been working five days a week since he got out of school at twenty-two. White collar. No children—the last was my rule, not part of the marking game. It was one thing to steal a woman's husband. Quite another to steal a father from his babies.

And he would have to have that look in his eye that I'd learned to identify a long time ago, back in Elk City. In those days, I didn't know what it meant. Now I did. It was a recognition of mortality, a slightly bewildered and panicked understanding of the fact that yes, you, too, will die. And you're not a movie star or a bank president or even all that important. You're just another body that'll be forgotten by humanity the second you're in the ground.

Don't ask me why women are not as frightened by this realization when it comes creeping into our heads. And it does, of course. Every thinking person feels it. Most women don't seem to need a new man or a new car or to prove that they won't die. Maybe we're just more sensible.

Most women, anyway.

The rest of it is pretty much true as I've told it to the girls all these years. I met Don at the Tropicana, and I saw immediately that he was the one. He filled all the requirements, but there was more: I liked him. His sapphire-colored eyes, and his little chuckle. His hands were badly chapped and needed hand cream, which I wanted to put on him. To my surprise, I didn't have to pretend to enjoy his kissing. It was tender and passionate and his lips fit mine in a good way. He told me he was married before he touched me and I liked his honor. I told him it didn't matter. That I'd never met anyone like him and I just wanted him to hold me.

And I don't tell this part, but Don knew it. When he made love to me in his room, where the air smelled inexplicably of chocolate cake, I wept softly. When he held me, all night, his arms around my body, I wept some more. I confessed that I'd lost someone important to me, and he kissed my shoulder and told me he hoped he could help me heal that wound as much as I'd helped him heal his own.

We spent three days together. Inseparable. We wandered the Strip holding hands and drinking Cokes with ice. He took me to a show. We ate eggs in the morning and steaks at buffets in the night. In between, we made love and made love and made love.

I will admit it was quite pleasurable. He was as good a lover as a kisser.

At the end of his conference, Sunday morning, we held each other and cried. I didn't have to fake tears, either. I was exhausted and pregnant and praying this would work. He was also a big, sturdy man and he knew how to hold me. He loved me, he said, but his wife loved him and would be lost without him.

I said I understood.

He said he would never forget me. That I had changed something in his heart and he would always be grateful.

I said I loved him, too. And oddly, when I said it, I meant it.

I let him go. I wished him a nice life. I told him, with tears running down my young and beautiful face, splashing down on my plump breasts, that if he ever changed his mind, he knew where to find me.

~

Of course he did not call. I called him once, at his job, and said, "I just want you to know that you are the most wonderful man I ever met."

He choked. "Eldora, I need to see you."

"I don't think that would be a good idea, Don. You are too good a man. It would ruin you."

Sometimes I think now, *How did I know it wouldn't ruin him? What if he'd self-destructed? What if, in his guilt, he'd fallen to drink or despair?*

The truth is, though, I gave him a reason to do what he most wanted to do: I was pregnant. He had no children. He lusted for me most desperately, but he couldn't have left his wife because of lust. He needed a higher motive.

I wrote him a letter and told him I was pregnant. I said I didn't expect him to take care of me or anything like that, but I thought he should know. I said I had a good job as a secretary at a bank and that I'd been wearing a wedding ring since I got there so nobody would think I was a single mother.

He came to Las Vegas three days later. When he arrived at my apartment, haggard but joyful, I promised myself that he would never, ever know that my child did not belong to him. He would never, for one second, believe anything less than I absolutely adored him. I vowed to take care of him for the rest of his life.

And so I did.

CHAPTER
THIRTY-EIGHT

India

When my mother stops talking, I say with some sharpness, "Well, except for that one little breach when you stole his daughters and took off across the country with somebody else."

She bows her head, nods. Cigarette smoke catches on a breeze, heads my way, then zooms off in the other direction as if it is alive. I stand. "Let's go back to the hotel."

Eldora follows me. Inside the car she says, "I just needed someone to know the whole story."

Furious, I spit the word: "Why?"

"I don't know." Her voice is thin. "Maybe I just needed one person on the planet to know who I really am."

"Who would that be, exactly, huh?" The words are in my mouth, ready to fall—slut? homewrecker? manipulating, lying Jezebel?—but I clamp my lips together hard.

"Who else could I tell, India?"

I turn toward her, eyes narrowed. "Don't you dare." Enunciating each word precisely. "Don't you make yourself into some victim of circumstance. Most of it, I got it, Mom. I got all of it up to where you had to take my father away from me."

She has the grace to bow her head, studies her hands. Red and blue neon flashes over her palms and wrists. "You might as well hate me for who I really am. You've been hating me all this time anyway."

"Oh, please. Grow up, Mom." I start the car with a slammed foot to the accelerator. When she's about to speak again, I hold up my hand. "Not another word tonight. Not one more."

She's quiet.

But I can't be. "How can you live with it, Mom? All the pain you caused those women?"

"What choice do I have, India? I mean, I live with it or I die." Her voice is low and resonant when she says, "How can a person undo sins committed thirty years ago?"

Scowling, I say, "I'm forty. Forty years."

"Yeah, those, too."

∾

I call Jack on his cell phone and he answers with the sound of slot machines binging and pinging in the background. "We're back at the hotel. Take your time."

"Is everything all right, India?"

"Fine."

But of course it isn't. Nothing is fine. And when Jack arrives forty-five minutes later, that's what I tell him: "My mother is a bitch, my sister is crazy and missing, and my father is not really my father."

He crosses the room, concerned, and puts his hands on my arms. "India!"

I can't stand the touch, and move away, pacing the length of the hotel room. He steps back, leans one hip against the wall. "What's this about?"

"My mother the liar. The man who I thought was my father isn't. So, that's one more thing I thought I had and life has taken. I'm tired of it. What's the point in wanting anything?"

"India, you're upset. Come here. Sit down. Let's talk."

"No, you don't get it. I'm pregnant and my twin sister suffers from schizophrenia, which means this baby might very well be prone, but I was still sort of dreaming about it, anyway, you know. But now I don't even know who my natural father was, what his family was like, anything. She's lied to me all these years. Lied to my dad." Overwhelmed with fury, I sink down on the bed and put my hands against my eyes. "Why did she have to tell me?"

He settles behind me, his legs and waist against my back, his hands on my shoulders. He doesn't speak, just rubs my shoulders.

The vision of that cottage in the west of Ireland, not a real place, but a symbol of what I want—Jack walking along the sea with the border collie he longs for, and our little girl between us—rises.

"It'll be all right, India."

"No," I say. Shattering that vision is my sister, wild-haired and wild-eyed. My mother, watching her lover's blood pour out of his body into her lap; my dear, dear father's blue eyes laughing as we made chocolate-covered cherries—his favorite and mine, and something my sister could not eat on a bet.

"Don's eyes are blue. How did I avoid putting that together? That my blue-eyed mother and blue-eyed father had brown-eyed daughters?"

"He's your father." His accent is pronounced, lilting. I think now that this is how English should sound, that all English should be spoken in this accent. How can I ever stand to hear it another way? "He's the one who raised you, took care of you, loved you."

I feel nauseous. "I guess."

"India, I've been tryin' to give you the space you seemed to want, but I love you. I want to be with you, take our chances with our child, love each other. Would it be so hard?"

He doesn't understand. "Have you ever known anyone who suffered from schizophrenia, Jack?"

"No."

I nod, rub my arms.

"Did you hear me at all, India?"

"I can't do it, Jack. I want to, but I can't. My grandmother suffered from schizophrenia, too. Did I tell you that?"

"No. It doesn't matter, India."

"Yes, it does. You don't understand how awful it is, Jack. You've never seen Gypsy when she's been lost for a couple of months, delusional. I don't know what happens to her or how she survives, and it makes me sick to imagine it." I raise my head. "I cannot do that to a child."

"To yourself you mean."

I bow my head. "Maybe."

"So that's the way of it then." He lets me go, heads for the door. "I can't live this way, never knowing when your walls will go up."

I can't think of anything to say. Bite my lip. My stomach is upset and I don't know how long it's going to be until I have to run for the toilet.

"I love you, India," he says, and I close my eyes. "I didn't intend to. I didn't want to take a chance, either, and risk the sorrow again. But it's good with us. It could be good always. You have to choose."

He opens the door and pauses a moment, looking at me, and walks out.

I let him.

Feeling overheated and disoriented and sick, I run for the toilet and throw up. When I come out, washing my face with a cool cloth, I can't stand to think of anything else tonight. Not the lump in my heart, the loss of Jack, my sister, my mother, anything. I order two bottles of Pellegrino from room service and when it's delivered, I sit on the bed in the dark, the curtains open and showing me the expanse of lights and movement below. Every color of light sparkles in the darkness. Cars move on the streets. Somewhere in the casinos, someone has just lost his life. Somewhere someone else has just won one. In the hotel rooms, people are making love and having fights and sleeping.

I sip my Pellegrino and stare into the darkness and feel dead. There's nothing in me at all.

~

At one point in the night, I awaken in a sweat, the sense of my sister so acute that I sit straight up in bed and call her name, "Gypsy?"

Of course she's not there, but I close my eyes, breathe in the sense of her, opening up a center that's her, and she speaks in my mind, *Remember the code. Come get me.* There is a sense of danger, of cold feet, a man with a silver tooth. I fight the sleep creeping in, knowing I'll lose her once I fall asleep all the way, but the lure is too strong and sucks me under. There's a tangle of dreams: Gypsy lying with the man with the silver tooth, and it gets mixed up with my mother and the bloody tale of her lost lover, and Jack, sailing away to Ireland, with me standing on the shore, weeping. It threads through my mind that the only time my mother wept this whole trip was when she spoke of my father, Don.

I awaken early, tangled in the sheets, exhausted but not sick to my stomach, finally. The dream reminds me to call the voice mail on my cell and house phone to see if Gypsy has called in person the way she called in my dreams, but the circuits are busy. I wonder, with a frown, if there's an earthquake or something. I'll call later, I think, and drift into sleep again.

~

My mother arrives at my door at ten a.m., looking a little swollen-eyed but none the worse for the wear. "I was up all night," she says without preamble. "C'mon and let me buy you breakfast, little girl."

"Mom, don't."

Eldora raises an eyebrow. "You can't hide from it, baby."

"You know what, Mom? I used to wish I had a normal mother. Somebody who baked brownies and wore polyester pantsuits instead of red dresses to school plays."

She nods without rancor, taps her unlit cigarette against the back of her hand. "I know. Sorry."

"Don't be. My father never regretted loving you for one single hour of his life. I have never known a man to love a woman the way he loved you. Do you know that?"

Eldora sighs. "Are you gonna spend your whole pregnancy being sentimental? Because I'll just fly to Florida until your eighth month."

"I'm not keeping this baby."

"Maybe not." She links an arm through mine. "Let's go eat, sweetie."

"No. I'm exhausted. I want to go to sleep for a year."

She tucks her arm around mine again. Stubbornly. "Sorry. We're gonna have a talk, little girl. I'm still your mama, and you still have to listen."

I glare at her. But I go.

In the hotel restaurant, there is, for once, no line. The waitress is a plump, graying woman in her early sixties who trundles over, coffeepot in hand, creamers coming out of her pockets with an expert hand. "You want a few minutes, girls?"

We order eggs Benedict. I'm impressed with the waitress, who winks at me, listens to our choices of potatoes and toast styles, and knows there are two tables coming into her section. She's probably been doing this a long time, and seems to still enjoy it. I watch her move away, wondering what that would be like, to be a waitress for forty years in Las Vegas.

Then my mother clears her throat. I look up at her.

"You, India Redding, are a control freak."

I raise my eyebrows. "This is supposed to be a revelation?"

"You need to learn how to let go and let life carry you through whatever you're going to experience."

"Like you?" I snap. "No, thanks."

She simply gazes at me. It irks me to no end that she's not contrite or apologetic or anything like that. She's just my mother, as always.

Herself. "God, Mother," I say in a low voice. "Are you even a little bit ashamed of all the things you've done?"

She narrows her eyes, scans the ceiling as if for an answer, then looks back at my face. "Shame is the wrong word. I wish I could change a few things. I really wish I could undo a couple of them. But shame? What good would it do now?"

I sigh. "I don't know." I am so tired I can't even hold up my head. I can't imagine going to have an abortion, but I can't imagine having a child, either. "I need Jack in my life," I say in a broken voice. "And that's scaring me to death, Mama." The word slips out. "I just don't know how to live with that risk."

"What risk, India?"

"I don't know . . . that he could fall out of love with me, leave me, die, change."

"One of those things will likely happen, baby. Sooner or later."

I don't want to cry and I bend my head and press my hands together very hard until I feel them go away. "When I lost Gypsy I felt like somebody took my lungs out of my body. I just didn't know how I'd live through it. And then, you were talking about when you have a baby and you have this hostage to fortune, I freaked, too. I'd love Jack and the baby and that would double my terror."

"India, would you send Gypsy back?"

"What?"

"If you could go back to the time before she was born and be God and say whether or not she was born, what would you have told God? Yes or no?"

"Yes!"

"Even though loving her has caused you pain?"

"It has given me joy, too!" I cry. "It's not that I wouldn't want her born, it's that I'd want her born without the disease!"

"I know, honey," my mother says patiently. "But that's not the choice you get to make. You get her as she is, or not at all."

I bow my head. State the obvious. "As she is."

The waitress, with impeccable timing, lays our breakfasts before us. "Anything else y'all need?"

"Looks terrific, thanks. Oh, but how about some vinegar pepper sauce for the eggs? Y'all have any? You know what I mean?"

"Sure, sweetie." The waitress chuckles, pulls a pencil from behind her ear and heads off toward the wait station. In two seconds, she's back, carrying the vinegar, and puts it down.

When Eldora reaches for it, the waitress doesn't let go. "I'll be damned. It is you. I would have known sooner, but you look a lot younger than the rest of us, Eldora, damn you."

My mother peers at the waitress, looks at her name tag. "Kitten?"

"Not quite as well-preserved as you, kiddo," the woman says, "but yep. Give me a hug, woman!"

And my mother, who is not at all given to public displays of affection unless the receiver happens to be male, leaps out of the booth and throws her long arms around the round, graying waitress, and squeals. "Kitten! I can't believe it!"

I'm intrigued, but the eggs are finely arranged, the sauce steaming and lovely, and I pick up my fork, cut a delicate piece of egg and Canadian bacon and swirl it around the exquisitely smooth Hollandaise sauce. "Oh," I exclaim softly. "That's good!"

Eldora laughs, turns her friend around. "Kitten, this is my daughter India. She drove me here."

"Is that right?" Her eyes are twinkling brown and merry, and for a flash of a second, I can see the young woman she must have once been. "I'm real glad to meet you, sweetheart."

I take her plump, worn hand, see the big diamonds on her left hand. "Nice to meet you, too."

"Kitten, do you have some time later? What time do you get off? Maybe we could go get some supper somewhere, catch up?"

"I'm way out in Henderson, Eldora. How about in a couple of hours? We could get some coffee somewhere."

"That'd be fine. Oh!" My mother bends down and hugs her friend again. "I am so happy to see you!"

Kitten is fierce. "Me, too. I've wondered about you every day of my life, just about." She rubs my mom's arm and something about the gesture makes me hurt slightly. "Looks like it all turned out all right."

"I'd say so," my mother agreed. "You, too, huh?"

The food is lovely and I'm watching them like they're the floor show. They are so full of secrets and depth my nostrils quiver with the scent of it.

"I'm off about one-thirty. Come back here and we'll go find some coffee."

My mother squeezes her hand. "Will do."

"Wow," I say as my mother scoots back into the booth. "Who was that?"

"She was my friend," my mother says, smiling softly. "She was with me the night I met your father."

A walnut of bitterness sticks in my throat, and I scowl, looking down at the plate. "Which one?" I spit out.

Eldora straightens, her nostrils flaring. "I deserve that. But I meant your daddy Don Redding."

"Did you even love him at all, Mom?"

Her Elizabeth Taylor eyes darken to a deep violet. "I didn't know how much," she says, "until he was gone."

The heat of disappointment and anger fill my chest cavity once again, and I realize I cannot sit here with her. "Are there any other revelations you want to pile on me before I go? Speak now or forever hold your peace."

"India—"

"No. I don't want to hear it. I understand why you had to tell me about your mother. Maybe some of the other stuff. I'll never forgive you for taking away my daddy. That wasn't fair."

She bows her head. "You're right."

I stand, tossing down my napkin. "I'm going to find Jack and talk to him about all of this. We'll find you later on."

Eldora nods. She doesn't say anything as I walk away.

CHAPTER THIRTY-NINE

India

I call Jack on his cell phone. He says he'll be there in a few minutes, which tells me he must not have ventured too far away this morning.

Not that it matters. A shard of headache sears the space above my right eyebrow and I punch in the numbers to my house phone voice mail. No messages. I'm dialing my cell number when Jack comes to my room with his coat on. His gray eyes are wary as he sits down in the chair opposite me. I hang up the phone, fold my hands, and look at him, and it sends a pain like a fist through my middle.

"I'm sorry I was a bitch last night," I say.

He nods, still wary. The scar above his eye gives me a pang, and I want to lie down next to him, stroke his brow.

I look at my hands, see in the gesture my mother's way of readying herself for a confession. "The chances that this baby will suffer from schizophrenia eventually are much higher than the normal population. I really need to know that you understand what that means, Jack."

"I'll do my best, darlin'. That's all I can do."

"No, I need you to feel this, on a gut level."

He sighs, exasperated. "India, what does it matter? Do you want the child?"

The vision of my little girl, black-haired with Jack's mouth and blue eyes bolts through me and I almost feel her move inside of me. I can't look at him. Nod, very slightly. "But we can't," I whisper. "You just don't know how terrible it can be."

"What if she isn't sick?"

I raise my eyes. "What if she is?" I hold up a hand when he would have spoken. "Maybe I can show you." I pick up the phone and dial my home number. I'll play him the messages from Gypsy, the happy one where it sounds like she's on vacation, and the other one, that ends with her sobbing. "You can hear her messages."

He gives me an exasperated sigh, and flips that heavy lock of hair from his forehead, slumping back with his feet in front of him, and I see a dozen other times he's done this with me.

Something in it shifts my world and I give him a grin. "You think I'm—"

I break off and bend my head to listen as the voice mail robot says, "You have one new message. Two saved messages." I press "one" to hear the message, my heart suddenly pounding very hard.

God please don't let it be the police the morgue the state anyone calling to say she is dead God please let her still be alive don't let me hear that I will never see her again.

"Hello, Ms. Redding, this is Katie Piers at the Gallup Homeless Shelter. Your sister is here. It's about two a.m. Saturday morning. Give us a call. She's mildly injured but otherwise well. They gave her a sedative at the hospital and sent her over to us, and she's sleeping."

Relief like a tsunami crashes through me. I drop the receiver and bend over, all the tears rushing through me, out of me. "It's Gypsy," I manage to choke out. "She's okay." I sink into myself and the tsunami crashes, over and over, on the shores of my heart.

Jack is beside me, arms around me. "It's all right, India. We'll go get her." He rocks me gently, my sobs shaking my entire body. "It's all right, love. It's all right." He kisses my hair.

~

When I've pulled myself together, washed my face, I call the homeless shelter to get a status report on my sister. The same woman I spoke to in person says Gypsy was still sleeping and likely would be for a while.

"You said minor injuries?" I ask.

"Uh, yeah. It's nothing serious. Stitches in a couple of spots and a broken arm. Not sure what happened. She showed up and we got her to the emergency room. There were no beds available thanks to this flu outbreak, so we brought her back here."

"Thank you," I whisper. "We'll be there as soon as we can." When I hang up the phone, I sigh. "It's a long drive. I think I need to rent a car. I can't stand to be in that Thunderbird one more minute."

Jack gives me his best sideways grin. "I have a better idea. C'mon. We'll go get her right now."

"You don't have to get all wrapped up in this. You're on vacation. Enjoy yourself."

He rolls his eyes. "Don't be daft. Let's go."

~

His idea is brilliant, actually. We call around to the various sightseeing helicopters listed in the yellow pages and find one who will fly us to Gallup. We're landing in early afternoon. I still haven't reached my mother by phone.

"Okay, this is the hard part," I tell Jack, putting my hand on his chest before we go into the shelter. "You've only seen her when she's stable."

"What do you think I am?"

I nod. "But you need to know what to expect. The drugs are hard on people. They cause a lot of weight gain, so she's sometimes kind of fat. And she's lost her teeth because the drugs dry out your mouth and then she's on the streets and—" I shrug.

He takes my hand. "I'm not going to judge her. I promise."

The woman leads us into the shelter, to my sister.

At last.

She's sitting up, groggy and swollen-eyed, one eye ringed with green and purple bruises. Her left arm is in a green cast up to the elbow and it appears to be giving her some irritation, because just this minute, she's tugging at it, scowling, shaking her head, and muttering. Her hair, yards of it, tumbles around her like a cloak, tangled and ratted, but I can see from long experience it's combable. Her fingernails are very long and dirty, but her hands are clean. Her shoes are missing, and her feet are wrapped in cloth, like a medieval beggar.

"Gypsy," I say.

She lifts her head and sees me and gives me a huge, toothless smile. "India!" she says. "You came."

"Of course." I fall to my knees and take her into my arms, seeing that she's been sedated and is not particularly delusional.

Her arms, solid and real, go around me, and now it's her turn to let the relief wash through her. She weeps on my shoulder, her body shaking and shaking. "You found me," she says. "You came."

"We did." I pull back, brushing hair from her face. "Do you have your bag?"

"Right here." She pats it, the green backpack my mother and I pack with goods. "Can we go home?"

"How about Las Vegas for tonight? Mama's there."

She nods, exhaustion plain in her every movement. I help her up gently. "This," I say to her, "is Jack. You remember him?"

Her expression clears. "Yes."

He offers his hand. "Shall I carry your bag?"

"Here," she says, patting the spot between her eyes. "I saw you here. They told me you were coming."

He smiles at her, very gently, and helps her to her feet. In his gray eyes I see compassion, love, pity, all the things that make him, in so many ways, like my mother. "Come, love," he says. "Let's get you somewhere you can have a good sleep, eh?"

CHAPTER FORTY

Getting Gypsy through the casino into the elevators proves a challenge—at first she won't go through it at all—but we both hold her hands and tell her to keep her eyes down to avoid the visual confusion, and we get her upstairs to my mother's waiting embrace. I know from experience that Eldora will take over now; she can't stand to let anyone else do this part: She gently brings Gypsy into her rooms, takes off the bandages on her feet.

As if someone has pulled a plug on her energy, Gypsy falls sideways on the bed, touching my mother's shoulder. "Mom," she says with a heavy, heartfelt sigh.

My mother raises her eyes to me, nods. I take Jack's hand and lead him out to the hall, leaving my mother to her ritual of reclaiming. She'll skim away the old, malodorous clothes and put Gypsy in a hot bath, then tenderly wash her. "My baby," she'll say. "My sweet girl. I'm so glad to have you back safe again. I missed you so much." It's like an incantation she uses to bring Gypsy back into the fold.

In the hallway, Jack says, "Let's find something to eat, shall we?"

"Away from the casino, though. The noise is really bothering me."

"I could do with a walk," he says. "Shall we get out and see what we find?"

"Sounds good."

It's been a long day, so it's odd to get out into the day and realize it's only late afternoon, and it might as well be summer—the air is warm and dry, the sunlight angling down in lemon meringue slices through the tall buildings. The sidewalks are busy with tourists; as we walk I see a crowd of young Asian people mugging for each other's cameras in front of the Bellagio lake. "It really does look like Italy," I comment.

"About the way McDonald's looks like a hamburger. Everything is in the right places, and the ingredients sound right—bun, burger, pickles—but it somehow doesn't really taste like anything."

"It tastes like McDonald's," I counter. We hold hands, two more tourists on the busy Las Vegas streets. "I'm unexpectedly charmed by this excess. It's so over the top, how can you help but love it?"

He smiles ruefully. "I don't think I could stay more than two or three days. I'd be spitting and hostile with all the noise."

We walk for a long time, long enough that we're past the Riviera, out of the main crowds. We don't need to talk the whole way, but there are moments of sporadic conversation, triggered by the sights, the oddities, the amazements—a man with a true ten-gallon hat walking along with a woman whose breasts appear to each be about the same size as the hat; a pair of guys in showgirl drag, hobbling up the sidewalk in glossy high heels behind a family of rotund tourists from the Midwest. I don't know how I know they're Midwestern, any more than I knew the girls were Irish, but they are.

"You've said your sister has a normal life when she takes her medications. How normal?"

I lift a shoulder. "Very. She responds well to drug therapy, and she's learned how to recognize the delusions, so she pretty much lives like anybody else. And as long as she's taking good care of herself, she can be like that all the time."

"How long does it take before she's stabilized again?"

"The sedatives will help her pretty fast, but the antipsychotics take about four to six weeks, usually."

"Where will she go?"

"She stays with my mother. Mostly, my mother is the one who steps in when Gypsy hits a rocky stretch; it's just that she was grieving this time and could barely take care of herself."

"I had the impression it was your father who offered care."

"He did, when Gypsy was younger. Once she had her first break, it was a lot more difficult for him. My mother is extremely good with her." I pause. "I guess I know why now."

"She's had a challenging life, your mother."

"Mmm."

We finally stop at a seventies-style coffee shop. "This will do," I say suddenly aware that I'm getting dangerously dizzy. "I need food right now."

"You should have said something sooner. Come on then, let's get you something to eat."

We order simple steaks and they come with a line-up I haven't had for a long time; bowl of soup—choice of chicken or minestrone; iceberg lettuce adorned with two cherry tomatoes, drowned in dressing; a baked potato with butter and sour cream; carrots; white rolls and butter; choice of iced tea or coffee for $9.99.

"My father would have loved this place," I say with a chuckle, digging into the salad.

"Mine, too," Jack says. "Wonder how often they can burn the fireplace, though, don't you?"

I chuckle. "I feel like I'm time traveling. We should be able to turn on the television and see The Partridge Family singing."

"Who?"

"You know, David Cassidy, Shirley Jones—they were a singing TV family."

He looks blank. Shrugs. "Sorry. That one must not have made it across."

"Probably just as well."

We never mention the baby, or Gypsy, or even my mother. It's peaceful. A reminder of how it is to be with him, just to be at peace.

Would it always be that way? Would we get on each other's nerves? Grouse about trivialities?

There is chocolate cake for dessert. Just plain old chocolate cake with frosting. I haven't had any in years and years. I lick the fork with satisfaction. "My mother used to bake cakes for my father."

"She loved him."

I look at the shiny tines of my fork. "What's sad is that I'm not sure she knew it until he died."

"That's the way of it, isn't it?"

"What do you mean?"

He bends his head over the cake and his hair falls forward on his brow. Light shines along the crown. I think, if I never looked at his nose again, it will be something I miss the rest of my life. "You think you've got it all figured out at fifteen. You'll study this, follow that, marry well and wisely, have children and whatever." He raises his eyes.

"Yeah?"

"Life comes along and changes the script, doesn't it?"

I think, with a pain, of my mother deciding, so coldly, to go out and find a man to fall in love with her and marry her so she could pass off her baby as his. It's both practical and horrible, and how can I condemn her? The man she picked so very well was my father for forty years. "My father's first wife died by suicide. Did I tell you that?"

"No."

"Yeah. I feel terrible for her, but it's impossible to imagine my life without my dad. So was it fate and she just wouldn't accept it? Or was it some evil that my mother put into play? Or is life just some stupid, random spin of the dice?"

Jack takes my hand. "I don't know."

"I was supposed to be the one who grew up and became a mommy," I say. "Gypsy was going to be the world traveler, the famous artist, and I was going to hold the fort and keep her children when she had to go somewhere."

He holds my gaze steadily until a girl in a wedding dress comes in, followed by a small knot of well-wishers. The groom is painfully thin, with an Adam's apple like a pyramid. "They're babies," I say softly. "So brave."

"It used to be easier," Jack says, "to imagine doing something foolish and wild for love, wasn't it?"

"Is that what you did?"

"Not really. I wanted to, when I was seventeen."

"I haven't heard this story. Who did you want to run away with?"

"Fiona Fallon. She had the most beautiful hair, all the way down her back, and the sweetest heart in all of Ireland."

"So why didn't you?"

"She wanted a ring, which I couldn't afford, but I think that was only an excuse, since she married another lad not six months after."

"Oh, poor you!"

"I was afraid to take chances. Always have been." His eyes held something strong and bright. "So then I picked a sure bet of a woman, who cheated on me and made my life a living hell until I finally got rid of her. And now, here I am, and you're more frightened than I am."

"Jack . . ."

He takes my hand across the table, and presses something cold into it. "I'm not so poor I can't afford a ring nowadays. Will you wear it for me, India?"

I open my hand. It's not a diamond or anything elaborate or fancy. It's just a simple gold band. Tears well in my eyes so suddenly and sharply—damn this emotional state!—that I have to lower my lids. "Oh, Jack, I'm so afraid."

"I know, sweetheart." He holds my hand fiercely, a great deal of public display for him. "But it's right between us. It is, India, you know it."

Frozen in my wanting, I whisper, "Jack, you saw my sister."

"I did." He takes money out of his wallet and tosses it on top of the bill. "Come outside. I can't talk here."

I follow him out. The sun is beginning to set, making the sky a rosy gold, with blue mountains cutting across the horizon. The sight makes me homesick for Pikes Peak. "Where will we live, Jack?"

"One question at a time." Taking my hands, he says earnestly, "If our child becomes ill, we'll care for him, India. That's all. Some things are simple."

I look at him, the ring clasped in my palm. "What if you break my heart?"

"What if you break mine?"

"What if you die?"

"I'm going to eventually."

"Me, too." It's hard to breathe. I have never wanted anything so much in my life as I want to marry this man and have him with me every night when I go to sleep. "What about your work? And where we live? And—"

He grins down at me. "Will you marry me, India?"

"Yes," I whisper.

"Forever and ever?"

"And ever and ever."

He looks over his shoulder. "Now?"

I see the Eternal Love Wedding Chapel, flashing in pale blue-and-pink neon. "You can't be serious."

"Why not?"

"Are you afraid I'll back out?"

"Maybe." He takes my hand. "Maybe it's just time for both of us to do something impulsive."

I can tell that I'm really going to do it. I raise my eyebrows and smile. "Okay."

"What about your mother? Shall we call her?"

"She won't leave Gypsy. And I wouldn't want her to." An idea comes to me. "Do you have your cell phone?"

He pulls it out of his jacket pocket and I dial the Flamingo, ask for my mother's room. Cars whiz by on Las Vegas Boulevard. In the distance, the lights of the Strip seem to be growing brighter. "Mom," I say when she answers, "where did you marry my dad?"

"Oh, India, I'm so happy for you!"

"Me, too, Mom. Now where?"

"The Eternal Love Wedding Chapel."

"You're kidding."

"I wouldn't joke about that."

"I'm standing right in front of it." There's a sign that says, "Established 1959."

Eldora gives her throaty, husky laugh. "Some things are just fated to be, sweetheart."

I look at Jack, at his gentle, steady gray eyes, and touch my belly. "I love you, Mom," I say.

"I love you, too, baby. More than you'll ever know."

Hanging up the phone, I look at Jack. "The minute I saw you, I fell head over heels in love. It's been killing me ever since."

He grins, slowly. "I've had the same trouble."

"Could we have a cottage on the west coast of Ireland? Not to live there all the time, just sometimes?"

He steps close, puts his arms around me. "That could be done."

"Let's marry then."

He bends his head to my neck. "This means I can sleep with you many nights, instead of just one or two a month, doesn't it?"

I laugh. "Many."

"You have no idea how I've prayed for blizzards."

"Me, too."

He raises his head, puts his hand on my face, and kisses me right in public, on the street in Las Vegas. "I love you, India."

"Let's get married."

So we do.

EPILOGUE

Eldora

It's a sunny August morning and I've got a box sitting on the passenger seat as I drive out to Evergreen Cemetery. India lets me drive as long as I don't drink. First I stop by Don's grave to inspect the headstone, which is a big cross, Celtic in design, and it looks beautiful—his birth and death, and "Beloved Husband, Beloved Father." When I go, I'll have the plot next to his. We picked them out a long time ago, two gravesites high on a hill, overlooking the sky and the mountains. It's a beautiful view and I think he must like it here. I've brought some fresh carnations for the vase, and I stick them in to show he's well loved, this man.

I know India will come here, too, on her daddy's birthday, which is in a couple of weeks. She and Jack have been splitting their time between New York and Colorado. Jack is arranging to have a second office of his magazine opened in Colorado Springs, and they're buying a house with a guest cottage in back. It's empty at the moment, but it has two bedrooms.

In the graveyard, I wander toward another section, to another grave. It's a fair hike to the south, over an up-and-down road that loops around a section of ex-soldiers and a section of children's graves from long ago, which always makes me sad. I think of the graveyard in Truchas and wish there was some of that life and color here. That sense of celebration, even in death.

Sometimes there isn't a lot you can do to put right what you've done wrong. I should have picked a man who wasn't married.

But I didn't. There is nothing I can do to make it up to Bea Redding, to make her life better, but ever since our trip to Las Vegas, I've been working on a way to at least tell her I'm sorry without making it a big production that's all about me. It's anonymous, but it's beautiful and I've worked real hard on it.

It's a *descanso*. I didn't think it would be okay to put one up for a suicide in a house where people might or might not know anything about it, but there's nothing wrong with a good cross in a graveyard. I collected about a hundred little things about Bea—pictures from Don's scrapbooks, and things clipped out of the newspaper, and bits and pieces from her church newsletter—I was so proud of myself for thinking of that!—and glued them all onto a sturdy wooden cross I made from cedar because the man at the hardware store said it lasted longest. In the middle of the cross, I put a picture of Bea and Don when they were happy, and I put it beneath glass so it would always be beautiful. The girls and I used to do decoupage and that's the technique I used, a good shellac over the top so it'll last longer.

It's not that much, you know, to make up for stealing her life. I know that. I know it's only a gesture, but it felt like I needed to do it anyway, to know her and show her—just her—that I really was sorry. The only thing I could do was take the time to know what her life was about and how much she loved Don and her church and even my little girls.

I planted it on the ground of her grave, face up to the world, a thing of color and beauty to mark the fact that she lived in this world and she loved and she was loved in return.

When you get right down to it, that's all there is. Love. Not the neat kind you put in a card and spritz with cologne, but all of it, the big messy mucky kinds and the imperfect kinds and the improper kinds.

That'd make a good neon sign, wouldn't it?

All love. All the time.

In the bright day, I admire the photo of Bea, and I hope people will stop sometimes to admire her, the cross, think about her, and how beautiful she once was. "I'm sorry, Bea," I say.

Then I put on my sunglasses and head back to my car. It's a beautiful day, and they're expecting me at the homeless shelter, which is one place nobody cares if you smoke or have a checkered past. All they need is the simple stuff—a good coat, some cigarettes, a bed with a pillow, a smile on a bad day. That's what I'm there for.

All love, all the time. Easy enough.

ACKNOWLEDGMENTS

I have so many thanks to offer this time. Thanks to Bill Stevenson for rocky road ice cream and keeping me company on research trips down Route 66, to Las Vegas and Santa Fe; thanks for all the walking and talking out plot points and reminding me that books only get written when writers sit down and do it. Thanks especially for the graveyard at Truchas, three days after El Dia de los Muertos—a sight I will never forget. Thanks to Teresa Hill, for repeated reads and reassurances and asking the right questions when I needed it; Christie Ridgway and Elizabeth Bevarly for discussions and focusing issues; the whole of RomEx, for thousands of hours of support in both life and writing. Thanks to Jackie and Kitten Hair for a wonderful evening in Las Vegas, and a special wave to my uncle Bill Hair, now departed to the great casino in the sky, because some of the seeds of his life grew into this tree. And always, thanks to my agent and editors: Meg Ruley, Linda Marrow, and her assistant, Arielle Zibrak. The one thing I know for sure is that I couldn't do it without you guys.

ABOUT THE AUTHOR

Photo © 2009 Blue Fox Photography

Barbara O'Neal is the *Washington Post, Wall Street Journal, USA Today,* and Amazon Charts bestselling author of more than a dozen novels of women's fiction, including the #1 Amazon Charts bestseller *When We Believed in Mermaids* as well as *The Starfish Sisters, This Place of Wonder, The Lost Girls of Devon, Write My Name Across the Sky,* and *The Art of Inheriting Secrets.* Her award-winning books have been published in over two dozen countries. She lives on the Oregon coast with her husband, a British endurance athlete who vows he'll never lose his accent. For more information, visit barbaraoneal.com.